James B. McMillan:
Essays in Linguistics by his Friends and Colleagues

James B. McMillan: Essays in Linguistics by his Friends and Colleagues

EDITED BY
James C. Raymond
AND
I. Willis Russell

THE UNIVERSITY OF ALABAMA PRESS
UNIVERSITY, ALABAMA

Library of Congress Cataloging in Publication Data

Main entry under title:

James B. McMillan : essays in linguistics by his friends and
    colleagues.
    "Publications on the English language by James B.
McMillan": p.
    Bibliography: p.
    Includes index.
    CONTENTS: Raymond, J. C. and I. W. Russell. James B.
McMillan.—Dialectology: Allen, H. B. The linguistic
atlas of the Upper Midwest as a source of sociolinguistic
information. Duckert, A. R. The winds of change [etc.]
    1. English language—Addresses, essays, lectures.
2. McMillan, James B., 1907– I. McMillan, James B., 1907–
II. Raymond, James C., 1940– III. Russell, I. Willis, 1903–
PE1072.J35   410   77-7169
ISBN 0-8173-0503-3

Contents

James B. McMillan

JAMES C. RAYMOND AND
I. WILLIS RUSSELL

To the world at large, James Benjamin McMillan—Jim McMillan to his many friends—is known as a scholar of the first rank. But to those who have known him well for any length of time, he is a great deal more than that. He is the "man thinking" of Emerson's great essay, and it is that man that this essay will attempt to sketch.

Jim McMillan was born on August 24, 1907, in Talladega, a small city located in the eastern part of Alabama. His elementary and secondary education was obtained in Talladega. It is not without interest that his Latin teacher was Mitford M. Mathews. After receiving his high school diploma, he spent a year in Davidson College, from which he went to the Alabama Polytechnic Institute—now Auburn University—which granted him the B.S. degree in 1929. The following year, he went to the University of North Carolina, receiving his M.A. in 1930.

The next year found him teaching at Judson College, and from 1932 on till his retirement in 1975 he was a full-time member of the faculty of the University of Alabama. Hence his subsequent graduate work was sporadic: The Johns Hopkins University during the summer of 1932, Columbia University in 1935, and the University of Chicago at various times later. It was the University of Chicago that awarded him his Ph.D. (with honors) for a dissertation directed by James R. Hulbert entitled "Phonology of the Standard English of East Central Alabama" (synopsized in H. L. Mencken's *The American Language, Supplement II,* pp. 130–31).

Besides Hulbert, at Chicago Jim studied under several other greats of a generation ago. Probably foremost among these was

Leonard Bloomfield, whose *Language* was already looking like a classic in the field of linguistics. Jim, never one to yield to unbridled enthusiasms, once said that he was always in his place in Bloomfield's class well before the beginning of the class period: every utterance of his was pure gold—if our metaphor seems extravagant it appears to be the way Bloomfieldians felt about the man. Then there was Sir William A. Craigie, fresh from the triumph of the *OED,* under whom Jim not only took courses but participated in the work on the *Dictionary of American English,* then in progress, of which Sir William along with Hulbert was editor.

Four other men at Chicago had a formative influence on Jim: Julian Bonfante (Indo-European dialects), B. F. Skinner (verbal behavior), John M. Manly (bibliography), and C. E. Parmenter (experimental phonetics), who is footnoted in Jim's first publication, "Vowel Nasality."

As has already been suggested, most of the graduate work just recounted and the writing of the dissertation were done along with a full load of teaching and administration. Jim served as instructor, assistant professor, and associate professor in the English Department of the School of Commerce and Business Administration until 1946. Made a full professor in that year, he joined the faculty of the College of Arts and Sciences, where he became Professor of Linguistics and Chairman of the newly formed Department of Linguistics. In 1962 linguistics was absorbed by The Department of English, when Jim was appointed Professor of English and Chairman of the Department. He held the latter post until 1971. He became Professor of English Emeritus in 1976.

Jim's long teaching career at the University of Alabama was interspersed with three visiting professorships: at the universities of Florida and Chicago and at Georgetown University. The Georgetown post is of special significance because as visiting professor he served as Director of the Georgetown University English Language Program at the University of Ankara in Turkey, where he was thrown directly into contact with Turkish, a Ural-Altaic language with structural features not found in Indo-European languages. He once wrote from Turkey about one of the problems in H. A. Gleason's *Workbook* dealing with (to Americans) a complicated rule of infixing in Turkish; his terse dry comment: "And Turkish children of six do it automatically every day."

Many never publish because they never ask questions; Jim's bibliography is ample evidence of a mind that never ceases to ask questions, to unsettle common assumptions. An almost unbroken series of publications from 1939 to 1976 has built for him a solid reputation as a scholar in virtually every aspect of the English language. He had published more than a dozen articles before completing his dissertation; the dissertation itself was simply another item, and an important one, in a productive and scholarly career already well under way.

Among the most important of his early works is "Vowel Nasality" (1939), the expansion of a term paper written in C. E. Parmenter's course in Experimental Phonetics. It reads like the work of a mature scholar rather than the first publication of a comparatively young man, and it is frequently cited by students working on the Linguistic Atlas of the Gulf States. His dissertation, "Phonology of the Standard English of East Central Alabama," has taken its place in the literature of the phonology of Southern American speech. "Five College Dictionaries" (1949), occasioned by the recent appearance of the *American College Dictionary* (edited by Clarence L. Barnhart), established the technique for evaluating dictionaries of the same kind through a comparison of their treatment of such matters as pronunciations, etymology, and definitions. Robert Chapman recognizes and builds upon this technique in his essay in this volume.

In the same year (1949) appeared another significant article, "Observations on American Place-Name Grammar," perhaps the most perceptive and seminal piece of Jim's entire career. The title is disarming, as is evident in the opening sentence of this properly placed lead article in *American Speech:* "When Americans consistently put *the* before *Susquehanna River* and just as consistently omit *the* before *Murder Creek* and *Lake Ontario,* when they unerringly trim *Mountain* to *Mount* if it precedes the specific name, a system of grammar is operating efficiently without benefit of handbook rules and without much notice even in special treatises on place names."

This is his style at its best: compact, terse, fluid, and as satisfying to read as an essay of Bacon's. Those of us for whom writing is arduous would like to think that Jim, too, works as hard at his prose; but he is remembered as saying once, in the company of scholars complaining about the difficulties of composing letters, "I just think of what it is I want to write and then write it." This is a gift Solomon might have asked for had he had more wisdom to begin with.

Among his more recent work, the *Annotated Bibliography of Southern American English* (1971) has been lauded by scholars as an important research tool. And "A Controversial Consonant" (1974), a typescript of some twenty pages, deals exhaustively with the consonant /ž/; with its complete review and analysis of all that has been said about the sound, it will certainly become the standard treatment of the subject and the starting point for any future study.

Jim characterizes himself as a teacher and a popularizer. Though the preceding section and his list of publications show that he has regularly replenished Thomas Arnold's reservoir of knowledge from which we all draw, he has been very concerned with the dissemination of knowledge. He has coauthored two textbooks; and in 1952 he revised the famous Foerster and Steadman *Writing and Thinking.* He has been a frequent consultant and has served on many panels, such as the CCCC panel "Linguistics for Teachers of English" in St. Louis in 1954, "Seminar for Southern Appellate Judges on Opinion-Writing" in Tuscaloosa in 1967, and USOE Livingston State Faculty Workshop on Transformational Grammar" in Livingston, Alabama, in 1970.

For nearly 20 years Jim addressed a wide audience through the NCTE English Usage Committee, of which he was a member from 1939 to 1958 and chairman from 1942 to 1949. In his pieces in the "Current English Forum" in *College English* and the *English Journal,* he not only answered queries made by teachers but at times explained to them how they could answer their own questions by observing the usage of cultivated speakers and writers: "We have no source of information about the English language except the English we hear and read."

One index to the importance of a scholar's work is the number of times he has been reprinted. Five of Jim's studies have been reprinted: "Vowel Nasality," "A Philosophy of Language," "Mispronunciation?," "Summary of Nineteenth Century . . . Linguistics," and "Dictionaries and Usage." "A Philosophy of Language" has appeared in no less than five collections and was included in the Golden Anniversary *College English* "Sampler from the Past" (November 1960) as one of twelve essays "presented as a sampler of both the high quality and the wide-ranging interests maintained through the years." Here seems to be a good place to mention the very fine statement of the "Contribution of the Liberal Arts" (*Collegiate Education for Business*, University, Alabama, 1954), abstracted in *What the Colleges are Doing* (January 1955).

The regard with which Jim and his work are held is indicated in yet another way. He has served on committees of and held posts in a number of organizations, including the American Dialect Society, the Modern Language Association of American, the National Council of Teachers of English, the Southeastern Conference on Linguistics, the South Atlantic Modern Language Association, the Center for Applied Linguistics, the Alabama Historical Association, and the American Association of University Professors.

He has also served on the editorial boards of *American Speech, College Composition and Communication,* the *National University Extension News,* and the *Harcourt-Brace School Dictionary,* and was managing editor of the *Alabama Review* for 16 years. At present he is serving on the advisory boards of *Abstracts of English Studies,* the *Britannica World Dictionary,* the Funk and Wagnalls Dictionaries, and the Linguistic Atlas of the Gulf States, and is Managing Editor of the *Publication of the American Dialect Society.* Since 1974 he has been a consultant on the *Oxford English Dictionary Supplement.*

During his long career Jim has held a variety of important administrative posts, at least two in areas that seem far afield from his area of language and literature, a fact that merely testifies to his versatility and wide interests: "homo sum; humani nihil a me alienum puto." His first administrative post, Acting Director of the Bureau of Business Research in the School of Commerce and Business Administration (1942–1945), was not only an indication of his breadth of interests, but also a recognition of his critical grasp of business problems and operations.

When the University of Alabama Press was set up in 1945, Jim was appointed its first director, a post which he held until 1962. Students of language will be interested in knowing that it was Jim who formulated the first agreement between the Press and the American Dialect Society which relieved the Secretary-Treasurer of chores the Press was better equipped to handle and allowed him more time to run the Society and edit its journal.

From 1943 to 1945, Jim, assisted by a remarkable group of colleagues, served as Director of Instruction of the Air Force Training Program and ASTR Program at the University of Alabama. Administrative resiliency was a must to handle directives that often arrived at the eleventh hour. Any suggestion useful for the program was welcomed and usually adopted. If the administrative structure was not set up for it, the structure was modified.

As Chairman of the Department of English from 1962 to 1971, Jim again displayed the creative leadership which encourages a group to do its best both in teaching and in research. Every professor had at least one course in his research specialty. There was no status quo. Committees, standing and ad hoc, continually reviewed the curriculum and reported to frequently held departmental meetings.

No account of Jim McMillan's career would be complete without mention of his immediate family. In 1932 he married Antoinette Brannon, known to all her friends as Anne. They have one daughter, Cynthia M. Lanford, and three grand-children. With their son-in-law, William (Bill), it is a warm family. The McMillan hospitality is legendary.

The foregoing account—by no means complete—will reveal why we think Jim McMillan deserves the very special birthday present which this volume constitutes. Others besides ourselves share our admiration: a wide circle of friends and colleagues, especially those who have generously contributed the essays that make up this volume; the Department of English, whose chairman, Dwight Eddins, has put the resources of the Department at our disposal; the College of Arts and Sciences, which, through its dean, Douglas E. Jones, contributed handsomely to the subsidy of the volume; and the University, whose former Vice-President for Educational Development, Neal Berte, was instrumental in obtaining the considerable initial subsidy which got the project moving; and the University of Alabama Press, whose staff has been at all times helpful.

And now it but remains for us all to wish you a very happy birthday, Jim, with many happy returns, the while you continue replenishing that reservoir of knowledge whose level you have substantially helped to maintain and whose water you have drawn upon and used so effectively.

JAMES C. RAYMOND
I. WILLIS RUSSELL

The University of Alabama

Publications on the English Language by James B. McMillan

1939: Vowel Nasality as a Sandhi Form of the Morphemes -nt and -ing in Southern American. *American Speech* 14:120–123.

1939: A Small Plea for Fact Before Legislation. *College English* 1:70–71.

1940: Review of The Effect of Stress upon Quantity in Dissyllables, by Norman E. Eliason and Roland C. Davis. *South Atlantic Bulletin* 6:11–12.

1941: A Word for the Oxford Dictionary. *Words* 7:74.

1941: 'Sleepy Hollow' and 'Trumeau Mirror,' *American Speech* 16:231–232.

1942: 'OK' A Comment. *American Speech* 17:127.

1943: Lexical Evidence from Charles Sealsfield. *American Speech* 18:117–127.

1943: Review of The Science of Grammar, by Wilson Clough. *College English* 5:108–109.

1945: New American Lexical Evidence. *American Speech* 20:34–39.

1945: LCL Again. *American Speech* 20:73.

1945: The Descriptive Grammarian's Point of View. *English Journal* 34:395–396.

1945: Review of The Psychology of English, by Margaret M. Bryant and Janet R. Aiken. *College English* 7:52–54.

1945: 'Who' and 'Whom.' *College English* 7:104.

1946: Review of The American Language, Supplement I, by H. L. Mencken. *English Journal* 35:164–165.

1946: The Pronunciation of Foreign Names. *English Journal* 35:274.

1946: Historical Notes on American Words. *American Speech* 21:175–184.

1947: Charivari as a Verb. *American Speech* 22:74.

1947: (with I. Willis Russell) Supplementing Word Lists. *Publication of the American Dialect Society* 8:39–41.

1948: A Philosophy of Language. *College English* 7:385–390.

1948: Review of The Place Names of Dane County, Wisconsin, by Frederic Cassidy, and West Virginia Place Names, by Hamill Kenny. *Modern Philology* 45:280–282.

1949: Five College Dictionaries. *College English* 10:214–221.

1949: Mispronunciation? *English Journal* 38:287–288.

1949: Observations on American Place-Name Grammar. *American Speech* 24:241–248.

1950: Review of Africanisms in the Gullah Dialect, by Lorenzo D. Turner. *Alabama Review* 3:148–150.

1951: Review of A Word Geography of the Eastern United States, by Hans Kurath. *Language* 27:423–429.

1952: (with Norman Foerster and John M. Steadman) Writing and Thinking (fifth edition), Boston: Houghton-Mifflin Co.

1952: Review of Indian Place Names in Delaware, by A. R. Dunlap and C. A. Weslager. *American Speech* 27:190–191.

1952: A Further Note on Place Name Grammar. *American Speech* 27:196–198.

1953: Review of Words and Ways of American English, by Thomas Pyles. *American Speech* 28:40–42.

1953: The Origin of 'Everglades.' *American Speech* 28:200–201.

1954: Review of Our Storehouse of Missouri Place Names, by Robert L. Ramsay. *Language* 30:173–174.

1954: Nineteenth Century Historical and Comparative Linguistics. *College Composition and Communication* 5:145–149.

1955: President's Report. *Publication of the American Dialect Society* 23:51–53.

1956: Review of Place Names of Franklin County, Missouri, by Robert L. Ramsay. *Midwest Folklore* 6:248.

1960: (with Lalia P. Boone et al) Communicative Arts, 4 vols. Washington: Colonial Press.

1964: Dictionaries and Usage. *Word Study* 39, No. 3.
1964: Pronunciation, in Standard College Dictionary. New York: Funk & Wagnalls.
1967: Doubling Consonants Before Suffixes. *American Speech* 42:235–236.
1968: Regional Pronunciation, in Harcourt-Brace School Dictionary. New York: Harcourt-Brace.
1969: Southern Speech, in A Bibliographical Guide to the Study of Southern Literature, ed. by Louis D. Rubin, Jr. Baton Rouge: L.S.U. Press.
1969: The Study of Regional and Social Variety in American English, in Language and Teaching: Essays in Honor of W. Wilbur Hatfield, ed. by Virginia McDavid. Chicago: Chicago State College.
1970: Four Place Name Studies. *Western Folklore* 29:138–140.
1970: Of Matters Lexicographical. *American Speech* 45:288–292.
1971: Annotated Bibliography of Southern American English. Coral Gables: University of Miami Press.
1971: Of Matters Lexicographical. *American Speech* 46:138–141.
1971: Review of The First Lincolnland Conference on Dialectology, and The Second and Third Lincolnland Conferences on Dialectology. *American Speech* 46:159–160.
1972: Review of Vocabulary Change, by Gordon R. Wood. *Mississippi Quarterly* 8:101–104.
1972: Of Matters Lexicographical. *American Speech* 47:261–265.
1974: Review of Variant Spellings in Modern American Dictionaries, by Donald W. Emery, and A Comparative Study of Spellings in Four Major Collegiate Dictionaries, by Lee C. Deighton. *American Speech* 49:134–137.
[1974]: A Controversial Consonant, in a Festschrift ed. by Walter Meyers (forthcoming).
[1975]: Lexis, in Current Trends in the Study of American English, ed. by John Algeo (forthcoming).
[1976]: Dialects, in Encyclopedia of Southern History, ed. by David C. Roller and Robert W. Twyman (forthcoming).

[1976]: Infixing and Interfixing in English (forthcoming in *American Speech*).

[1976]: Review of The Barnhart Dictionary of New English Since 1963, ed. by Clarence L. Barnhart, Sol Steinmetz, and Robert K. Barnhart, and 6,000 Words, A Supplement to Webster's Third New International Dictionary (forthcoming in *American Speech*).

[1977]: The Naming of American Dialects, in Papers in Language Variation, ed. by David Shores and Carole P. Hines. University, AL: The University of Alabama Press.

Directory of Contributors

John Algeo
University of Georgia

Harold B. Allen
University of Minnesota

R. W. Burchfield
Chief Editor, The Oxford
English Dictionaries and
Editor, *A Supplement to the
Oxford English Dictionary*

Frederic G. Cassidy
University of Wisconsin

Robert L. Chapman
Drew University

Audrey R. Duckert
University of Massachusetts

Matthew Marino
University of Alabama

Raven I. McDavid, Jr.
University of Chicago
University of South Carolina

Virginia McDavid
Chicago State University

Raymond K. O'Cain
University of South Carolina

Lee Pederson
Emory University

Mary Gray Porter
University of Alabama

DIALECTOLOGY

The *Linguistic Atlas of the Upper Midwest* as a Source of Sociolinguistic Information[1]

HAROLD B. ALLEN

When, nearly fifty years ago, Hans Kurath included a three-point social dimension in the selection of field informants for the Linguistic Atlas of New England, he provided a precedent that increasingly has brought to light significant social variation in American English.[2] The phonological analysis prepared for the third and final volume of the *Linguistic Atlas of the Upper Midwest,*[3] along with the treatment of the lexicon and the grammar in the first two volumes, now adds measurably to the sociolinguistic data available not only to dialectologists but also to students and teachers of usage, to textbook writers, and to sociolinguists themselves.

The *Linguistic Atlas of the Upper Midwest (LAUM)* covers the states of Minnesota, Iowa, North and South Dakota, and Nebraska. Its primary function, like that of other American regional dialect atlases now in process, is of course the presentation of regional differences in American English. But, also like the other atlases, it follows Kurath's lead in giving information about ascertained social differences as well. It specifies the social

range and sometimes even the register of many linguistic items:
lexical, grammatical, and phonological. The use of the term
"range" must not be overlooked. Although the data are presented as summarized frequencies with each of the three informant classes, they are not to be interpreted as absolute frequencies for the classes as such. A frequency distribution of,
say, 72% for the relatively uneducated speakers in Type I, of
22% for the better educated high school group of speakers in
Type II, and of 6% for the cultivated college group in Type
III means simply that there is a fairly sharp decline in the use
of a given item or form as one looks at people along the educational ladder, a ladder which at the time of the field work could
in the Upper Midwest be reasonably equated with the social
ladder.

Two important limitations, then, restrict the interpretation of
the data. First, the information is for a particular region, the
Upper Midwest, and hence is suggestive and not definitive with
respect to other sections of the country, where the distribution
might be quite different. It demonstrates principles and procedures only so far as other areas are concerned. Second, the
information was gathered at the midcentury point and hence for
at least certain items is not to be taken as reflecting the current
situation, more than a quarter of a century later. It may be noted,
furthermore, that the information is derived from interviews that
in themselves offer variation ranging from an occasional fairly
formal register to the usual informal and sometimes even casual
style. But the language reported is always living English, never
the edited variety analyzed in studies of the printed page.

Although within the 800-item corpus of the Upper Midwest
worksheets more attention is given specifically to the vocabulary,
the lexicon is not very significant in exhibiting social contrast.
The selection of vocabulary items was made primarily to reveal
differences in everyday words, not levels of personal lexical
choice. Yet even with this limitation some vocabulary matters do
manifest social range. For example, only a handful of the Type I
and Type II informants use bus or railroad *station* exclusively,
but 25% of those in Type III use only that word. Its prestige
is suggested by the informant who calls *depot* "improper," and

by another informant who during the interview corrected himself by saying "station" after he had first replied with "depot," and then commented, "That's the right word." "The sun *rose*" is preferred by all the college graduates and by 83% of the high school group but by a smaller 70% of the Type I informants, with the others choosing *came up*. A slightly higher proportion of the cultivated speakers select *dishcloth* (58%) and a corresponding proportion of the Type I's prefer *dishrag*. Of the 18 informants out of 208 who offer *widow woman* instead of simple *widow*, fourteen are in Type I, four in Type II, and none at all in the college-trained group III. *Relations* instead of *relatives* is preferred by 37% of the least educated, 18% of the high school group, and none of the Type III informants. More than one-third of the Type I speakers use *learn* in the sense of *teach*, but only a few Type II informants do, and none at all in Type III. It may be additionally noted that of the many colorful equivalents of *tired, vomit,* and *jilt,* nearly all are offered by Type I and Type II speakers and only a meager few by those in Type III.

But it is with respect to grammar and pronunciation that the *LAUM* field records are most revelatory of social contrast. Specifically, for more than half a century repeated educational research has found the irregular verbs to be the source of most of the so-called grammatical errors in the writing of school children. It is not surprising that they reveal the greatest social differences in the actual field investigations in the Upper Midwest. Nor is it surprising that, as the not infrequent total of more than 100% indicates, some informants are so insecure that they shift back and forth from one form to another.

Although textbooks and usage manuals usually posit a rather sharp division between the correct and incorrect, the acceptable and the inacceptable, in actual practice the contrast is rather one of varying frequency on a sliding scale or range. Three points on the range can be taken as summaries of sections of the range as a whole. Of the thirty-seven worksheet verb forms listed below, for example, only five are not used by at least one college graduate. Thirty-two of them are in use throughout the complete social range, though of course with increasing or decreasing frequency between one end of the range and the other. As social markers, they can be held significant, then, only insofar as they occur with other social markers. Neither the presence nor absence of a given form in the speech of one informant is sufficient evidence to categorize him as a Type I, II, or III speaker.

"He *come* yesterday," for example, though clearly the dominant choice of Type I informants with 75% frequency, still is used in the speech of nearly one-half of the high school group, and by a perhaps surprising 19% of the college-trained informants. Similarly with "He *run* into me," in which the base form *run* appears as a preterit in the speech of 65% of those in Type I, 36% in Type II, and even with 19% again in Type III. Likewise, *give* occurs in a past time context in "He *give* it to me yesterday" for most of the Type I informants but also with decreased incidence in the speech of those in Types II and III. The converse, a preterit form used as past participle, exhibits a similar range in the 59% frequency of "I've never *drove* a horse" among Type I speakers but only 19% among the college informants.

Even "He *done* it" does not turn out to be an entirely illiterate expression if language itself is not used as the criterion. One-fourth of the high school group has it along with one college-trained speaker.

Lie and *lay* are even less inclined to fit into the rigid dichotomy implied in textbook prescriptivism. The distant loss of any *Sprachgefühl* for the special sense and function of preterit causative verbs long ago led to such confusion that today it is a fifty-fifty chance whether an Upper Midwest college graduate will say "She *lay* in bed all morning" or "She *laid* in bed all morning." But Type I speakers are not in doubt as to which is the right form. Eighty-five percent of them are confident that it is *laid*. The infinitive is only slightly less a problem to the Type III informants, 81% of whom have the orthodox "I'm going to *lie* down." Of greater value as a social marker is the preterit of the simplex of the analogous verb pair, *sit* and *set*. Although more than one-third of the least educated speakers have *set* as the preterit in "Then they all *set* down," all but one of the Type III group have the standard "They *sat* down." The remaining verbs in the following list likewise offer evidence supporting the existence of a continuous range or continuum along which social contrast is to be measured.

Irregular verbs

	TYPE I %	TYPE II %	TYPE III %
bitten	45	81	68
climbed, *pret.*	73	86	100
clum	25	12	0
clim	9	1	0
come, *pret.*	75	41	19
did	57	81	94
done, *pret.*	63	27	6
drank, *ppl.*	92	78	47
drunk	8	27	60
driven	65	80	94
drove, *ppl.*	41	13	6
drownded, *ppl.*	29	8	0
give, *pret.*	52	19	13
gave	66	94	94
lie, *infin.*	60	70	81
lay = lie, *infin.*	52	40	19
laid, *pret.*	77	69	47
lay, *pret.*	15	28	53
ridden	48	82	81
rode, *ppl.*	59	21	19
ran	63	90	100
run, *pret.*	65	36	19
saw	73	82	87
see, *pret.*	42	27	13
sat	60	88	94
set = sat	37	15	6
swam	85	97	100
swum, *pret.*	18	5	0

(continued)

Continued from page 7.

	TYPE I %	TYPE II %	TYPE III %
tore, *ppl.*	42	26	7
torn	60	75	93
threw	77	94	100
throwed, *pret.*	31	9	6
awoke	6	20	19
wakened	6	6	25
woke (up)	84	73	56
written	79	92	100
wrote, *ppl.*	22	9	0

Several of the miscellaneous grammatical items recorded during the interviews provide more positive social markers than do the strong verbs. Concord with *be,* for example, is rigorously observed by the college informants. Not one of them favors the construction accepted by a majority of the Type I speakers, *we was* or *they was.* Nor did any of the college informants use *Here's* followed by a plural subject, such as *your clothes,* although most of the Type I speakers and more than one-half of the Type II's apparently treat *Here's* as an unchangeable formula to be used before either a singular or a plural noun in the predicate.

"I *ain't* going to" is likewise missing in the speech of the college group, although it is in the speech of one-fourth of the Type II's and of one-half of the least educated informants. "I *ain't* done it" is even more clearly a social marker, as it is not only abjured by informants in Type III and used by only nine percent of the high school Type II but is accepted as normal by more than one-third of the Type I's.

The controversial inverted negative interrogative of *be* offers a different picture. The historically normal phonetic development of *Am not I?* is *Ain't I?,* but the latter has acquired such a pejorative aura that in the Upper Midwest only nine percent of the Type III speakers will use it occasionally in contrast with 45% of the Type II informants and 63% of the Type I's. Conversely, two-thirds of the Type III informants use the stilted *Am I not?* in contrast with only 29% of the Type I speakers, while a surprising 27% of the college group take refuge in the bizarre and illogical *Aren't I?*—although none would seek such consistency as would exist if they should say "I are going too, aren't I?"

Third person *don't* is not so distinctive a social marker as usage manuals would imply. *He don't* is the customary locution not only for almost all the Type I informants and more than one-half of the Type II's but also for nearly one-half of the college-trained group. A similar social gradation appears in the distribution of *way* and *ways*. While *a long way* is preferred by twice as high a proportion of educated informants as by the least educated, the seeming plural *ways* (historically the adverbial genitive in -*es*) is the majority choice of all three types.

Still greater inconsistency appears in the contrast between two locutions in which a numeral precedes a modified noun. Only 15% of the Type I informants and a bare seven percent of the Type II's accept the locution *two pound,* as of flour or sugar; not one college graduate has it. But with the historically parallel *two bushel* the incidence in Type I rises to 62%. Nearly one-half of the Type II speakers have it, as do even 13% of the Type III's. The former is clearly a sharp though minor social marker; the latter, despite its being analogous, is only suggestively so.

Although in the somewhat unusual interview situation nearly one-half of the cultivated informants use the formal *It wasn't I* (preponderantly the female speakers), only 20% of the Type II informants have it, and only four percent of the Type I's. In all three types the majority say simply *It wasn't me.* When all three types are examined it appears that 80% of those who say *It wasn't I* are women. The relation of this fact to the current concern with sexism in language remains to be studied.

Two syntactic constructions with relative clauses yield variants providing rather sharp social contrast. In the non-restrictive relative clause modifying a noun with the + human feature, as "He's the man REL PRO...", more than three-fourths of the Type I speakers select *that,* as do nearly that many of the Type II's; but only one-fourth of the cultivated speakers choose it. Conversely, only one-fifth of Type I select *who,* but three-fourths of those in Type III have it. A minor social marker is the zero or omitted relative as subject, castigated in usage manuals, as in "He's the man brought the furniture." One-tenth of the least educated informants have this construction, as do two percent of the high school group, but none in Type III. The genitive relative pronoun bemuses one-half of the Type I informants. In the possible context "He's the boy whose father..." they replace *whose* with *that his* (30%) or *that the* (9%), or with simple *his* and no relative pronoun (9%). Each of the three minor variants is a clear social marker.

A well-known social contrast between *those* and *them* as adjectivals before a plural noun is expectedly attested in the Upper Midwest. *Those boys* is the only locution reported for the college group; *them boys* is used by 60% of the Type I informants and by 22% of the Type II's. Several additional social markers are listed in the following chart, where it is shown that these language matters as well occur with greater frequency in the speech of the least educated: *poison* as a predicate modifier in "Some berries are poison;" *sick at the stomach* and *sick in the stomach; in back of* (the door); *died with* rather than *died from,* and *towards* and *toward.* When in the following chart percentages total more than 100, the indication is simply that an informant uses more than one form.

Grammar miscellany

	TYPE I	TYPE II	TYPE III
We/they was	60%	30%	0
We/they were	53	76	100
Here are N PL	24	49	100
Here's N PL	81	59	0
I ain't going to	46	26	0
I'm not going to	58	83	100
Ain't I?	63	45	9
Am I not?	29	45	64
Aren't I?	5	15	27

(continued)

Continued from page 10.

	Type I	Type II	Type III
I haven't done it	72	97	100
I ain't done it	38	9	0
He doesn't	26	51	77
He don't	88	60	46
a long) way	24	30	47
a long) ways	86	82	73
two) bushel	62	49	13
two) bushels	43	52	87
two) pound	15	7	0
two) pounds	89	94	100
He's the man that...	77	65	27
He's the man who...	19	42	73
He's the man 0	10	2	0
He's a boy whose father...	49	79	87
He's a boy that his father...	30	11	7
He's a boy that the father...	9	5	0
He's a boy his father...	9	5	7
Some berries are poisonous	47	67	93
Some berries are poison	55	32	7
those boys	61	90	100
them boys	60	22	0
sick at the stomach	32	26	13
sick in the stomach	13	3	0
sick to the stomach	52	68	94
back of (the door	26	27	31
in back of (the door	8	7	0
behind	71	73	75
toward	40	54	100
towards	63	48	0
died from	31	33	44
died of	45	59	63
died with	29	8	0

Although certain gross matters of pronunciation have sometimes been labeled "incorrect" in the schools, the three-point social range investigated in dialect research provides a sounder description of the social contrasts discernible in phonological variation. While most of the phonological differences revealed in the field records of the Upper Midwest survey are only regionally significant, a number manifest social contrast as well. They occur in several categories.

Stress variation exhibits social correlation in a few words. Among Type I and Type II informants, for instance, the proportion favoring initial stress in the verb *address* is twice as high as among those in Type III. Nearly one-half of the least educated speakers have initial stress in *umbrella,* but only one-fifth of the college group do. One-fourth of the Type I's have primary or secondary stress on the second syllable of *theater,* but only 6% of the Type III's. A conspicuous example is the pronunciation of *genuine.* The least educated speakers strongly favor heavy stress on the final syllable; the cultivated speakers favor zero stress, with corresponding reduction of the vowel to /ɪ/. A similar contrast occurs with *guardian,* with 34% of the Type I informants favoring /gɑrdín/ while all the cultivated speakers have /gárdìən/.

Stress variation

		TYPE I	TYPE II	TYPE III
address, *vb*.	/ǽdrès/	26%	25%	11%
genuine	/jɛ́nyuɪn/	17	47	86
	/jɛ́nyuwàɪn/	83	54	14
guardian	/gɑ̀rdín/	34	15	0
theater	/θí-êtɚ/	23	8	6
	/θìətɚ/	64	78	63
	/θɪətɚ/	13	14	31
umbrella	/ə́mbrèlə/	44	24	19

Vowel variation may create social markers. *LAUM* reports that the pronunciation of *root* as /rut/, although accepted by one-third of the Type I and Type II speakers, is preferred over /rʊt/ by only 13% of the college group. The same checked vowel /ʊ/ in *soot* is the choice of one-half of the least educated speakers but by nine out of ten of the Type III's. None of the latter group has the pronunciation /sət/, the choice of one-third of the Type I speakers. A few of the Type I's have adopted what must be a spelling pronunciation, /sut/. Two variants of *yolk,* /yɛlk/ and /yʊlk/, are favored by Type I speakers over the customary /yok/. The pronunciation /rɛdɪš/ is normal for one-third of the least educated but rare among college-trained speakers. The form /kæg/ for *keg* is a minor social marker, with 15% preference in Type I and no use at all by Type III's. In Minnesota and North Dakota /ɑnt/ and /ænt/ have become social markers, with the former pronunciation of *aunt* preferred by 32% of the Type III speakers and even by 15% of those in Type I. And for speakers stressing the first syllable in *theater* there is a choice of free and checked vowels. More common is /i/, but twice as high a proportion of Type III's selected checked

Vowel variation

		TYPE I	TYPE II	TYPE III
aunt	/ɑnt/	15%	21%	32%
keg	/kæg/	16	5	0
radish	/rɛdɪš/	33	22	6
root	/rut/	33	35	13
	/rʊt/	76	66	87
soot	/sut/	18	8	13
	/sʊt/	51	73	88
	/sət/	34	18	0
yolk	/yɛlk/ } /yʊlk/	31	19	6

/ɪ/, a pronunciation apparently associated by these informants with the French and British spelling *theatre.*

Even an unstressed vowel in terminal position manifests socially correlated variations. All the college-educated informants have final /o/ in *minnow* (excepting one with /u/), but the folk speech /mɪni/ is found in the speech of one-fourth of the Type I's. A few of them also have the variant with final /u/. For *meadow* and *widow* a pronunciation with final /ə/ is a minor social marker; for *tomato* it is much more significant, with its use by more than one-half of the Type I speakers.

Terminal reduction Vowel

		TYPE I	TYPE II	TYPE III
meadow	/mɛdo/	78%	93%	92%
	/mɛdə/	14	2	0
	/mɛdu/	9	8	8
minnow	/mɪni/	25	12	0
	/mɪno/	67	83	100
	/mɪnu/	10	12	6
tomato	/təméto/	46	62	73
	/təmétə/	54	38	27
widow	/wɪdo/	55	71	82
	/wɪdə/	14	4	0
	/wɪdu/	30	25	18

An apparent epenthetic or anaptyctic vowel exhibits social contrast. It seems to be induced by initial stress in *umbrella,* for the same speakers have both, nearly always in Type I. A similar vowel in *mushroom,* however, is actually historical, as the French etymon is *mousseron* and orthographic variants with medial *e* have persisted since the early 15th century. It is preserved in the speech of one-fourth of the least educated informants, but is rare in the speech of the others. Incidentally, a final

n instead of *m*, likewise historical, is also preserved largely by
Type I speakers, 55% of whom have it beside only 20% of the
college group. Another example of the epenthetic schwa may
actually be a reduced form of the pronoun *it*. For the injunction
Look here! 42% of the Type I speakers have either /lʊkəhir/ or
/lʊkɨthir/, with the incidence dropping to one-third in Type II
and only 14% in Type III.

A nonhistorical excrescent /t/ is a sharp social feature. It
occurs after /s/, with 26% of the Type I informants and 14% of
the Type II's adding it to *once* and *across* (but no college graduates), and after /f/, with 18% of the Type I informants and eight
percent of the Type II's adding it to *skiff, cliff,* or *trough* (but no
college graduates).

Although replacement of terminal velar /ŋ/ by alveolar /n/
is common in the verbal ending *ing*, its presence in the words
nothing and *something* is much more definitely of social significance. More than one-third of the Type I's say /nɔ́θɨn/ but
only 6% of the Type III's. One-fourth of the Type I's say
/sɔ́mθɨn/ or the assimilated form /sɔ́mpʔm/, but only 13% of
the Type III's.

Addition and replacement

Look here!		TYPE I	TYPE II	TYPE III
Look here!	/lʊkəhɪr/ /lʊkɨhɪr/ /lʊkɨthɪr/	42%	33%	14%
mushroom	/mɔ́šrum/	46	75	87
	/mɔ́šrun/	55	23	20
	/mɔ́šərun/	23	9	6
nothing	/nɔ́θɨn/	35	17	6
something	/sɔ́mθɨn, sɔ́mpʔm/	25	20	13
umbrella	/ɔ́mbərɛ̀lə/	44	24	19

The historical tendency toward the reduction or simplification
of consonant clusters manifests itself with greater strength among

the uneducated, except perhaps for the initial cluster /hw/.
There the unaspirated variant /w/ is becoming more acceptable
to many speakers in Types II and III, as in *wheel, whetstone,
white,* and *whip,* though apparently not in *wheat.* Generally
Upper Midwest speakers seem to retain initial /h/, especially
in Minnesota and North Dakota. But the initial cluster /hy/ has
been reduced to simple /y/ for more than one-half of the Type I
informants, largely in Iowa and Nebraska, and for one-fifth of the
college group.

The final *sts* cluster in several words tends to be retained by
cultivated speakers. *Fists,* for instance, is /fɪs·/ or /fɪs·t/ for
75% of the Type I speakers but for only 44% of the Type III's.
In two words, *library* and *secretary,* simplification may have been
reinforced by the tendency toward dissimilation. *Library* is simply
/laibɛri/ for 28% of the Type I informants but for only 12% of
the Type III's; and *secretary* is /sɛkɨtɛri/ for 57% of the Type
I speakers, and for more than one-fourth of the Type II's, but for
only six percent of the Type III's. The cluster /nd/ in *hundred*
is reduced to /n/ in the pronunciation /hə́nəˑd/ recorded in
the speech of 18% of the Type I and 15% of the Type II informants. No Type III informant was heard to use it.

Cluster simplification

		TYPE I	TYPE II	TYPE III
fists	/fɪsts/	28	44	56
	/fɪs·t/	19	5	13
	/fɪs·/	56	13	31
humor	/yumɚ/	54	29	20
	/hyumɚ/	43	70	80
hundred	/hə́nəˑd/	18	15	0
library	/laibrɛri/	70	75	94
	/laibɛri/	28	21	12
secretary	/sɛkrɨtɛri/	39	74	94
	/sɛkɨtɛri/	57	27	6

Spelling pronunciation, the use of the visual form as a guide to the oral form, does not always result from the same factors in yielding a social contrast. The school emphasis upon spelling as the criterion may cause a change in the pronunciation of a familiar word, or sudden encounter with an unfamiliar word may lead to a plausible but nonhistorical pronunciation.

Of the several notable instances in *LAUM*, one, the pronunciation of *mongrel* with visually-suggested /ɑ/ rather than the historical /ə/ otherwise accepted unquestioningly in such words as *money, monkey*, and *wonder*, is usual among college graduates but chosen by but not much more than one-half of the less educated informants. But other examples of spelling pronunciation illustrate a readier acceptance of spelling as a guide by folk speakers. Although one-half of the college informants are sufficiently bemused by the *phth* combination in *diphtheria* to pronounce the obvious first letter and overlook the second, 95% of the Type I informants accept the same solution to the problem with the pronunciation of the first syllable as simple /dɪp/. Nearly one-half of the least educated follow analogous *earth* in their pronunciation of *hearth;* only seven percent of Type III do. One-fourth of the Type I informants have a spelling pronunciation of *palm* with the voiced /l/; only seven percent of the college speakers do. Nearly one-fourth of the Type I's have /s/ in *raspberries* instead of /z/; none of the college informants does.

Spelling pronunciation

		Type I	Type II	Type III
diphtheria	/dɪfθɪryə/	5	18	50
	/dɪpθɪryə/	95	82	50
hearth	/hɚθ/	44	26	7
mongrel	/mɔ́ŋgrəl/	43	31	18
	/mɑ́ŋgrəl/	57	69	82
palm	/pɑlm/	25	29	7

Although too sporadic to be relied upon as social markers, a number of aberrant pronunciations appear almost exclusively in the speech of Type I informants and hence do have some value in supporting social categorization. One is the pronunciation /čímbli/ for *chimney;* another is the use of the affricate in either /rınč/ or /rɛnč/ for *rinse.* Two lisped pronunciations of /θ/ occur as /f/ in /drauf/ for *drouth* and in /mæfyu/ for *Matthew.* And the Midland preterit or participial ending /t/ rather than /d/ is preserved almost entirely by Type I informants in their versions of *boiled, spoiled,* and *scared.*

Sociologists have quite ignored such data as this article presents in their various attempts to define social classes and subclasses by means of educational and socioeconomic criterions. Sociolinguists have neglected the rich source of relevant data in linguistic atlas field records. In the teaching of English little attention has been placed upon this kind of information. But perhaps now the more readily accessible facts in *LAUM* will be found useful by them in their studies of social mobility and their sometimes imperfect recognition of a range or dimension rather than neatly tiered social classes and usage levels.

NOTES

1. This is a revised version of a paper orally presented at the regional meeting of the American Dialect Society in St. Louis, Missouri, November 4, 1976.

2. Although Jakob Jud and Karl Jaberg had incidentally included a few informants from different social classes in their *Sprach und Sachatlas Italiens und der Südschweiss* (1928–1940), Kurath was the first dialectologist to build social range into a systematically surveyed population of a dialect project. As early as 1948 Raven I. McDavid, Jr., drew attention to the significance of the resulting social data for the social scientist. Observation of social contrast appeared in Kurath's *Word Geography of the Eastern United States* (1949) and in his and McDavid's *Pronunciation of English in the Atlantic States* (1961), although it was not detailed and quantified. More detailed statements are in E. Bagby Atwood's *Survey of Verb Forms in the Eastern United States* (1958), a study subsequently extended in two University of Minnesota dissertations by Virginia Glenn McDavid in 1954 (Verb Forms of the North Central

States and Upper Midwest) and Jean Malmstrom in 1958 (A Study of the Validity of Textbook Statements about Certain Controversial Grammatical Items in the Light of Evidence from the Linguistic Atlas).
    3. Harold B. Allen. *The Linguistic Atlas of the Upper Midwest.* Volume 1: *Handbook and Lexicon,* 1973. Volume 2: *Grammar,* 1975. Volume 3: *Pronunciation,* 1976. Minneapolis, Minnesota: University of Minnesota Press.

The Winds of Change[1]

AUDREY R. DUCKERT

It was one hundred years ago, in 1876, that Georg Wenker sent his set of forty sentences to some 40,000 German schoolmasters, asking them to transcribe the literary language in which they were written into the local dialect. It was eighty years ago, in 1896, that the last of the nine parts that formed volume I of *Dialect Notes* was published. And it was forty-five years ago, in the early fall of 1931, that the fieldworkers for the Linguistic Atlas of New England project began the first extensive survey of American English. Though the first fieldworkers for the Dictionary of American Regional English project took off in their word-wagons in 1965, the pilot work on the questionnaire and fieldwork began as the Wisconsin English Language Survey in 1949—25 years ago.

Anniversaries, anniversaries—of passing interest in themselves, but what do they really mark? The results of these projects and of the many other related ones continue to appear; the hundredth birthday of the American Dialect Society in 1989 will surely witness great wealth.

A look through the "wrong" end of the telescope may be revealing. The apocryphal story has it that as Gertrude Stein lay dying, the faithful Alice B. Toklas asked her, "Gertrude, Gertrude, what is the answer?" and that Gertrude Stein's last enigmatic words were, "What is the question?"

"What is the question?" is indeed a good question. Dialectologists are fond of saying that the time to make the questions is when the survey is complete and it has become clear at last what should have been asked and how. *Dialect Notes*, Vol. I, Pt. 1, published in Boston in 1890, the year after the ADS was founded, contained three articles of collected material: "New

England Pronunciations in Ohio," "Contributions to the New England Vocabulary," and "Various Contributions,"—all of them collections of observed usages and pronunciations, sometimes followed by bracketed remarks from the editor, E. S. Sheldon, who obviously couldn't resist. In his role as Secretary of the Society, Professor Sheldon contributed a "Plan of Work" to the same volume, with an early version of the International Phonetic Alphabet and instructions for collecting vocabulary in which one reads this startling sentence: "Many school-teachers might contribute lists of words and phrases which they perhaps have to teach their pupils not to use."[2]

Children of our times that we all are, we will have to look forward to being held by our own successors to be quaint, outdated, or even wrong-headed. Let us then be charitable to our predecessors who worked in the beginning without the refined version of the IPA, and who, until the transistor was put into practical use in the 1950s, had recording equipment that was either incredibly cumbersome or nonexistent. Like Dorcas, they did what they could—and so do we. What follows here is a series of observations, not a critique. Taking Georg Wenker to task for lacking the sophistication of Hans Kurath would be a bit like scolding Beethoven for not getting a hearing aid.

To keep these remarks finite, begin with the *Linguistic Atlas of New England*[3] (hereafter *LANE*), the first systematic survey of American English on an extensive and intensive basis. The fieldworkers were provided with worksheets rather than questionnaires; they knew which terms they were to elicit and were more or less left to choose the best framework, the best way to get the response.[4]

Relics and disappearances

Like dictionaries, questionnaires are perforce derivative and will continue to be; but like all good dictionaries, they must reflect life—the dictionary that of the living language, the questionnaire that of the language-livers. Some of the terms investigated by the New England *Atlas* are now simply out of public ken, no matter what the region or who the speaker; *LANE cog wheel* (map 158), *dairy* (map 107), didn't yield well even in the 30s, and though many informants then knew the terms *off* and *nigh* in relation to horses and oxen (map 175), fewer knew which was which. In the early 50s, a rural Wisconsin informant wrote: "I wouldn't know him from *Adam's all fox.*" It is possible that the current oil crisis may bring a return to the *woodbox* and *lid-lifters* and *warming ovens*, but the once-productive variants of *coal hod/scuttle/bucket/pail* are unlikely ever again to be familiar words. The questionnaire that was, after revisions, ultimately to serve as the information base for the Dictionary of American Regional English (hereafter DARE) is not free of regional, cultural, or temporal bias.[5] There are still too many cows in it, and not enough street smarts. But this may not be all bad—farm talk has a way of holding its own; it is deep in the American vocabulary, in proverbs and speech figures that may be used by speakers with little idea of the appearance or nature of the source: to *kick over the traces, thresh* out a problem, *make hay,* be part of a *peck(ing) order* are a few examples.

Fieldworkers are likely to seek out the oldest speakers in a community, and this gives rise to the myth that dialectology is the study of quaint, old-fashioned, unusual speech. Not so, not so. The older speakers, their words and sounds are sought most earnestly because they are the landmarks (or, better, the sound-marks) in the history of the language. Still, it may be a mistake to assume we will have speakers now in middle age with us long enough so that we can collect their speech when they are retired and have the time to talk to us.

Ladies' Day

The effect, or non-effect, of attempts by some of the more strident feminists to change the English language is beyond the scope of these words; the dialectologist is concerned with natural variations and changes in the language, not with artificial ones. Still there is no denying that certain features strike the current reader of *LANE* and its *Handbook*[6] that might not have been so conspicuous in 1943. The suggested phrasings in the worksheets are generally masculine in tone, from eliciting the ordinal nu-

merals: 1.6 (maps 62−63) the first (*man,* the second (*man* ... to
103.6 (map 713) I haven't seen *him*) since Monday and 103.7
(map 719) *He* did it) on purpose. The feminine ones are cul-
turally dictated and natural: 25.1 (map 357) Here are your clothes
[*mother* to child], 26.7 (map 457) *She* has a) prettier (dress;
though 74 offers: *She* is) quite lively... , *She*) didn't use to...
and *She's* too) slovenly (for me... In all fairness, let it be observed that both *my husband* and *my wife* are elicited in the
context "I must ask..." (63.1 (map 374), 63.2 (map 375). We can
never know whether or how much the dominance of masculine
examples influenced the responses; chances are, the influence
was minimal because the questions were put in a natural way to
people who were far less pronoun-conscious than we. An interesting adventure might be to determine whether there are in the
49 field records done by Rachel Harris or the 13 done by Mar-
guerite Chapallaz any characteristics that do not appear in those
done by the men. But that must wait for another occasion.[7] The
Women's Movement might be unhappy with the clearly male
orientation of suggested phrasing in the *LANE* worksheets, but
let it be remembered that 124 of the 416 *Atlas* informants were
women whereas only three of the 75 Guy Lowman interviewed
for the South of England Survey were.

The passing of certain taboos

The common speech of the 1970s evidences a much more explicit and less self-conscious vocabulary in the area of sex,
though it has tighter restrictions on the use of racial and religious
slurs. *LANE* sought for *bull, stallion, ram,* and *boar* three categories of response: those used by farmers, those used in the
presence of women, and those used by women themselves.
Rachel Harris's customary way of getting the *bull* terms was to
ask about the "animal that is cross and goes for you if you wear
red."[8] Lee Pederson, in the Linguistic Atlas of the Gulf States
survey a generation later seeking words for *stallion,* asked:
"Years ago did women use that word? Would men say it in the
presence of women? [If not] what did they say?"[9] His context
of time past is telling and true. The first version of what ul-

timately became the DARE questionnaire was markedly pure in heart, but not because its authors were prudish or unaware. The Wisconsin English Language Survey (WELS), which served as a pilot operation and field trial for DARE, was conducted by mail, answered by 50 informants throughout the state, most of whom stuck with it for the entire 1800-item questionnaire. It was not until the follow-up interviews were conducted by F. G. Cassidy that there was any direct personal contact with the informants, which meant that the confidentiality a fieldworker can often establish was missing. Questions about male domestic animals were asked much in the style of *LANE;* also included were questions about castration and udders. On the human side there were questions on illegitimacy, shotgun weddings, the outhouse, and the chamber pot—but that was as far as it went. And perhaps that's as far as it could go, given the context of a mailed questionnaire being sent out in Wisconsin during the period when the late Senator Joe McCarthy was riding his roughest. The question of how much a scholar really needs to know is a difficult one. In the atmosphere of the early 50s, it certainly seemed reasonable to omit a handful of somewhat delicate questions rather than offend informants or risk having the entire project purged by an anti-intellectual "crusader." (One wonders, by the way, considering the taboos, why they seem to cleave to the male; why, e.g., a woman who could speak bluntly about a cow's *bag* or a clogged *tit* referred to a bull as "the animal.")

The final DARE questionnaire, which will be published along with the dictionary, has forthright questions on menstruation, homosexuals, and female breasts.[10] But there remains a gray area, one we shall probably never define precisely. Where does dialect stop and slang begin? If obscenities vary regionally and diachronically, are they also dialect?

Meanwhile, the euphemisms of one generation become the taboos of the next. The *insane asylum,* literally a safe place for the not-well, became a snake-pit and was replaced by *sanitarium* (if private) or a new euphemism like "mental health care center" (if public). And so it was perhaps inevitable that an overheard conversation between two women talking about a third who was in just such a place went, in part: "Oh! I never thought *she* was the kind of person to have mental health.'' It might be noted that questionnaires deal gingerly with these matters. Over and over the original WELS questionnaire uses the words "joking words for" intended not to collect humor but to release the informant from attributing to himself serious use of terms like *nut-house* or *booby-hatch*.

Innovations

Most of the terms just dealt with changed because attitudes did; now for a few Wörter und Sachen concerns. When *LANE* was in the making, ice cream was still a special treat, often home-made and hand-cranked for summertime family reunions; 45 years later, variants like *cabinet, frappe, frosted, milkshake,* and *velvet* are widespread for a mixture of ice cream, milk, and flavoring. *Milkshake* now bids fair to take over nationally, but there is still enough diachronic and synchronic evidence to make it includible in future questionnaires.

The language changes; the variation remains. *LANE* dealt in *buggy-shafts/shavs/fills/thills;* its successors deal in *rotaries/traffic circles/circuses.* As the *thank-you-ma'am* fades, the *speedbump* emerges; and instead of worrying about *mud-time,* travellers are concerned with winter roads becoming *slippery/slick/greasy.* There are some important distinctions among the comings and goings. (1) Diachronic variation on a linguistic level only—the designatum remains essentially the same. A *riddle* becomes a *sieve* or a *collander;* a *foot-feed* becomes an *accelerator; infantile paralysis* becomes *polio(myelitis).* In the area of medicine, some of this seems to involve the introduction of more clinical-sounding and therefore perhaps less threatening or personal terms—a kind of euphemism by distance. Thus: *quinsy sore throat > peritonsillar abscess; St. Vitus dance > chorea; the shingles > herpes.*[11] (2) The designatum changes in ways that may seem to call for a new name, but retains its basic place, function, or purpose: *ice chest/ice box > refrigerator/fridge; radio, victrola > hi-fi, stereo.* (3) The designatum becomes a fly-in-amber because it is increasingly less a part of everyday life; its once-variant terms recede with it: *slop pail/orts pail/swill pail* (or *bucket*) are simply going out. (4) In the trickiest and meanest

of all, the unqualified designans remains the same and the designatum changes markedly. This has been going on for a long time.
Engine currently implies an internal combustion engine, not the
kind of device the Lilliputians used to move Gulliver; a *truck*
now has wheels and a motor; a *tire* is made of rubber, not metal;
a *lamp* is powered by electricity. All of these changes come into
the ken of the dialectologist, all must be kept up with; but since
they are relatively tangible, they can be explained.

Another kind of change, harder to chronicle, is a shift in awareness or perception in the users of the language which then reflects
itself in usage. A basic one is surfacing in weather terms, especially but not only among city dwellers. This may be one area
in which the often-predicted leveling of dialects with the on-
slaught of mass communications may be taking place. Pandemic
preoccupation with the weather means that most people watch or
listen to forecasts and hear and then use the likes of *Bermuda
high, cold Canadian air mass, thunder showers, snow flurries* . . .
and out the window go *muggy days, cold snaps, electrical storms*
(or the even older *tempests*), and the first *skift of snow*. A second
factor in weather word changes is the limited amount of personal
observation. The old-time farmer traditionally stepped out the
door at bed-time to check the sky; his grandson gets the word on
television, or he may look out the window of his city apartment
to see what the signal on the John Hancock tower is flashing.
His days may be spent in a windowless place, and a word like
lowery, so aptly descriptive of a dark and ominous sky that could
yield up almost anything—including evil spirits—is one he will
not use or know, any more than he can smell the coming of the
snow or feel the give of *limber ice.*

Weather-talk may be an exception, for the reasons just noted,
to the general persistence of regional and diachronic variation in
American English. It may be that, or it may be a portent; the
less man experiences directly, the more likely he is to adopt some
form of the language of those who inform him about what his
grandfather used to know at first hand.

For the moment, however, the winds of change blow variably
and from interesting directions; they bring and take, and the rest-
less evidence they bear is also the reason dialectology is perhaps
the liveliest of the linguistic arts.

NOTES

1. That James B. McMillan is seventy years old seems impossible, but since it is merely a chronological fact having little to do with who and what the man is, let it be noted. The occasion it has provided is a happy one. Many of the changes sung and rung have taken place during Professor McMillan's long and distinguished career, and he has played an active role in more than one.

2. *Dialect Notes* I, Part I, p. 25.

3. The *Linguistic Atlas of New England* (ed. Hans Kurath, et al. Providence, R.I.; American Council of Learned Societies, 1939–43) *passim.*

4. For specifics on elicitation methods used in *LANE* and later Atlas projects, see *A Manual for Dialect Research in the Southern States* (2d. ed., ed. Lee Pederson, Raven I. McDavid, Jr., Charles W. Foster, and Charles E. Billiard. University, Alabama: University of Alabama Press, 1974) pp. 35–60, 99–208 *passim.* (Hereafter cited as *MDR*).

5. The first published version of the questionnaire, revised from the one used in the Wisconsin Survey, appeared in 1953 in F. G. Cassidy with A. R. Duckert, *A Method for Collecting Dialect,* in *Publication of the American Dialect Society,* No. 20.

6. *Handbook of the Linguistic Geography of New England* (ed. Hans Kurath et al., 2d ed., New York: AMS Press, 1973) *passim.*

7. Julia Bloch, though she made no field records, was, of course, closely connected with *LANE* and its editing. Dialectology has always been hospitable to women scholars, and three women's names appear among the original 158 in *DN* I.

8. *MDR,* p. 134.

9. *MDR,* p. 135.

10. A functionary in the office of the U.S. Office of Education, which provided some of DARE's early funding, objected to the field questionnaire having the possible responses to the question on breasts printed in it; so, in 1965, several hours were spent blacking out the offending terms. This, of course, had the net result of drawing more attention to the question as it appears on the page, and Mrs. Grundy wins a pyrrhic victory.

11. The common symbol for an obsolete or obsolescent form, +, does not appear to have a common corollary to indicate an innovation. A request for suggestions from a class brought several, two of which may have possibilities. one is ⌒, a stylized sunrise, if you will; the other is ⼂ a modification of the +.

"Existential" *there* and *it:* An Essay on Method and Interpretation of data

RAVEN I. McDAVID, Jr., AND RAYMOND K. O'CAIN

I

Whatever road one sets out to follow in attempting to explore the English language, he is likely to find that Jim McMillan has been there before him. Jim learned serious objective linguistics at Chicago under Leonard Bloomfield, and an awareness of the perils of challenging those who lack such objectivity. He was a working lexicographer on the *Dictionary of American English,* under the eyes of Sir William Craigie and James Hulbert, and in the company of such good men as Woodford Heflin and Allen Walker Read. He explored the potentialities of instrumental phonetics as a means of resolving phonological questions. He has read widely and deeply in works dealing with the English language, and has assembled an exhaustive and indispensable bibliography of Southern American English—of which his own doctoral dissertation is one of the early landmarks. He has done as much as any teacher to develop a new generation of competent scholars, and has generously collaborated with professional colleagues and their students—always insisting that there is no substitute for objective data, honestly recorded. This little offering in his honor owes much to all these aspects of his career, touching as it does on a subject where there has often been a dearth of light and a plethora of heat.

II

One of the troublesome details of idiomatic English syntax is the inverted sentence with an empty *there* preverbal, in the normal subject position. Observers have frequently noted two variants of this construction: (1) *there* may become indistinguishable from the third person plural nominative pronoun, so that *there are* and *they are* become homonymous;[1] (2) *there* may be replaced by *it*, yielding such sentences as *it's lots of beer in the refrigerator.* In some sociolinguistic investigations, those who lack day-to-day familiarity with these alternatives—who have not grown up in communities where these are common—are likely to label them as characteristic of, or even restricted to, specific social groups. It is the purpose of this paper to show the recorded distribution of these variants along the Atlantic Seaboard, and to suggest an explanation of this distribution. The materials under consideration are the field records for the *Linguistic Atlas of New England* (1939–43; reprinted 1972), and the *Linguistic Atlas of the Middle and South Atlantic States* (editing in progress). The presentation is descriptive, not polemic; those who have encountered other interpretations are welcome to draw their own conclusions from the data as presented.

III

Although the methods of the American regional linguistic atlases have been frequently described, a little redundancy is not out of place, since many students of American English are not as familiar with these projects as they should be.[2] Like their predecessors in Germany, France and Italy, these atlases are part of historical linguistics. They aim to provide a body of data against which earlier observations of regional speech may be measured, from which historical comparisons may be drawn, and by which the development of new dialect patterns, as in urban areas, may be interpreted.[3] In other words, their purpose is not to solve, but to provide a basis for solutions; they do not constitute a hypothesis but a method of investigation, though the data assembled

will permit the making of hypotheses about particular details of
the language. They are not committed in advance to any interpretation of any aspect of the language, as used by any social
group; their purpose is to present the evidence and let the conclusions be what they may.

The methods of inquiry are basically those as set forth by Jules
Gilliéron for the *Atlas linguistique de la France* (1902–1910):

1. A selection of communities for study, somewhat biased in
the direction of rural and small-town communities, as most likely
to preserve the older forms of the language, but (an innovation of
American investigations) generously sampling urban areas as
well.

2. A selection of representative local informants, with as many
generations of family residence as possible. The informants are of
three basic types: (1) old and uneducated (2) moderately sophisti-
cated (3) cultivated. Again, the first type is over-represented from
a purely statistical point of view, in order to get as much as
possible of the older type of usage. The inclusion of the two other
types is an innovation in American dialectology; the European
atlases have largely restricted themselves to the first type, as the
only true speakers of "dialect," and some European observers
have felt that American atlases have erred in not so restricting
their coverage.[4]

3. A questionnaire of specific items of pronunciation, vocabulary and grammar, familiar to most informants interviewed, easy
to introduce into a conversational situation and known or sus-
pected to have significant regional or social variants. Again, the
historical purpose of the investigation is reflected in a bias toward
rural and small-town life and an emphasis on older ways of living.

4. Trained investigators.

5. Interviewing in situations familiar to the informants.

6. Presentation of the responses in finely graded phonetic notation. Down to the early 1950s the transcription was customarily
made as the interview progressed; more recently, the interviews
have been recorded on tape and the transcriptions made at a later
time—often by someone other than the interviewer. The use of
tape recordings has both advantages and disadvantages.

IV

In all interviews along the Atlantic Seaboard—some 400 in New England, 1200 in the Middle and South Atlantic States—investigators were instructed to seek responses of the type *there are/there is/there's* (lots of them). In addition, they often—though not invariably—recorded other occurrences of introductory *there* in free conversation. The difference is especially noticeable between the two principal investigators for the Middle and South Atlantic States, Guy S. Lowman, Jr., who conducted some eight hundred interviews (in addition to 158 in New England) and Raven I. McDavid, Jr., who conducted some three hundred. Lowman's interviews were fairly direct, held closely to the items in the questionnaire, contained relatively few items from free conversation, and rarely skipped an item; McDavid's were more discursive, often exploratory of matters of local cultural interest, contained a very large number of conversational responses, but often omitted syntactic items rather than suggest or force a response. For items like the one examined here, the two styles of interviewing must be taken into account. In addition, McDavid transcribed from tapes some fifty interviews conducted by other investigators; this experience provides a basis for comparing the older and the more recent types of interviewing.

In examining the responses, the original plan was to include only replacement of *there* by *they* or *it*. However, the frequency with which the pronunciation /ði/ occurred, especially in New England, led to the inclusion of this variant. Other variants, however, were set aside, including replacement of *there* by zero. What patterns these other variants may show are left to future investigators.

It is recognized that there is a wide range of phonic variation in the syllabic of such words as *there* when the syllabic is followed by consonantal [-r], vocalic [-ɚ] or [-ə]. Furthermore, in weak-stressed pronunciations, the syllabic of *there* may be [ɚ, ə, ɪ]. All such variant pronunciations were set asied; the study is limited to stressed forms of *there,* with unequivocal /e/ or /i/.

Finally, all examples suggested, forced, or reported as heard from others have been disregarded. Only direct or conversational responses were included. However, responses which informants consider old-fashioned but normally use were included, as representing an aspect of natural usage.

These precautions may not remove all danger of misinterpreting the data. But they do suggest that the variants studied are at least as common in the areas investigated as the field records would indicate.[5]

V

The distribution of the variants examined is shown on the accompanying maps.

In New England (Map 1) /ðe/ is common in Vermont and on Cape Cod, and moderately common in the Berkshire area of western Massachusetts. There is a small clustering in western Connecticut (but no occurrences in Fairfield County, New York City commuting territory), another in York County, Maine, and scattered examples in eastern Massachusetts and northern Maine. It is not found on Long Island, in New Hampshire, or in Rhode Island, though there is one occurrence on the Massachusetts side of Narragansett Bay. In contrast, /ði/ is restricted to northeastern New England, especially Maine, except for one occurrence in the Edgartown area of Martha's Vineyard.

In the Middle and South Atlantic States (Map 2) /ðe/ is very common in South Carolina and Georgia, somewhat less common in Upstate New York. There is a small clustering in northwestern North Carolina, another in eastern North Carolina, still another in eastern Kentucky.[6] It is not found in the Hudson Valley, New Jersey, Maryland, Delaware, the Northern Neck of Virginia, the Shenandoah Valley, southwestern Virginia, eastern Ohio, or Pennsylvania outside the strip of Yankee settlement; and there is but one occurrence in West Virginia. There are only seven occurrences of /ði/: five scattered across Virginia, one in the Erie "chimney" of northwestern Pennsylvania, and one in southeastern North Carolina. *It*, not found in New England, is used by a majority of the informants on Maryland's Eastern Shore, and by over a third of those in West Virginia. There is a generous scattering in the Coastal Plain and Piedmont, from Baltimore to the Neuse. There are five examples in Georgia, four in Pennsylvania (three of them near the West Virginia line), four in eastern Ohio opposite West Virginia, one in New Jersey, one in South Carolina, and one in Florida.

VI

Since these variants are popularly associated with uneducated speech, they are predictably rare in the usage of the cultivated. But there are examples of all three forms in the speech of educated informants, especially in the South. Nor is there any pronounced racial patterning where black and white informants were interviewed in the same community. Occasionally it is the black informant who has the variant, but in one community—Somerset County, on Maryland's Eastern Shore—both whites have *it* and the uneducated black has only *there,* with neither of the pronunciation variants in question.

VII

The problem of origins of these variants must remain, at present, in the speculative stage. For Lowman's wide-meshed survey of Southern England (1937–8), Kurath omitted *there are/there is/ there's* from the questionnaire; it is also lacking in the Dieth-Orton *Questionnaire* for the *Survey of English Dialects* (1962–71). Nor is there any evidence on /ðe, ði/ in the *Oxford English Dictionary,* Wright's *English Dialect Dictionary,* or the first volume of Jespersen's *Modern English Grammar.* On *it,* which apparently preceded *there* in impersonal clauses, both the *OED* and the *EDD* have many examples, dating from the fourteenth century, chiefly from Northern England and Scotland;[7] the American evidence suggests that the form may have been brought from Northern Britain or Ulster, since West Virginia was heavily settled by Ulster Scots and the Eastern Shore was one of the earliest strongholds of Scottish (and Ulster) Presbyterianism, and most of the other communities where *it* occurs have Ulster Scots prominent among the early settlers. Yet some communities do not fit this description, notably those of Tidewater Virginia; and *it* is

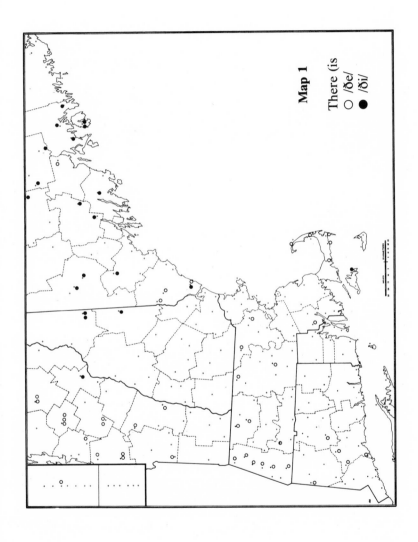

Map 1

There (is

○ /ðe/
● /ði/

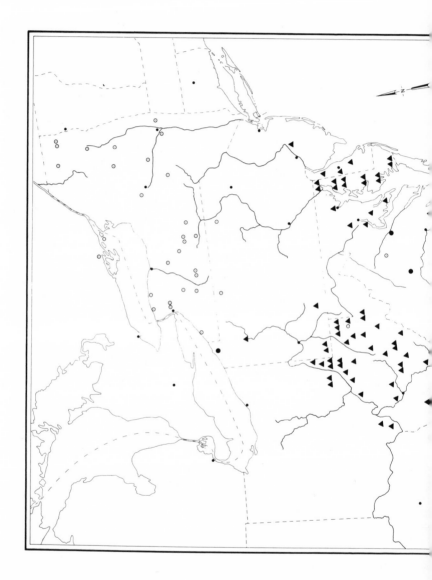

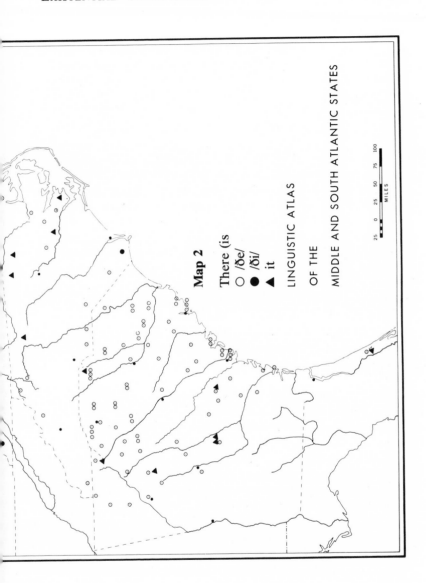

Map 2

There (is

○ /ðe/
● /ði/
▲ it

LINGUISTIC ATLAS

OF THE

MIDDLE AND SOUTH ATLANTIC STATES

MILES

25   0   25   50   75   100

lacking in the Highlander settlements of the Cape Fear Valley. For /ði/ the concentration in northeastern New England suggests East Anglian affiliation; /ðe/ would seem to have had wide distribution in southern England.[8] But these remain speculations for the moment.

VIII

Some differences in the relative frequency of the responses seem derived from differences in field techniques. In New England, Bernard Bloch was more active than Lowman in recording variants from free conversation, and a large number of the occurrences of /ðe/ were recorded from free conversation in Bloch's territory. Yet Rachel Harris, who ranked very high in recording conversational responses, has only one example of /ðe/ in her territory. Where Lowman and McDavid covered the same territory—South Carolina, Georgia, Upstate New York—McDavid recorded many more examples of /ðe/, as would be expected from his practice of listening for the item in free conversation, whether or not he elicited it directly. His records also show numerous variants for *there are/there is/there's* that fall outside the scope of this study.

IX

This evidence also suggests the value of recording interviews on tape and reviewing the tapes afterward. There are problems with this technique. It is always good to transcribe as much as possible during the interview, as insurance against power failures or obtrusive background noises; a passing truck, a ticking clock, or a squawling child is more likely to interfere with the perception of sounds when the tape is played back than during the actual interview. And tape recorders cannot be responsible for adequate recording levels or intelligent putting of questions. But they will gather far more conversational evidence than even Bloch or Harris could write down in a live interview.

It is not surprising, therefore, that the proportion of the variants we have discussed are somewhat higher in taped interviews than in others. Five of the twelve taped interviews in Upstate

New York and eastern Ontario yield examples of /ðe/. And four of the examples of *it* from South Carolina, Georgia, and Florida are found in the taped interviews. This last fact suggests that the tapes pick up more examples of conversational forms but make a variant like *it's lots of them* more obvious. It is also probable that the frequent assertion by sociolinguists of the restricted ethnic status of *it* made McDavid more alert to this construction at the time he was transcribing tapes. In all probability, had every South Carolina and Georgia interview been taped, there would have been more examples of *it*—though one must remember that there is not a single example in Lowman's thirty-odd interviews in South Carolina and Georgia, nor in any of his North Carolina records south of the Neuse and west of the Yadkin.

The distribution of these variants clearly needs further study, especially in tapes of informal conversation. There are several places one may look:

1. The Hanley Tapes, dubbed by Frederic Cassidy and his staff from aluminum recordings made in the 1930s, chiefly in New England. They are now being studied, for grammatical evidence, by Betty Jacobsen, of the Illinois Institute of Technology.

2. The DARE tapes, made by Cassidy's investigators for the Dictionary of Ameican Regional English. Each of some thousand informants is represented by a generous sample of continuous speech.

3. The samples preserved by the Survey of English Dialects.

4. The interviews taped by Rex Wilson and his associates for the dialect survey of the Maritime Provinces.

5. The folklore archives of the Memorial University of Newfoundland.

Clearly we have not said the last word on "existential" *there* and its variants; like all the work done and sponsored by Jim McMillan we provide fewer definitive answers than questions for the next generation of scholars to explore.

NOTES

1. For an earlier treatment of a related problem, see R. I. McDavid, Jr., "/r/ and /y/ in the South," *Studies in Linguistics* 7:18–21 (1949).

2. *The Linguistic Atlas of New England*, first section of a proposed

Linguistic Atlas of the United States and Canada, appeared in 1939–43, when the energies of reviewers and readers were occupied with the problems of World War II. Subsequently, linguistic geography in the United States took a back seat in comparison with teaching of English as a second language, machine translation, and applied sociolinguistics— and the theoretical approaches of structuralism and transformationalism. Though several regional atlases are in the editorial stage, only Harold Allen's *Linguistic Atlas of the Upper Midwest* has achieved publication, and that a quarter century after his field work began. Although the atlases have drawn a great deal of criticism from younger linguists, few of the latter have ever seen the atlases themselves.

3. Of course, the regional atlases do not preclude other types of investigations, using other methods and interviewing other kinds of populations. Each kind of investigation must be ordered in terms of its purpose: a study of the language of school children in a metropolitan area would necessarily require the interviewing of recent arrivals in the community, who would never be considered by a linguistic atlas.

4. Since World War II, various social forces have altered the notions of prestige in many a community, and consequently induced new directions of linguistic change. The inclusion of several types of informants in the regional atlases permits a more careful assaying of these new directions of change than would have been possible had only one class of informants been interviewed.

Needless to say, the Atlas records do not purport to give an exhaustive sociolinguistic description of any community; they provide only a framework—but a useful framework.

5. This practice—and the concluding statement—are derived from E. Bagby Atwood, *A Survey of Verb Forms in the Eastern United States* (Ann Arbor, 1953).

6. Although *there are* and its congeners were not included in the shorter questionnaire used in eastern Kentucky, McDavid recorded the item when it appeared in free conversation. Scattered other examples appear throughout the North-Central area.

7. *It* became traditional—or continued as traditional—in the ballad; not surprisingly *it* in this context appears in the first line of the *Ancient Mariner*.

8. New England drew heavily from East Anglia and the Home Counties; the coastal South from southwestern England.

The Social Distribution of Selected Verb Forms in the Linguistic Atlas of the North Central States

VIRGINIA McDAVID

The decade of the 1970s is a bright one in American dialectology. The *Dictionary of American Regional English,* long the major project of the American Dialect Society, is nearing completion under the editorship of Frederic G. Cassidy, and some portions of it should appear by 1980. The *Linguistic Atlas of New England* was reprinted in 1972 and its *Handbook* in 1973, the latter with the addition of a Word Index and Map Inventory by Audrey Duckert. Under Raven I. McDavid, Jr. editing has been completed for the Linguistic Atlas of the Middle and South Atlantic States, and final copy is being prepared for printing by the University of Chicago Press. The first fascicles will appear in 1978. Fieldwork for the Gulf States has been completed, and editing has begun, with Lee Pederson directing the project. The *Linguistic Atlas of the Upper Midwest* has appeared (1973, 1975, 1976), the culmination of a project begun in 1947 by Harold B. Allen.

The last two years have also seen the resumption of active editing of the materials of the Linguistic Atlas of the North Central States, which comprises Wisconsin, Michigan, Illinois, Indiana, Kentucky, Ohio, and southern Ontario. This area is a crucial one and tantalizing for dialect study because dialect patterns reflect settlement patterns, patterns which generally reflect a movement from east to west. Just as the material from New England and the Middle and South Atlantic States can help explain what is found in the North Central area, so the North Central data can provide a foundation for understanding what is found in areas further west.

The Linguistic Atlas of the North Central States was begun by Albert H. Marckwardt in 1938 as one of the regional atlases into which the originally planned Linguistic Atlas of the United States and Canada was to be divided. Most of the fieldwork was completed between 1938 and 1957, some before this period and more after it. Until 1975 these materials had largely lain fallow with little active editing or use of them.

In June 1975 a small conference with Marckwardt as chairman was held at the University of Chicago to discuss plans for editing and interpreting the material. The Linguistic Atlas of the North Central States will not present the data in list manuscript form, as in the Linguistic Atlas of the Middle and South Atlantic States, but rather in summary volumes, closer in format to those of the Linguistic Atlas of the Upper Midwest. These under their separate editors will describe the phonology, grammar, and lexicon of the area and be accompanied by a handbook. After Marckwardt's death later in 1975, Raven I. McDavid, Jr., the principal fieldworker in the North Central area, became editor.

Much has been accomplished since the 1975 conference. The final inventory of the records is nearly finished. The Atlas will include nearly 500 complete records and 50 partial ones, some 44,000 pages. All records have been renumbered, a procedure made necessary by the inclusion of substantial amounts of new material, especially in Illinois. The most important development has been the publication of each record in the original forms in which the fieldworker transcribed it. These *Basic Materials,* as they are now known, are part of the University of Chicago *Microfilm Collection of Manuscripts on Cultural Anthropology,* edited by Norman McQuown, and are available either in microfilm or on Xerox prints. Editing of the grammatical materials has now begun.

While the preliminary work was continuing, some studies were made of verb forms. The conclusions are admittedly tentative. The Ontario materials have been omitted because it had been

Table 1

Average number of responses per item: 444. The number of responses is given in parentheses following the percentages.

Type I, 49% (218); Type II, 42% (185); Type III 9% (41).

	AVE.		I		II		III	
bitten, ppl.	34%	(152)	27%	(61)	38%	(72)	51	(19)
bit	66	(296)	73	(163)	62	(115)	49	(18)
came, pret.	46	(251)	35	(98)	52	(116)	84	(37)
come	54	(294)	65	(182)	48	(105)	16	(7)
did, pret.	48	(223)	32	(76)	55	(98)	92	(49)
done	52	(244)	68	(159)	45	(81)	8	(4)
driven, ppl.	55	(238)	41	(83)	62	(115)	93	(40)
drove	45	(194)	59	(121)	38	(70)	7	(3)
gave, pret.	51	(228)	40	(91)	57	(106)	97	(31)
give	49	(217)	60	(135)	43	(81)	3	(1)
ran, pret.	40	(194)	27	(64)	45	(94)	82	(36)
run	60	(294)	73	(172)	55	(114)	18	(8)
shrank, pret.	16	(50)	15	(20)	10	(14)	40	(16)
shrunk	84	(258)	85	(109)	90	(125)	60	(24)
torn, ppl.	59	(243)	42	(85)	74	(125)	87	(33)
tore	41	(166)	58	(116)	26	(45)	13	(5)
threw, pret.	63	(302)	51	(118)	69	(143)	98	(41)
throwed	37	(179)	49	(114)	31	(64)	2	(1)
written, ppl.	71	(300)	59	(124)	84	(142)	87	(34)
wrote	29	(120)	41	(87)	16	(28)	13	(5)

thought that additional Ontario records would shortly be added, an incorrect assumption. The Indiana materials are now being retranscribed from the original tapes with the resultant emergence of much new grammatical material. Some changes in the conclusions presented here are therefore likely after the materials in their final form have been studied. The average number of responses per item in this group of ten verbs was 444. Of these 49 percent, an average of 218 responses, are from Type I informants; 42 percent, an average of 185 responses, are from Type

Table 2
Use of Standard Forms by Types of Informants

	I	II	III
0–10%		shrank	
11–20%	shrank		
21–30%	bitten		
	ran		
31–40%	came	bitten	shrank
	did		
	gave		
41–50%	driven	ran	
	torn		
51–60%	threw	came	bitten
	written	did	
		gave	
61–70%		driven	
		threw	
71–80%		torn	
81–90%		written	came
			ran
			torn
			written
91–100%			did
			driven
			gave
			threw

II informants; and 9 percent, an average of 41 responses, are from Type III informants.

The data for the preterit or past participle form of ten verbs—*bite, come, do, drive, give, run, shrink, tear, throw,* and *write*—are presented here. These ten were selected because the use of the "correct" or "standard" preterit or past participle form is regarded, both popularly and in usage guides, as a reflection of social and educational status. For these ten a clear pattern of distribution appears: the standard forms are used least commonly by the oldest and least educated informants and most commonly by the youngest and most highly educated informants. Statistically these differences are overwhelming (See Tables 1, 2, 3, and 4).[1]

There are regional patterns for these verbs as well (see Table 5), but they are not considered here. Kentucky, for example,

Table 3
Binomial Test of Significance,
Assuming the Null Hypothesis

The statistics for all items *not* marked with an asterisk (*) are significant at the $\alpha = .05$ level. In other words, for items not marked there is one chance in twenty or less that the result would occur under the null hypothesis. Under the entry *bitten, bit,* .0001 means that there is less chance than one in 10,000, and .0016 means that there are less than sixteen chances in 10,000, that these results would occur by chance.

	I	II	III
bitten, bit	.0001	.0016	*.9268
came, come	.0001	*.4592	.0001
did, done	.0001	*.2040	.0001
driven, drove	.0078	.0010	.0001
gave, give	.0034	*.0672	.0001
ran, run	.0001	*.1646	.0001
shrank, shrunk	.0001	.0001	*.2058
torn, tore	.0286	.0001	.0001
threw, throwed	*.7948	.0001	.0001
written, wrote	.0108	.0001	.0001

Table 4
Results of Chi-Square Test

This table gives the result of a chi-square test for the significance of the variation in the use of standard as opposed to nonstandard forms as a function of informant type. In each of the columns I, II, and III the left figures are the number of responses actually heard, while the right figures are the number of responses which would be expected under the hypothesis that there is no relation between response and informant type (the null hypothesis). In the rightmost column are the chi-square statistics for each item. All are significant at the 0.005 level, which means that there is one chance in 200 of the observed results occurring under the null hypothesis. All except *bitten-bit* are significant at the 0.001 level, which means that there is one chance in 1000 of the observed results occurring under the null hypothesis. Under the null hypothesis the smallest expected number of responses is 6.494, so the chi-square test is appropriate here.

	I		II		III		Total	
bitten	61	76.000	72	63.446	19	12.554	152	
bit	163	148.000	115	123.554	18	24.446	296	
	224		187		37		448	$X^2 = 11.236$
came	98	128.954	116	101.782	37	20.264	251	
come	182	151.046	105	119.218	7	23.736	294	
	280		221		44		545	$X^2 = 43.078$
did	76	112.216	98	85.475	49	25.308	223	
done	159	122.784	81	83.525	4	27.692	244	
	235		179		53		467	$X^2 = 45.030$
driven	83	112.389	115	101.921	40	23.690	238	
drove	121	91.611	70	83.079	3	19.310	194	
	204		185		43		432	$X^2 = 45.855$

(continued)

Table IV (*continued*)

	I		II		III		Total	
gave	91	115.793	106	95.811	31	16.396	228	
give	135	110.207	81	91.189	1	15.604	217	
	226		187		32		445	$X^2 = 39.784$
ran	64	93.820	94	82.689	36	17.492	194	
run	172	142.180	114	125.311	8	26.508	294	
	236		208		44		488	$X^2 = 50.806$
shrank	20	20.942	14	22.565	16	6.494	50	
shrunk	109	108.058	125	116.435	24	33.506	258	
	129		139		40		308	$X^2 = 20.544$
torn	85	119.421	125	101.002	33	22.579	243	
tore	116	81.579	45	68.998	5	15.423	166	
	201		170		38		409	$X^2 = 50.349$
threw	118	145.663	143	129.967	41	26.370	302	
throwed	114	86.337	64	77.033	1	15.630	179	
	232		207		42		481	$X^2 = 36.613$
written	124	150.714	142	121.429	34	27.857	300	
wrote	87	60.286	28	48.571	5	11.143	120	
	211		170		39		420	$X^2 = 33.511$

has a generally lower use of standard forms, and other studies with North Central materials reveal a higher use of relic forms there.

Consideration of the past participle of *bite* (*bitten* or *bit*) and the preterit of *shrink* (*shrank* or *shrunk*) should be separated from that of the forms of the other eight verbs because with these two the traditional standard forms are used with strikingly less frequency. *Bitten* is used by one-fourth of the Type I informants, 40 percent of the Type II informants and 51 percent (statisically nonsignificant) of the Type III informants. The forms *dog-bit* and

48   V. McDavid

Table 5
Percentages of Responses by States

	WI		MI		IL		IN		KY		OH	
bitten, ppl.	47%	(24)	37%	(27)	40%	(49)	15%	(7)	25%	(21)	34%	(24)
bit	53	(27)	63	(46)	60	(74)	85	(41)	75	(62)	66	(46)
came, pret.	38	(25)	42	(39)	57	(87)	43	(19)	33	(34)	54	(47)
come	62	(41)	58	(54)	43	(65)	57	(25)	67	(69)	46	(40)
did, pret.	29	(17)	54	(42)	56	(74)	34	(13)	39	(33)	57	(44)
done	71	(41)	46	(36)	44	(57)	66	(25)	61	(52)	43	(33)
driven, ppl.	51	(27)	53	(33)	65	(82)	59	(30)	36	(26)	61	(40)
drove	49	(26)	47	(29)	35	(45)	41	(21)	64	(47)	39	(26)
gave, pret.	55	(31)	47	(33)	63	(84)	25	(7)	35	(29)	59	(44)
give	45	(25)	53	(37)	37	(50)	75	(21)	65	(54)	41	(30)
ran, pret.	32	(19)	27	(20)	53	(70)	40	(21)	31	(31)	46	(33)
run	68	(41)	73	(53)	47	(62)	60	(31)	69	(68)	54	(39)
shrank, pret.			10	(6)	21	(23)	5	(2)	20	(9)	17	(10)
shrunk			90	(52)	79	(85)	95	(36)	80	(35)	83	(50)
torn, ppl.	55	(23)	64	(38)	71	(84)	50	(24)	46	(36)	59	(38)
tore	45	(19)	36	(21)	29	(34)	50	(24)	54	(42)	41	(26)
threw, pret.	67	(34)	65	(50)	70	(92)	62	(32)	49	(48)	64	(46)
throwed	33	(17)	35	(27)	30	(40)	38	(20)	51	(49)	36	(26)
written, ppl.	79	(41)	83	(53)	78	(88)	64	(32)	47	(33)	75	(53)
wrote	21	(11)	17	(11)	22	(25)	36	(18)	53	(37)	25	(18)

The number of responses is given in parentheses following the percentages.
The preterit of *shrink* was not recorded in Wisconsin.

snake-bit, found in Kentucky and southern Indiana and Ohio, were not included here.

Shrunk is the most common preterit for all informants of all types. *Shrank* is used by 40 percent of the Type III informants, but again no conclusion can be drawn from this figure. Current dictionaries recognize divided standard usage for the forms of these two verbs, giving both *bitten* and *bit* and *shrank* and *shrunk*.

These data support that decision, but if the first form listed in dictionaries is intended to be the more common one, the order should be reversed to read *bit* and *bitten* and *shrunk* and *shrank*.

The other eight verbs may also be grouped together because of the similarity of the data. In all, the standard forms—*came, did, driven, gave, ran, torn, threw,* and *written*—are much more common in the speech of the more highly educated informants.

Came: About one-third of the Type I informants use *came,* one-half of the Type II informants, and 84 percent of the Type III informants.

Did: One-third of the Type I informants use *did,* a little more than half of the Type II informants, and more than 90 percent of the Type II informants.

Driven: Two-fifths of the Type I informants use *driven,* three-fifths of the Type II informants, and 98 percent of the Type III informants.

Gave: Two-fifths of the Type I informants use *gave* and 97 percent of the Type III informants. The statistics for the Type II informants are nonsignificant.

Ran: Fewer than one-third of the Type I informants use *ran* and 82 percent of the Type III informants. The statistics for the Type II informants are nonsignificant. A lower percentage of all types of informants use the standard form of this verb than of any other.

Torn: Two-fifths of the Type I informants use *torn,* three-fourths of the Type II informants, and nearly 90 percent of the Type III informants.

Threw: About one-half of the Type I informants use *threw,* 70 percent of the Type II informants, and nearly all the Type III informants.

Written: Nearly 60 percent of the Type I informants use *written,* a higher percentage of use of the standard form among Type I informants than for any other of the eight verbs. About 85 percent of the Type II and Type III informants use *written.*

Table 2 reveals the increasing use of the standard forms as one progresses from Type I to Type III informants. If *bitten* and *shrank* are excluded, more than 80 percent of all Type III speakers use the standard forms *came, did, driven, gave, ran, torn, threw,* and *written.* More than 61 percent of the Type II speakers use *driven, threw, torn,* and *written;* between 41 and 60 percent *came, did, gave,* and *ran.* Between 41 and 60 percent of the Type I speakers use *driven, threw, torn,* and *written,* and between 21 and 40 percent use *came, did, gave,* and *ran.*

Phrased somewhat differently, between 21 and 40 percent of the Type I informants use *came, did, gave,* and *ran,* and between 41 and 60 percent of the Type II informants. Between 41 and 60 percent of the Type I informants use *driven, threw, torn,* and *written,* and between 61 and 90 percent of the Type II informants. More than 90 percent of the Type III informants use all eight forms.

What general conclusions can be drawn from this small study based on the North Central data? One conclusion never doubted but here confirmed is that these materials can and do contribute significantly to our knowledge of social variation in American English. A further conclusion is that dialectology, and specifically the findings of the linguistic atlases, have real and serious implications for education, especially the study of English usage, which has too long been a record of prejudice rather than of fact.

NOTE

1. The author wishes to acknowledge her indebtedness to Glenn T. McDavid, programmer/analyst, First National Bank of Chicago, for his assistance in the preparation and interpretation of the statistical data and tables.

GRAMMAR

Grammatical Usage: Modern Shibboleths

JOHN ALGEO

When the Greeks, who showed us the way in language study, as in much else, thought about linguistic variation, they distinguished between *Hellēnismós* 'good Greek' and *barbarismós* 'foreign mode of talk.' The basic distinction was between "us" and "them," between the insiders who speak properly and the outsiders who stammer and babble. Essentially, that is still the basic distinction made in usage study, although nowadays it is usually phrased more delicately.

Every language has various ways of saying the "same" thing, that is, different expressions for the same referential meaning. Usage study, in a broad sense, has as its object those variations. In this broad sense, it thus encompasses dialect geography (or areal linguistics), social dialectology, stylistics, and all other such branches of language study as focus on variation. In a narrower sense, however, usage study is concerned with the establishment of norms within a community. The community may be all those people who interact by means of the language, or it may be a subset that is defined geographically, socially, educationally, or otherwise.

The primary task of usage study, narrowly considered, is therefore to establish norms and to define the group for whom the norms are established. This is a descriptive activity, and any statement about usage must rest on such activity if it is to merit attention. In practice, the kinds of description that support usage statements are extremely varied, ranging from surveys of the scope of the *Oxford English Dictionary* to ipse-dixits that record only the impressions of the describer. When the describer is a well-informed and sensitive observer of the linguistic scene, his impressions may be worth attention, but they necessarily lack the authority, as description, of a more general survey. The group whose norms are being ascertained may range, then, from English speakers at all times and places to a single speaker fishing in his own pond (as the use of introspection has been dubbed)—from the panchronic language to an idiolect.

A second task of usage study is to project the norms that have already been established, on whatever basis, back upon the community as an ideal to which members of the community should aspire. This is a prescriptive activity. The controversy over description versus prescription that began during the first half of this century and still continues under slogans like "the students' right to their own language" has resulted in a good bit of confusion on the part of those who have not clearly understood the issues. Descriptions establish norms, and norms are at least implicit prescriptions. The question is not whether prescription as such is good or bad—education generally and language teaching specifically are prescriptive by nature. The question is rather what kinds of prescription are offered. Every prescription is a norm of some degree of generality. The norm may reflect what is statistically average and typical for a large group; this is what used to be called the whatever-is-is-right approach to usage but now might be called the right-to-one's-own-language approach. On the other hand, the norm may express an ideal of linguistic behavior that is actually practiced by only a small minority within the total speech community; this might be called the ad-astra-per-aspera approach. One kind of norm is democratic and leveling; the other is elitist and discriminating. The choice between such norms is one of value and taste, not of truth and morality, although the intensity with which a choice is defended often suggests otherwise.

Some Twentieth-Century Studies

Whether students of usage ostensibly describe the norms of some language community or prescribe norms as a linguistic model, they are doing the modern equivalent of separating *Hellēn-ismós* from *barbarismós;* they are defining the language of a group, and thus in turn defining the group by its language. Students of language have been doing this since at least the days of the Greeks. The vigor with which such studies are pursued varies, however, from time to time. Like the vast meteorological cycles that produce now an ice age and now an epochal summer, linguistic history has its lesser cycles during which a concern for standards intensifies or relaxes. A time of more intense activity began during the social and political revolutions of the eighteenth century, both in Britain and in America, and has continued to our own day. About one-third through our century, the pace quickened, with the National Council of Teachers of English leading the way. In 1932, Sterling Leonard's *Current English Usage* appeared; and in 1938, Marckwardt and Walcott's *Facts about Current English Usage.* In the following year, the Committee on Current English of the National Council began to edit "Current English Forum" as a regular department of *College English* and the *English Journal.* The "Forum" answered questions and presented short articles about disputed points of usage from a descriptive viewpoint. During the first ten years of its publication, James B. McMillan was one of the leading contributors of columns noted for accuracy, clarity, and common sense. In 1940, Charles Carpenter Fries published his *American English Grammar.* The period of the 1930s and 1940s was the high point of the Council's interest in substantive matters of usage, although a more general interest continues to the present time.[1]

Council publications were directed primarily at members of the teaching profession. Other usage studies have addressed themselves to a more general audience. One of the early examples of the latter sort was J. Lesslie Hall's 1917 *English Usage,* which reported for 141 items of disputed usage both the opinions of contemporary usage guides and the facts of usage as gleaned from 75,000 pages of British and American belles-lettres. One of the more recent is William and Mary Morris's 1975 *Harper Dictionary of Contemporary Usage,* which gives advice about 2111 items of usage and whose dustjacket advertises it as "the most authoritative and comprehensive reference book on the state of the language today, with piercing, perceptive, and witty comments from 136 outstanding writers and editors from Auden and Asimov to Tuchman, Viorst, and Wouk.'' About 6 percent of the entries have comments from some of the usage panel. Although they vary considerably in perception and wit, they are an interesting record of the linguistic attitudes of men and women of letters.

Quite apart from the general attitudes toward usage and the opinions about specific issues expressed in those works addressed to the reading public, the questions that have been considered worth asking are noteworthy. Items treated in books on usage for the general reader have some claim to be considered symptoms that he would regard as diagnostic of the "us-them" dichotomy. What are the usage questions that the general reader will find treated in the books he presumably consults for advice about linguistic propriety? What, in effect, are the shibboleths of modern *Hellēnismós* versus *barbarismós?* The answer to this question, based upon seven American usage books, including the two just mentioned but omitting the very influential Fowler because of his Britishness, occupies the remainder of this study. The works examined are these:

J. Lesslie Hall, *English Usage: Studies in the History and Uses of English Words and Phrases* (Chicago: Scott, Foresman, 1917).

Margaret M. Bryant, *Current American Usage* (New York: Funk & Wagnalls, 1962).

Wilson Follett, *Modern American Usage: A Guide,* edited and completed by Jacques Barzun (New York: Hill & Wang, 1966).

Jerome Shostak, *Concise Dictionary of Current American Usage* (New York: Washington Square Press, 1968).

Theodore M. Bernstein, *The Careful Writer: A Modern Guide to English Usage* (New York: Atheneum, 1973).

Harry Shaw, *Dictionary of Problem Words and Expressions* (New York: McGraw-Hill, 1975).

William Morris and Mary Morris, *Harper Dictionary of Contemporary Usage* (New York: Harper & Row, 1975).

Each entry in these seven books was classified as a grammatical or nongrammatical item. Grammatical items comprise discussions of function words, word class, word order, inflections, concord, and syntactic categories such as number and gender—in general, questions involving selection from a closed system, order, modulation, or phonetic modification (to use the Bloomfieldian fourfold classification of grammatical features). Nongrammatical items comprise discussions of lexis—the spelling, pronunciation, meaning, or pragmatic use of open-class items, for example, *finalize, disinterested,* and *dock* (versus *pier* and *wharf).* The proportion of grammatical and nongrammatical items in the seven books is itself of some interest:

	TOTAL	GRAMMATICAL	NONGRAMMATICAL
Hall	141	92	49
Bryant	235	222	13
Follett	372	139	233
Shostak	2027	785	1242
Bernstein	1272	747	525
Shaw	1129	280	849
Morris	2111	378	1733
Total	7287	2643	4644

The proportion of items in Bernstein is somewhat misleading. Of the 747 grammatical items, 443 (nearly 60 percent) concern the selection of a preposition after a verb, noun, or adjective, for example, *lean on, upon,* or *against;* most of these, like the example cited, involve no problem for the native speaker, and the reason for their inclusion is obscure. Many usage guides have some favorite topic that is treated disproportionately—perhaps just to help distinguish them from all the otherwise remarkably similar books; prepositional complements are Bernstein's hobbyhorse. Apart from this anomaly, there is a clear pattern. The more academically oriented books by Hall and Bryant favor grammatical items for discussion (65 and 95 percent respectively); the more popularly oriented books are less concerned with grammatical items (ranging from 39 down to 18 percent). In fact, the number of grammatical items treated in any one book is not great. Shostak has the largest number of grammatical entries, but a great many of them (and the longest ones) are definitions of grammatical terms rather than treatments of disputed points of usage; grammatically, his book is as much a glossary of terminology as it is a dictionary of usage, terms being his hobbyhorse. There will be no further analysis here of the nongrammatical items in any of the books. The grammatical items, however, were further classified according to part of speech or general structural problem and were then subclassified to whatever degree of detail seemed appropriate for each group.

The seven books approach their subject in extremely varied ways. Hall's and Bryant's studies focus clearly and consistently on the facts of usage as they appear in the evidence on which the studies are based; that evidence has weaknesses, but theirs are the only ones of these studies to concern themselves with facts as distinct from imperatives of usage. The Morrises' book reports the opinions of its panel about a fraction of the items in it, but 136 subjective judgments do not equal one objective fact. The other volumes vary, from those that attempt to depict the facts of American usage as fairly as the author's knowledge allows, to those that specialize in curmudgeonly judgments seeking to out-Fowler Fowler. *What* these books say about usage items is not the main question here, however. Rather, the question is *which* items are covered and thus are presumably matters of concern to those who consult such books. It is impractical to describe all 2643 grammatical items covered in these volumes. Instead, those items of usage that are given main entries in at least half of the books are reported (and are called *shibboleths,* a term that thus has a stipulated technical sense here). What follows is a survey of the variants most often treated in these popular guides to usage.

Verbs

About 15 percent of the entries in the seven usage books are devoted to verbs, including about 7 percent devoted to the principal parts of irregular verbs. In the latter group, the shibboleths are *get* (specifically the past participle *got* versus *gotten*), *prove* (past participle *proved* versus *proven*), *dive* (preterit *dived* versus *dove*), *broadcast* (*broadcasted* versus *broadcast*), *hang* (*hanged* versus *hung*), and *light* (*lighted* versus *lit*). The choice of principal parts is also involved in discriminating the intransitive from the transitive-causative forms of *lie/lay* and *sit/set*.

Although the selection of inflected forms accounts for about half of the verb entries in usage books, there are other problems as well. There are three shibboleths among the modals: the choice between *shall* and *will*, the choice between *can* and *may*, and problems with *ought* (mainly its negative, whether *ought not* or *hadn't ought*, and the ellipsis of *to* in expressions like *ought not go*). The semimodals are given nearly as much attention as the modals, but there is only one clear shibboleth: the expression *had rather*.

In spite of, or perhaps because of, the fact that the past subjunctive is a moribund category in English, it is much discussed in usage books. Specifically, the choice of *was* versus *were* for first- and third-person singular subjects in contrary-to-fact clauses is the shibboleth. The treatment that usage books accord this construction is evidence, if evidence is needed, that they follow a tradition in their choice and discussion of topics. Six of the seven books discuss the use of *was* rather than *were* in contrary-to-fact clauses like "if Goldwater was President"; none gives consideration to the opposite and increasingly common substitution of *were* for *was* in simple conditions. A recent example is the comment by the NBC-TV reporter Judy Woodruff on 24 July 1976: "If Carter were sore today [after playing softball yesterday], he didn't show it." Usage books do not treat the hypercorrection because, however frequent it may be, it has not yet found a place in the received list of topics.[2]

Other verbal categories that usage books almost invariably treat are the passive voice and problems of tense. There is, however, no single construction or lexical item that is treated in a majority of the books. The perfect form of the verb has a shibboleth in *of* used for *have*, as in *would of, could of, should of*, and the like. It might be considered merely a spelling variant, but for constructions of the type "If I hadn't of heard it with my own ears, I wouldn't of believed it," in which the expression *had of* is doubtless influenced by the following *would of*. The existence of *had of*, whatever its origin, presents a descriptive problem for grammarians, as well as a usage problem, in that *had have* is ungrammatical. The usage books disagree about whether *of* should be regarded as a spelling variant of *have* in these constructions, but none recognizes the really interesting problem created by its extension to *had of*.

Infinitives have two shibboleths. First, the split infinitive is an almost inescapable concern of usage writers. Second, the use of *and* instead of *to* as an infinitive marker in expressions of the type *try and go* is even more widely commented upon. Six of the seven books deal with the split infinitive, but all of them discuss *try and*.

Substantives

Substantives account for 16 percent of the entries in the seven usage books: nouns for 10 percent and pronouns for 6 percent. Among nouns, the major concern is for plurality; 7 percent of the total number of entries concern the category of number. Foreign, and especially Graeco-Latin, plurals account for nearly one-third of the entries about number. The shibboleths are *datum/data, agendum/agenda, criterion/criteria, medium/media, memorandum/memoranda,* and *phenomenon/phenomena.* The use of a plural infix versus suffix in compounds is a problem that engages some attention. A paradigmatic case is that of nouns ending in *-ful (cupful, armful, glassful, handful, spoonful,* and the like), thus: *cupsful* versus *cupfuls.* Another shibboleth that involves the choice between alternative plural forms is *people/persons* as the plural of *person.* Several usage books discuss the creation of new singulars by back formation (for example, *kudo* from *kudos*), but no individual noun is treated in a majority of the books. Two shibboleths involve the use of the singular versus the plural form of a noun in particular collocations: *in regard(s) to* and *a long way(s).*

The system of countability, whose terms are mass and unit

nouns, is responsible for a good deal of usage variation in English. Two shibboleths are *less* versus *fewer* and *amount* versus *number* when constructed with plural unit nouns, thus "less/fewer than thirty dollars" and "the amount/number of freshmen."

The genitive gives rise to a number of problems, but only two are treated often enough to be shibboleths. One is the double genitive (for example, *a friend of my wife's*). The other is the use of the genitive versus the common form (or, for pronouns, the objective case) as the subject of a gerund. A typical instance is "Have you heard about Bob/Bob's leaving?" This shibboleth is part of the usage tradition; two of the longer and more detailed discussions, by Bernstein and Follett, begin by referring to Fowler's 1926 discussion in *Modern English Usage,* which is based on his earlier treatment in *The King's English* (1906). Yet it is also one in which there is real variation and considerable complexity of construction types; the problem is more involved than any of the books describe, even those with relatively full treatments, not to mention those that simply advise the reader to use the genitive.

Because gender in English is indicated primarily by pronoun selection, it is a category that overlaps nouns and pronouns. A majority of the usage books discuss some gender-related problems, such as the gender concord of pronouns or the existence of alternative forms of nouns to indicate sex (*fiancé/fiancée, actor/actress, chairman/chairwoman/chairlady*) but no individual item is discussed in enough sources to be considered a shibboleth. In this regard, even the most recent usage books are certainly out of date. The use of *man* and its congeners as unmarked forms for either sex is currently a lively issue. The failure of any of the books to give much consideration to the question is another indication that they address themselves mainly to an inherited list of problems rather than to real issues in contemporary English.

Pronouns offer a variety of minor problems and some major ones. Among the minor problems is the pronominal use of *such* in constructions like "He will not accept such" and "Such will be welcome." The treatment accorded *you all* is another indication that most usage books overlook significant current problems if they are not part of the inherited tradition of usage study. Three of the sources list *you all,* but two make only brief and con-descending remarks that are factually confused. Margaret Bryant's one-page treatment, on the other hand, is accurate and fair. The complexity in the uses of the form are such, however, that an even more extensive treatment is warranted. Perhaps the new emergence of the South in national politics will change the attitude toward its speechways of those who instruct their fellow citizens about the intricacies of usage.

A number of other minor problems involve the antecedents and referents of pronouns. Two uses of personal pronouns are shibboleths: editorial *we* and impersonal *you.* So is the use of relative *whose* for nonpersonal antecedents (rather than *of which*), as in "a book whose cover" versus "a book the cover of which." Another shibboleth of relatives is the choice among *that, which,* and *who,* the crucial problem being the use of *which* and *that* in restrictive and nonrestrictive clauses. Yet another is the false coordination of a relative clause—the *and which* construction, as in "trips beginning in zone A and which extend across two or more zones." The problem is typically one of faulty parallelism.

Pronominal genitives are the source of a number of usage problems and of one shibboleth: the genitive form of compound pronouns ending in *else,* for instance, *someone else's* versus *someone's else.* As with the plural of *cupful,* the question is about suffixation versus infixation, in this case, of the genitive particle. The persistence of this question in usage books is remarkable. There is not much evidence that the construction is the cause of uncertainty among English speakers or that there is significant variation in its use. Nevertheless it is treated both in the oldest usage book examined here (1917) and in one of the two newest (1975). Its status as a shibboleth can only be explained by the fact that it has come to be part of the tradition. There is doubtless genuine variation for one type of the construction, namely *whose else* versus *who else's,* but that type is hardly mentioned in the usage books.

The major problems, in terms of the amount of attention given to them in usage books, are the case forms of pronouns, which account for nearly two-fifths of all pronoun entries in these books. Although the accepted wisdom has it that English is an analytical language, with few inflections, case appears to be a major concern of usage writers. Perhaps, as with the subjunctive, the decline of a category creates uncertainty about its use. At the head of the list of shibboleths is the *It's me/I* construction, closely followed by the choice between *who* and *whom* or between *whoever* and *whomever* in interrogative and relative clauses. Other choices between the nominative and objective form of the pronoun are after *but* and *than,* as in "Everyone left but him/he" and "better than him/he." The analytical question in both cases is whether the connectives *but* and *than* are to be taken as prepositions governing the objective form of the pronoun or as conjunctions followed by elliptical clauses, with the form of the pronoun controlled by its function in the clause. The temptation for usage writers is to answer the analytical question first ("*than* is construed as a conjunction") and then to deduce an answer to the usage problem. The proper way of handling such matters is, of course, to ascertain the usage first and answer the analytical question accordingly. Use, as Quintilian knew long ago, gives currency to grammar as well as to the coinage.

Another shibboleth construction is the case form of a pronoun that is part of the coordinated object of a preposition. *Between you and I/me* is the paradigmatic example. A variant of this construction shows that the intricacies of English usage can play hob with even those who would be their master. The Morrises give the following entry for the lemma "infinitive, subject of the" (ellipses are in the original):

> The confusion about the use of "I" and "me" is reflected in such statements as "The first thing for somebody like you or I to do...." The *subject of the infinitive* "to do" must be in the accusative or objective case. Since the objective case of the first personal pronoun is "me," the statement should be "The first thing for somebody like you or me to do...." [p. 338]

In the statement cited, the subject of the inifinitive is *somebody; I* is rather part of the object of the preposition and for that reason, if one requires and proposes to follow reason in such matters, should be in the objective case. Quis docet ipsos doctores?

Related to the preceding problem, although with a history of some complexity, is the use of *self* forms in objective slots, such as *for her and myself/me.*

Adjuncts

Adjuncts account for 21 percent of the entries in the seven usage books. More particularly, adverbs account for 10 percent; qualifiers for 3 percent; descriptive adjectives and participles for 2 percent; comparative constructions (whether of adjectives or adverbs) for 3 percent; and determiners and other limiting adjectives for 3 percent.

The most often discussed adverbial problem is that of the choice between an adjective and its related adverb (usually one formed by the suffix -*ly*). There are four shibboleths of this kind: *first* versus *firstly* as a signal of position in a list; (*feel*) *bad* versus *badly;* (*feel*) *good* versus *well,* which has semantic complications; and (*go*) *slow* versus *slowly.* Other shibboleths of form are *anywhere* versus *anywheres,* the free extension of the suffix -*wise* to form denominal adverbs like *saleswise,* and adverbs in -*place* (*anyplace, everyplace, someplace, noplace*) versus those in -*where.* It is probably a syntactic blend that has created another shibboleth—*rarely ever*—by combining *rarely* with *hardly ever.*

The functions of adverbs are also a concern of the usage books. Various sentence adverbials in general and conjunctive adverbs in particular receive a good deal of attention, but no one of them is treated often enough to count as a shibboleth. *Hopefully* and *you know* or *you see* almost make it; they are likely candidates to be added to the traditional list of usage concerns. Redundant adverbs (as in *refer, remand, return,* or *revert back*) also are much commented upon, but no single combination attains shibboleth status, although *back* seems to be far and away the favorite redundant adverb of usage writers. When the attention of the guides turns to word order, however, *only* is an inescapable shibboleth.

Qualifiers (that is, adverbs of degree) are a popular class of function words among usage writers, but there are some surprises in the particular words that are most often discussed. One might expect to find *not too* and *not that* in the sense 'not very,' *good and* for 'very,' and *kind of* or *sort of* for 'rather.' Although all of those items are treated in some of the usage books, there are only four shibboleths: *pretty, nowhere near, mighty,* and *real* versus *really*. Perhaps the very abundance of qualifiers in current use makes it difficult for usage writers to agree upon individual ones for treatment.

Adjectives offer much less challenge to the usage writer than adverbs. There are fewer entries, and less diversity of kind of entry. Problems of form, a major concern for adverbs, are minimal. There is only one functional shibboleth: *for free*, in which an adjective serves as object of a preposition. Participles in adjectival use are responsible for two other shibboleths: the use of *very* as a modifier of participles and the dangling participle construction.

Problems relating to comparison overlap both major types of adjuncts. The most frequently discussed of these problems is that of incomparability—adjectives and adverbs whose meaning is such that they cannot be logically compared. Six of the seven usage books discuss the question (the most often discussed items being *unique, preferable,* and *perfect*), but there are no particular words cited often enough to be shibboleths. The second most frequently discussed topic is the choice between alternative forms, a problem for which there are two shibboleths: *further* versus *farther* and *last* versus *latest*. There are two other comparative constructions that engage the attention of a majority of the usage books. One is the ellipsis of the first pivot in conjoined comparisons of the type *as good* (*as*) *or better than*. The second is the redundant construction *equally as* (*good*), which is presumably the result of a syntactic blend of *equally good* with *as good*.

The determiner system spawns four shibboleths. Among the determiners proper, the choice between *a* and *an* is the most widely discussed problem; it is simply a question of phonetic modification, but one that still generates controversy.[3] The use of *most* for *almost,* as in "most every one" or "most all of the books," is certainly the result of aphesis and thus, historically at least, is also a phonological problem; many naive speakers, however, are doubtless like some usage writers in regarding the use as one of word substitution. The aphetic *most* is not limited to predeterminer position, to be sure; it occurs also as a qualifier, as in "most always." However, it is generally illustrated in the determiner context and is probably commoner there. Other pre-determiner items are *all* in adjunctive versus substantive use, as in "all the books" versus "all of the books," and the use of the indefinite article after *kind of,* as in "that kind of book" versus "that kind of a book."

Connectives

Connectives monopolize the attention of the seven usage studies in that there are more entries for them than for any other kind of item: 31 percent. The monopoly is, however, misleading, because 19 percent concern the choice of preposition after a verb, noun, or adjective—a subject that predominates in one of the usage books. With that idiosyncratic emphasis eliminated from consideration, connectives account for only 12 percent of the entries, a more realistic proportion.

Even though the bulk of entries for prepositional complements are from one usage book, there are still five shibboleths of this type: *blame on/for, center on/around, different from/than/to, inferior to/than,* and *wait on/for.* In the first of these shibboleths, the choice of preposition reflects a difference in structure, since one blames a thing on a person, but blames a person for a thing. In the other four, however, the choice is made on some other basis—logic, geography, style, or the like.

Other shibboleths are the use of the expressions *due to, per,* and *prior to* 'before' as prepositions and the choice among the forms *till/'til/until/'till, on to / onto,* and *toward/towards.* The redundant combinations (*at*) *about* and *off* (*of*) are two more. One matter of word order—the terminal preposition—is an inescapable usage item.

Among conjunctions, the use of a coordinating conjunction such as *and* or *but* at the beginning of a sentence is a shibboleth. The asyndetic combination *and/or,* as in "sugar and/or cream," is another. Parallelism of the structures following the correlative conjunctions *not only ... but* (*also*), *either ... or,* and *neither ... nor* is a matter for comment in most of the usage books. The last two correlatives also have problems of number concord with the verb when they connect subjects (as in "Either one or the other is/are") and of internal negative concord (that is, mixing of their parts, as in *neither . . . or*).

Subordinating conjunctions are the subject of more comment than coordinating conjunctions and include a larger number of shibboleths. The choice between *although* versus *though* and between *provided* versus *providing* is one kind of problem. Another is the use of *as* in the sense 'because,' *like* in the sense 'as if' or 'as,' *while* in the sense 'whereas, although,' and *without* in the sense 'unless.' Four shibboleths involve the choice of subordinating conjunctions to begin noun clauses. The choice between *if* and *whether* for indirect questions like "I wonder if/whether it will rain" is one problem. Two others are the choice between *that* and *if* (or *whether*) after *doubt*, as in "I doubt that/if/whether it will," and the choice between *that* and *because* in "The reason is that/because." The use of *when* or *where* to introduce noun clauses after the copula, as in "A grand slam is when/where you take all the tricks," has no simple option, but usually requires a change of sentence structure to provide an alternative. The coordination of subordinating conjunctions in *if and when* and *unless and until* is discussed as a question of verbosity.

Sentence Structure and Interclass Shibboleths

In addition to those problems that can be associated more or less firmly with one of the parts of speech, there are questions about the relationship between parts of speech and about sentence structure. Approximately 17 percent of usage entries concern such problems. One that potentially cuts across all parts-of-speech boundaries is that of class shift—the use of a word customarily associated with one part as a different part of speech. Three shibboleths are *above* as an adjective or noun (as in "the above paragraph" or simply "the above"), *loan* as a verb, and that bête noire of the Merriam-baiters, *contact* as a verb.

Number concord, usually between subject and verb, though also between such modifiers as show number and their headwords and between pronouns and their antecedents, is a prolific source of difficulty, if we judge by the attention paid to it. Verbal concord with a subject whose identity is confused produces two

shibboleths: *More than one is/are* and *one of those who is/are.*
In both cases, the semantic prominence of *one* apparently at-
tracts the verb into the singular despite the logical grounds for
choosing the plural. Another shibboleth is the use of *kind* as a
plural, as in "These kind are." Concord of verb and pronoun
with collectives (for example, "The committee have/has published
their/its results") is discussed in a majority of the usage books,
although no single collective noun is. There are similar concord
problems with the indefinite pronouns *each* and *none* (for example, "Each have/has their/his own"). Gender problems enter
into such constructions also, although usage writers have not yet
come to grips with the proposal advanced by those seeking to rid
the language of sexist bias that *each . . . their* is in fact superior
to its alternatives, which make use of a chauvinistic *his,* a legal-
istic *his or her,* or one of the novel but hardly serious coinages
like *hiser.* It is the fate of usage books to miss the really hot
controversies.

English grammars usually state that the number system of the
language consists of the categories singular and plural, but a third
term, the dual, creates several usage problems. The choice of
between versus *among,* depending on whether the object of the
preposition denotes two or more, is a hoary question that is still
treated in all the most recent studies. Similar are the choices between *each other* and *one another* and between *latter* and *last,*
as well as other instances of the comparative for two and the
superlative for three or more.

Negation is a popular topic. All the usage books comment on
the double negative; a shibboleth is *can't hardly.* Negative concord, the peculiar association of some words with negation, is the
basis for objections to the affirmative use of *anymore* (as in
"They do that all the time anymore"); only one of the usage
writers (Shaw) comments on the spelling variation of the term.
Another concord item is the choice between *so* and *as* in negative
constructions (as in "not so/as tall as"). Negative contraction
produces the archetype of all shibboleths—*ain't.* Of recent usage
writers, only Follett has no discussion of the form, presumably
because none of his readers would be expected to need any advice about it.

There are a good many other problems of sentence structure (about 4.5 percent of the total entries), but only two constructions are discussed frequently enough to count as shibboleths. One is *can't seem to* in the sense 'seems unable to,' for example, "He can't seem to find it." It can be regarded as transformationally related to the variant "It seems that he can't find it," but the illogicality of a literal reading of the form is probably what earns it a place in several usage books. The other shibboleth is the use of *for* to introduce infinitive complements, as in "I would like (for) him to." The construction is doubtless more common in the South than in some other sections of the country, but, as Bryant observes, "considering its frequency in speech, one can only wonder at its rarity in edited writing, and surmise that editors must disapprove of what some textbooks call the redundant *for*" (p. 136). All of the other usage writers who comment on it regard it as a tainted form, labeling it "colloquial" or "nonstandard."

Conclusions

The shibboleths listed here—which are for the most part the darlings of linguistic Comstockery—make a pretty florilegium, but they also suggest some conclusions about the nature of usage books.

First, there is a tradition of items to be covered in a usage study. The historical scope of this survey is much too limited to consider how old that tradition is; in many, perhaps most, of its details it is at least as ancient as the Republic. George Campbell's *Philosophy of Rhetoric* (1776) lists among its violations of "grammatical purity" many of the shibboleths of the twentieth-century usage books. One hardly knows whether to rejoice over the fidelity of our concerns after two hundred years or to lament that we seem to have made so little progress toward a more immaculate state of the language. Whatever one's judgment of the fact, it is apparent that usage writers read one another. DeWitt Starnes and Gertrude Noyes have suggested that the history of early lexicography was largely one of progress by plagiarism with the best lexicographer as "the most discriminating plagiarist."[4]

The copyright laws now prevent the cruder forms of unauthorized imitation, but anyone who compares usage books will recognize that they propagate by inbreeding.

Second, as a concomitant of their adherence to a tradition of disputed items, usage books often fail to capture the living issues of language variation. To some extent, this failure is the common weakness of all reference books—by the time of their publication they are out of date—but usage books as a whole seem to expend more effort than other reference works in looking back to other examples of their genre and less in looking outward at the facts they supposedly report.

Third, if "standard English" means something like the forms used today by educated speakers throughout the country, popular usage books treat almost exclusively variants within the standard language. Forms that are regionally or socially limited, such as invariant *be* or the deleted copula, are hardly considered. Thus the object of popular usage study is by no means the full range of variation within American English, but rather a sharply restricted set of stylistic variants in the speechways of the dominant culture. Usage books clearly assume that their readers understand perfectly well the gross differences that separate the sheep from the goats and want instead those fine distinctions that pick out the angoras from the scapegoats.

Fourth, although the focus here has been upon what items are covered rather than on what is said about those items, the method and content of usage books cannot altogether escape comment. Only two of the books (those by Hall and Bryant) make a serious effort to define the group for whom norms are being established or to be specific about the evidence for the norms. A third (the Morrises') does so to a very limited extent with its panel. As a whole, usage books must be identified as commerical enterprises rather than as scholarly pursuits.

The serious study of usage, to which James McMillan, C. C. Fries, Albert Marckwardt, and others made outstanding contributions during the 1930s and 1940s, now languishes in a state of neglect. In the absence of such serious study, commercialism fills the vacuum, with results that vary from the surprisingly good to the merely ludicrous. The popular usage book is doubtless like the poor in that we will have it with us always—though it certainly has made some of its producers rich enough. The popular usage book fills a need, and popularity is no fault. But if it is to fill that need well rather than shoddily, it must rest upon the kind of serious studies that have recently been all too rare. Perhaps now is the time for the American Dialect Society and the National Council of Teachers of English, as the two organizations most deeply concerned with usage, once again to take the lead in the kind of responsible usage study exemplified so well by the work of James B. McMillan.

NOTES

1. A convenient history of linguistic attitudes, including those toward usage, in the Council's publications from 1911 to 1963 is *An Examination of the Attitudes of the NCTE toward Language,* ed. by Raven I. McDavid, Jr., Research Report no. 4 (Champaign, Ill.: National Council of Teachers of English, 1965).

2. William M. Ryan, "Pseudo-Subjunctive 'Were,'" *American Speech* 36 (1961): 48–53, called attention to the construction fifteen years ago.

3. For example, Dwight L. Bolinger, "Are You a Sincere *H*-Dropper?" *American Speech* 50 (1975): 313–15.

4. *The English Dictionary from Cawdrey to Johnson* (Chapel Hill: University of North Carolina Press, 1946), p. 183.

Toward a
Modal Paradigm

MATTHEW MARINO

The syntax and semantics of the contemporary modal system is one of the least understood and most unsystematically described areas of English grammar. It has been traditionally suggested that the closed system of modals is syntactically simple and semantically chaotic. Modals were described by structuralists as simple slots in the expanded verb; such a view seems to have been confirmed by the early transformational-generative treatments. In the era of generative semantics, however, hard questions about the simultaneous representation of both the syntactic and semantic facts[1] are being put in answerable forms. Great stress must be laid on the fact that we are only at the beginning of an adequate syntactico-semantic description of the formal and conceptual aspects of the modal system. Although there have been numerous diachronic and synchronic studies of the semantics of modals,[2] these studies have not captured the subtle systematic diversities of the modal system. This lack of systematic treatment for semantic structure in what we intuitively perceive to be a system gives one pause.

The first problem in any study of modals is the problem of taxonomy—deciding which occurrences are modals and which are not. Indeed, whether or not a legitimate class exists may be the subject of much debate. Modals have generally been considered to be an intuitively satisfying cluster of language occurrences which exhibit sufficient structural affinities to justify inclusionary and exclusionary judgments. Five features are characteristic of at least eight of the words we intuitively class as modals: the lack of an overt morphemic marker for third person singular present tense forms, the immediate post-positioning of a zero infinitive form, the capacity to be the operative constituent in questions, negations and the like, the unique historical past and present form relationships, and the inability to co-occur with other class members.

(1) can   could
    may   might
    shall should
    will   would

If past/present pairing were an essential characteristic of modals, then *must* would have to be excluded from the class. It can be argued, however, that the others are not truly paired, because of the semantic and syntactic independence between the members of each pair. But even placement of *must* in a system of paired modals would only make for one mildly anomalous class member—a not unusual grammatical situation.

Ought to is the tenth and last member of the class which is usually considered to be clearly part of the closed modal system. The use here of *ought to* instead of *ought* begins to indicate the taxonomer's problem. The force of so many analogous occurrences of verbs plus marked infinitives suggests that the modal unit is *ought* and the *to* belongs to the following verbal matter.

(2) Ought he to go?
(3) He shouldn't ought to go.

Such tests as questionizing in (2) confirm the constituency, and in some dialects co-occurrence with other modals as in (3) seems possible, refuting its status as a modal. However, most native speakers respond to *ought to* as the modal unit, perhaps only as a false surface analogy, but this response does seem to place *ought to* in a class with the other nine modals.

Were it not for the questionable status of some other verbs which are usually represented by *dare* (*to*) and *need* (*to*), one would be strongly inclined to make the taxonomer's choice rest only on the most basic syntactic criteria. These verbs have well-documented ranges of occurrence which sometimes allow them to fulfill the usual criteria of modal verbs and sometimes to act like full verbs. Although some matters seem to be dialectal, most represent a wide variety of choices for any individual speaker. Many examples of conflicting criteria are possible in my dialect.

(4) Dare he go?
(5) *Dare he to go?
(6) Dared he to go?

While (6) is possibly a literature-induced archaism (i.e., main verb swing in questions), it seems more likely to represent the casual remark that grammars leak.[3] The phylogeny of the modal system does suggest that these younger members of the species might well end up clearly in the class at some point.

The auxiliary verb *do,* which is not usually classified as a modal, requires comment. *Do* does not satisfy most people's intuitive sense of the semantics of modality, but Michael Grady presents it in a list of modal verbs, apparently because it occurs with the zero infinitive following it.[4] Some other behavioral criteria are fulfilled by *do:* non-occurrence with modals and operative constituency in questions and negations. However, most other criteria do not indicate that *do* is a modal; even more importantly, the semantic field of modality does not seem to have a place for *do.* It does not result in what I have elsewhere called an "unrealized predicate."[5]

On the other hand, many verbs that are linked to modality by fulfilling some sort of semantic sense of modality tend not to obey most of the simple syntactic criteria of modality.

(7) He is to go.
(8) He has to go.
(9) He is going to go.
(10) He is about to go.
(11) He seems to go.
(12) He continues to go.

Only the first item in the series, *is (to),* does not freely occur with other modals. By the time one gets to (12), one finds that the ground has shifted to what is clearly a full complement verb not unlike some instances of *need (to)* and *dare (to)*. The semantic character of such verbs and the great variety of intermediate structures presented in (7)–(12) is a matter of much debate; I have elsewhere suggested that the semantics of both grammatical formatives and full lexical items might be coherently captured by a feature analysis.[6] And even though the wide range of syntactic occurrences does not suggest a clear hierarchical order from paired closed modals to full complement verbs, there appears to be a hard structural and semantic core of modality from which many types of occurrences diverge in varying structural and semantic ways. To examine a verb like *continue* may not be to examine a modal verb, but it may well inform the examination of modal verbs.

The basic thrust of structuralist semantic examinations of modals has been to set matrices of meaning that encompass as many of the textual occurrences of the modals as possible; the occurrences are defined by formal criteria like those mentioned above. W. F. Twaddell develops a schema which excludes the paired past tenses because they are in the relationship of non-reality and sequence-of-tenses; he does expositorially reintroduce some of the more frequent formal past occurrences. He postulates an axis of contingency which has three members: unrestricted, inconclusive, and morally determined. A second axis of potential is represented by prediction, possibility, and necessity. Many of the points on the axes have more than one term applied, but the result is a nine value system, of which eight have members.[7] Along the same lines, Martin Joos attempts to supply a vocabulary of modality in which "each modal is either *adequate* or *contingent,* and either *casual* or *stable;* and each either *assures* the event or specifies that it is *potential.*"[8] F. R. Palmer's listing of possible uses under each item is more directly in the long tradition of the study of modal semantics; his more expansive treatment tries to capture multiple meaning without reference to a semantic structure.[9] These useful categorizations are generally independent of syntactic occurrence, but they do help to supply a vocabulary for modality.

Frederick Newmeyer's effort to examine "aspectuality" places modal verbs in a broad deep structure category called aspectual verbs, which are "essentially lexical items whose semantic role is to function as one place predicates of arguments which contain entire propositions."[10]

(13) He happens to go.

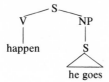

happen
S
he goes

(14) He may go.

may
S
he goes

The generalizations caught by such representations are very interesting, but the mechanics of such an analysis are not necessarily accepted by many linguists and that controversy is not the immediate problem. Newmeyer does however place modals in a clearly defined verbal category, in some ways a more discerning representation of the important statement of John R. Ross on the status of auxiliary verbs. Ross describes modals and other auxiliaries as main verbs which take their propositions as objects in the deep structure.[11]

Among transformational-generative grammars the least analytic position on modals is represented by Noam Chomsky in *Syntactic Structures* and even later in *Aspects of the Theory of Syntax:*

(15) Aux→ Tense (Modal) (have + en) (be + ing)

(16) Aux→ {Tense/Modal} (have + en) (be + ing)

Most structuralists and most early transformational-generative
linguists have used some close equivalent of the representation in
(15): the structuralist's simple verb expansion finds its generative
correlation in a simple phrase structure rule. However, a different
claim about the tense of modals is expressed by (16), but this only
seems to represent the problem of whether to treat the historical
past and present tense pairing as a synchronic feature or to consider each member of the pair as separate. The conceptual problem of tense is much more difficult; however, it is not simple-
mindedness that moves linguists like Chomsky to accept the
simple structures of (15) and (16). It is either an explicit or implicit acceptance of interpretive semantics rather than generative
semantics. Interpretive semantics with its separate semantic
component simply puts the problem of semantic description in an
ill-defined place. A holistic grammar will have to treat syntactic
and semantic matters in an integrated way; thus one returns to
syntactico-semantic descriptions.

The simple phrase structure rules that share a remarkable af-
finity with descriptive formulations by structuralists are chal-
lenged by Ross and later Newmeyer among many others, with
Ross arguing that auxiliaries must have atypical treatment in
order to be included in the phrase structure rules.[12] However, it
is not necessary to accept any of these positions, if we allow that
other methods of description will inform our knowledge of English. Even as the feature analysis mentioned above could either
be used by certain generative semantic models or might be part
of a semantic field theory, the focus here will be on the core
semantic characteristics of the paired modals. There will be no
hesitation to call on formal matters to support or control the
semantics of the data, but almost every procedural decision will
be to simplify in order to find what is at the center. Toward this
end, only the paired items in (1) will be examined.

The most basic taxonomic distinction in this analysis breaks
the modal system into two classes: epistemic modals and root
modals. T. Ronald Hofmann suggests that epistemic modals are
similar to epistemic passives, which have no corresponding active
sentences; but more importantly for this study, they both tend
to qualify the truth value of the predictions in their sentences.

He also observes that the root modals have some severe syntactic restrictions.[13] Neither Hofmann nor Newmeyer, who adopts the distinction and articulates some non-systematic syntactic differences, attempts to give a structured semantic analysis. J. Boyd and J. P. Thorne's commentary on the semantics of modal verbs, which utilizes the notion of speech acts, is a partial implicit representation of the epistemic concept, but they fail to note the systematic nature of the modal paradigm.[14] It may not be possible to create perfectly clear categories for all the occurrences in the modal system, but one might well be able to indicate the central structured description of their semantics.

Below is an anticipatory representation of what remains an insufficient vocabulary to describe the semantic field of the modals; a metavocabulary that is outside the bounds of natural language would probably be necessary, but would also be inexplicable. In general, the root occurrences must be understood to involve the speaker's modal perspective on the subject of the sentence and the epistemic occurrences refer to the speaker's modal perception of the whole proposition.

(17) root *can*   capacity
      epistemic *can*   propositional capacity
      epistemic *could*   conditional propositional capacity

      root *may*   permission
      epistemic *may*   propositional possibility
      epistemic *might*   conditional propositional possibility

      root *shall*   promissory intent
      epistemic *shall*   emphatic propositional future
      epistemic *should*   conditional propositional entailment

      root *will*   determination
      epistemic *will*   definite propositional future
      epistemic *would*   implied negation

In preparation for the semantic analysis, some of the most trenchant syntactic criteria which can be used to distinguish between epistemic and root modals will be discussed, but the derivational structures will not be treated.[15] (i) The animate subject that both Hofmann [16] and Newmeyer insist upon for root modals is probably better described as what the deep case grammarians would call an agent or even a secondary agent.

(18) John may $\begin{smallmatrix}\text{(propositional possibility)}\\\text{(permission)}\end{smallmatrix}$ enjoy the book.

(19) John may $\begin{smallmatrix}\text{(propositional possibility)}\\\text{(*permission)}\end{smallmatrix}$ like the book.

The modal in (18) could be either epistemic or root. In order for (19) to be read as grammatical, it must be epistemic. Since *John* is a deep case Dative, it makes the root modal reading ungrammatical. Such a restriction will also capture Newmeyer's apparently separate restriction that root modals must be followed by active verbs. (ii) Epistemic modals may take a perfective verb expansion, but root modals cannot.

(20) John may have enjoyed the book.

The perfective expansion of (18) to (20) disambiguates the sentence; (20) can only be the epistemic sense of *may*.[17] (iii) Newmeyer argues that epistemic modals may be paraphrased in the form 'it (modal) be S', and root modals cannot be.[18]

(21) It may be that John enjoyed the book.

Again (21) disambiguates the two possibilities that are presented by (18). (iv) Hofmann's claim that the present tense of the epistemic modal is represented by the progressive form seems too strong.[19]

(22) He may sing now.
(23) He may be singing now.

Certainly the second example must be epistemic, but the first is ambiguously root or epistemic. This minimal discussion of the permutations in syntactic behavior of the two occurrences of *may* should give the reader some idea what the differences between a root modal and an epistemic modal are.

The ultimate purposes of both the Newmeyer and the Hofmann studies are laudable but not central to this analysis; each study subordinates its commentary on modals to a different aim: Hofmann is interested in the syntactic phenomena of the formal perfective replacing the formal past tense as an indication of simple conceptual past in certain types of constructions, and Newmeyer is basically interested in showing that epistemic modals are aspectual in nature. Each item will be examined under controlled conditions in order to describe the central semantic thrust. All of the items have been tried out under the permutations which arise from combinations of questionizing, negating, past tense, and perfective forms. Even for this limited corpus, reporting such occurrences became repetitive and unconstructive, so that there is a focus on those variations which explicate the basic paradigm.

The root *can* suggests that the speaker perceives the subject of being capable of certain acts.

(24) I can speak German.
(25) I could speak German yesterday.

As with most occurrences of root modals, the simplest occurrence will normally be ambiguous. The reader must avoid substituting the semantic content of the epistemic representations so that the discussions of the root modals will make sense. Unlike the epistemic system, some of the root modals still maintain both the formal and conceptual past tense relationships in a very direct way. The *could* of (25) clearly does predicate the same modality as *can* in (24), but in a past time.

The epistemic *can* indicates that the proposition is capable of being fulfilled, generally in its physical aspect.

(26) It can happen.
(27)*It could happen yesterday.
(28) It [can not] happen.
(29) Can't it happen?
(30) It can [not happen].
(31) Can it not happen?

While a simple examination of (24) and (26) would lead one to say that they are the same modal, introspection would tell one that the root and epistemic ambiguity of (24) is not present in (26). Many of the tests mentioned above could confirm the differences in syntax that are indicative of the differences in semantics. The non-occurrence of (27) is one of the more direct indications. A persistent problem in these discussions will revolve around the topicalization of the negation in these putatively simple sentences. Without the square brackets (28) and (30) would look the same in writing and would have a good chance of being pronounced the same; it is possible to differentiate them by saying (30) with more stress on the modal and, if even stronger differentiation is required, by putting some sort of juncture between *can* and *not*. It can however be argued that in the main (28) and (30) can be mistaken for each other unless the speaker chooses to make the differentiation. For instance, a speaker is capable of making (28) unambiguous by using a contracted form of the negative; it could not then be (30). The questionized forms of the sentence are obviously not ambiguous as to the topicalization of the negation. Unless otherwise noted through the rest of this investigation, only those negations which are focused on the modals themselves will be of interest.

The epistemic *could* has at its center a description of the capacity of the proposition to occur under some condition or conditions.

(32) It could happen, if the conditions were right.
(33) It could have happened yesterday, if the conditions had been right.
(34) His going is to be expected.
(35) His having gone is to have been expected.

It is interesting to note in (32) and (33) that for most of the epistemic modals the perfect expansion creates a conceptual past tense. This is not without analogy in other parts of the verbal system as the gerundive and infinitive nominalizations of (35) show in their comparison with (34). The relationship of (26) to (32) is not temporal in any straight-forward way, so we might choose to regard (32) as the subjunctive manifestation of (26) if it were possible to establish what that means in modern English.[20]

(36) He says it can happen.
(37) He says it could happen.

(38) He said it can happen.
(39) He said it could happen.

However, the indirect discourse of (36)–(39) raises the same problem more directly for non-temporal analysis of the epistemic *can* and *could*. The embedded constituents in (36) and (37) raise no problem if we treat them as epistemic modals. (38) might seem strange but would be interpreted as meaning that the *saying* was prior to time of utterance and the *happening* was potentially any time after the *saying*. It is not immediately clear that (39) has two senses. Only in the context of the other sentences can one see that (39) is possibly the conceptual past of (36) or an independent statement of the epistemic *could* in the past; that independent statement may also only be disguised direct discourse. The problems of sequence of tenses are still ill-defined for modern English. It is possible that the formal past and present relationship exists even in the epistemic system when there are certain kinds of embedding like indirect discourse.

The speaker's recognition of granted permission for the subject is the core of the root occurrence of *may*.

(40) He may go to the ballgame.
(41) I may go to the ballgame.
(42) He might go to the ballgame yesterday.

The modality of (40) is obviously at least twice ambiguous because it might relate to the possibility of the predicate happening or it might be the case where the speaker has been granted permission. There is an added confusion which occurs because there is the possibility that a third party has granted the permission. However, the granting of permission by a third party surprisingly belongs to the epistemic sense because the modality is not in the granting but in the attendant possibility as seen by the speaker. The oddness of (41) as a root modal addresses the semantic problem of giving oneself permission, but as an epistemic modal there is no problem. There appears to be no easy explanation for the fact that the root has no past tense equivalent as the root *can* was shown to have. It is difficult to perceive (42) as the conceptual past of (40) although some informants do recognize it as such.

F. Th. Visser claims that historically the type 'He might do it, because he was a god' (1584) is "used to express permission or sanction in the past."[21] Few of his historical examples are unequivocal, and his 20th century examples simply do not seem to have the force suggested by the category.

The possibility that a proposition may be true is the core of the epistemic modality of *may*.

(43) It may rain.
(44)*May it rain?
(45) It might rain, if I'm right.
(46) Might it rain?

The oddness of the questionizing in the modality of the epistemic *may* must be related to the fact that the proposition is already once questioned by the truth value of the modality. In fact there is a tendency to read (44) as being a metaphoric version of the root modal. The likely questionized form of epistemic *may* would seem to reside in the epistemic *might*, which expresses a conditional propositional possibility. It would seem that the condition rather than the proposition is questionized so that (46) is conceptually the question for both (43) and (45). The resistance of *may* and *might* to forming a contracted form of negation suggests the difficulty that propositional possibility does not lend itself to modification.

The root *shall* indicates the speaker's view of the subject's promissory intention.

(47) I shall do my very best.
(48) I shall have done my very best.
(49) He shall do his very best.
(50)*I should do my very best yesterday.
(51) Shall I do my very best?

It is often hard to tell the epistemic from the root as in (47). Since (47) does not readily form the simple past tense as it might in (50), we should look at the possibility of (48) being the past. It is however clear that (48) is not promissory but belongs rather to the emphatic propositional future of the epistemic *shall*, in which this action has been completed. The possible non-epistemic

reading of (49) is interesting, even though it is not the usual
first response. It is possible to interpret it to mean 'I [the speaker]
promise you that he will do his very best.' Such a reading would
institute a root modal sense for (49). The single epistemic reading
of the questionizing in (51) indicates that the semantic content of
the root *shall* cannot be questionized because of the semantic
presuppositional nature of promissory intentions.

The epistemic *shall* has been the center of traditional debates
about its relationship with the epistemic *will*. Here, it is simply
characterized as an emphatic propositional future.

(52) The war shall end today.
(53) Shall the war end today?
(54) Will the war *really* end today?
(55) Shall we dance?
(56) Will we dance?

The semantic intention of (53) is very interesting because it does
not seem to represent what would be the simple questionizing of
(52). One needs to paraphrase as in (54) to get the semantically
equivalent question. The likely reading of (53) is that there is a
conspiratorial intent between speaker and addressee to extract
mutual promises of ending the war; in essence, we are forced
to take (53) as a special instance of a questionized root modal.
Much the same response would resolve the traditional dilemma of
what seems to be such radical semantic divergence in the questionized forms in (55) and (56) from the semantically similar
assertions that seem to formally underlie the questions. One cannot be both emphatic about a predication and questionize it, but
one can emphatically questionize a predication as in (54).

The epistemic *should* reflects a likely propositional entailment,
which is likely rather than certain by nature of some conditionality.

(57) The war should end today.
(58) Should the war end today?

The semantic force of the question in (58) is informative because it
shows that the topicalization of the question is not on the proposi-

tion itself, but on the conditionality. The question invites the respondent to offer a judgment based on conditions.

The speaker's attitude toward determination in the root *will* seems to reflect in part the historically discernible concept of volition that is associated with the item. It is useful to put emphasis on the modal to obtain a reading with the root meaning.

(59) I will go to the ballgame.
(60) I won't go to the ballgame.
(61) I would go to the ballgame yesterday.
(62) I would go to the ballgame on a day like yesterday.
(63) I wouldn't go to the ballgame yesterday.
(64) You will go to the ballgame.

Some small tradition has grown up for treating *won't* as a separate modal meaning refusal, but that seems unnecessary with this treatment of the root *will;* refusal is fairly equated with negative determination. The use of *would* in (61) does seem to exist in modern English, but it occurs almost exclusively with a tone of disgust, which is what makes the qualified (62) seem so much more possible. The occurrence of (63) is another argument for the treatment of *won't* as a separate modal. There seem to be no references in the scholarship to the effect of negation on the capacity of the root *will* to occur in its historical past tense form. It remains semantically involved with the determination of the speaker. The quality of an order in (64) is similarly involved with the determination of the speaker: the paraphrase is 'I will that you go to the ballgame.'

The epistemic *will* represents a definite propositional future.

(65) The war will end.
(66) Will the war end?
(67) The war won't end.

Its occurrence seems straight-forward; the questionized form and the negated form seem to be no more than the conceptually appropriate variations on the basic construct.

The epistemic *would* represents once again the difficulty of wording a conditionally affected definite proposition. The definiteness affects the conditionality in a very strong way, so that *would* seems to invite an implied negative clause. This appears to make epistemic *would* semantically remote for epistemic *will*, but it is closely related because it is a polar opposite.

(68) The war would end, but something prohibits it.
(69) Would the war end if something didn't prohibit it?
(70) Wouldn't the war end if something didn't prohibit it?

While epistemic *will* predicates something will happen, epistemic *would* usually predicates that it will not happen. The similarity between (69) and (70) that is suggested by the occurrence of the same answer to each question under the same conditions shows that the implied negation may be either overt or tacit.

We now have evidence that the core modal paradigm exists in a somewhat more complicated form than is usually shown.

(71)

Modal	Core Meaning	Past Form
root *can*	capacity	*could*
epistemic *can*	propositional capacity	*can* + perfective
epistemic *could*	conditional propositional capacity	*could* + perfective
root *may*	permission	semantically blocked
epistemic *may*	propositional possibility	*may* + perfective
epistemic *might*	conditional propositional possibility	*might* + perfective
root *shall*	promissory intent	semantically blocked
epistemic *shall*	emphatic propositional future	semantically blocked
epistemic *should*	conditional propositional entailment	*should* + perfective
root *will*	determination	*would*
epistemic *will*	definite propositional future	semantically blocked
epistemic *would*	implied negation	*would* + perfective

Both the epistemic *shall* plus a perfect expansion and *will* plus a perfect expansion exist, but they are not conceptual past tenses as is shown by (73) and (75).

(72) The war shall have ended.
(73)*The war shall have ended yesterday.
(74) The war will have ended.
(75)*The war will have ended yesterday.

The character of (72) and (74) would allow us to fill the hole in the paradigm formally, but would violate the semantic goals of this study. They seem to be true perfectives. The study sought to explain the semantic blocking of root *may* and root *shall,* but the semantic arguments must be weakly articulated. We are, however left with the historical fact of the disappearance of both conceptual pasts.

Such an analysis suggests that extensive work is still necessary to sort out the semantic structure of the modal system. We already have models of unstructured representations both historical and synchronic. We also have seen attempts at sorting out the syntactic behavior and deep structure representations of the modals, but the structural accountability in the study of the syntax of modals must be carried over to the varied and seemingly chaotic semantic evidence. This analysis has begun with the core of the semantic matters, and leaves the more difficult peripheral evidence to later studies.

NOTES

1. The general status of modal analyses is laid out in my "A Feature Analysis of the Modal System of English," *Lingua* 32 (1973): 309–311. Since all judgments about possible constructions and meanings are my own as verified by acquaintances, other readers may take exceptions to some of them—hopefully not too many.

2. F. Th. Visser, *An Historical Syntax of the English Language* (Leiden: Brill Co., 1969) presents a mass of material on the historical development of the syntax and semantics of English verbs; modals are treated particularly in *Part Three, First Half.* Yvan Lebrun's *Can and May in Present-Day English* (Bruxelles: Presses Universitaires de Bruxelles, 1965) represents the type of expansive investigation of particular modals that continues to be necessary, but it is of little help to this study because Lebrun finds that *can, may, could,* and *might* all have the same basic meanings.

3. There is more and more evidence that rules in grammars are not completely codifiable because indefinite quantities in rules, conflicting rules, and multiple grammars are all a basic part of natural speech acts; in current terminology, even a modal of competence is not completely competent.

4. *Syntax and Semantics of the English Verb Phrase* (The Hague: Mouton and Co., 1970), p. 19.

5. "Feature Analysis," pp. 311–12.

6. Ibid., p. 322.

7. *The English Verb Auxiliaries* (Providence: Brown University Press, 1960), pp. 10–12.

8. *The English Verb: Form and Meanings* (Madison: The University of Wisconsin Press, 1964), p. 149.

9. *A Linguistic Study of the English Verb* (Coral Gables: University of Miami Press, 1968), pp. 105–139; Madeline Ehrman's *The Meanings of the Modals in Present-Day American English* (The Hague: Mouton and Co., 1966) and William Diver's "The Modal System of the English Verb," *Word* 20 (1964): 322–353 are worthwhile exercises except that their existence simply emphasizes the proliferation of terms and systems when all the studies are taken as a whole.

10. *English Aspectual Verbs* (The Hague: Mouton and Co., 1975), p. 8.

11. "Auxiliaries as Main verbs," mimeographed, M.I.T., 1967.

12. Ibid.

13. "Past Tense Replacement and the Modal System," *Report No. NSF-17*, Mathematical Linguistics and Automatic Translation to National Science Foundation (Cambridge: Harvard University, 1966), pp. (VII-2)–(VII-3).

14. "The Semantics of Modal Verbs," *Journal of Linguistics* 5 (1969): 57–74.

15. Shuan-fan Huang, "On the Syntax and Semantics of English Modals," *Working Papers in Linguistics*, No. 3 (Columbus: The Ohio State University, 1969), pp. 159–181, is a good attempt to derive surface structures from deep structures, but it ends up explaining little about the systematic semantics of modals.

16. "Past Tense Replacement," pp. (VII-12)–(VII-13).

17. *Aspectual Verbs*, p. 73; Newmeyer wrongly argues in addition that root modals don't have overt past tense forms.

18. Ibid., pp. 73–74.

19. "Past Tense Replacement," p. (VII-14).

20. Wayne Harsh's *The Subjunctive in English* (University, AL: University of Alabama Press, 1968) shows the difficulty of trying to set up either formal or conceptual criteria for the subjunctive.

21. *Historical Syntax*, p. 1767.

Grassroots Grammar in the Gulf States

LEE PEDERSON

Sixty-seven years after Mencken's call for a descriptive grammar of American common speech,[1] more echoes than answers have been heard. To be sure, shelves are filled with useful information about American speech, but all of that together makes no national grammar. Although Mencken's enthusiastic charge—like the onomastic chutzpa in the title of his best book—reflects an imperfect understanding of a large problem, the idea of a grammar of Spoken American English endures as a worthwhile task to be completed. This demands individual and collective efforts: native competence that is operational in every region and among every significant social organization to provide the information and understanding needed to determine the ranges of dialectical variation, the rules of grammar, and the standards of correctness, and long-term projects that extend local studies across dialect areas and explore every aspect of the communication process. Nothing less will suffice to produce the kind of work that Mencken had in mind, a description of the linguistic habits of the most socially complicated people in the history of civilization.

Within the Southern states, the work of James B. McMillan is a classic individual effort of just that kind. His description of phonology and morphophonemics is an authoritative reference for the speech of the Interior South, and his *Annotated Bibliography of Southern American English* is a model regional index. The current Linguistic Atlas of the Gulf States (LAGS) Project responds to questions implicitly raised in the pioneering work of McMillan and others. His latter work, for example, is a discriminating guide to more than 1400 titles, but only 62 of these directly concern morphology and syntax, with nearly half of those involving personal pronouns in the second person—*you all, you-uns,* and *youse.* When similar, if not comparable, bibliographies are compiled for other regions of the United States, the problem can be stated with elegance at a national level of concern. Students will know the kinds of information needed for a morphology and syntax of the spontaneous speech of the American people, a grassroots grammar. Meanwhile, following McMillan's lead, the LAGS Project approaches the investigation in the Interior South to suggest some possibilities in an area where a substantial foundation has been laid.

Atlas data from most sections of the country provide baseline evidence for the inductive study of regional phonology, morphology, and vocabulary. Lightweight, sensitive, and dependable reel-to-reel tape recorders now offer a means to complement atlas collections with as much syntactic data as a regional grammarian might need for transcription and study through replays that are virtually instantaneous and limitless. Indeed, it is the tape recorder, more than innovative sampling, analytical, or descriptive procedures, that has advanced current sociolinguistic investigation.[2]

Conventional dialectology today with its emphasis on conversational discourse records and preserves every word spoken in the interview to provide a rich corpus of thoroughly verifiable data. Such material can be treated as cursorily or elaborately as the grammarian chooses, but the evidence stands and must be ultimately accounted for in a comprehensive fashion. Broad generalizations of phrase structure and overviews of syntactic patterns must at some time be substantiated with context sensitive interpretations of grammatical forms based on microlinguistic analyses of all elements in the communication process.

The LAGS Project is designed to give the descriptive grammarian some of that information by organizing and indexing a corpus of regional American English—approximately 4,000 hours of tape-recorded conversational speech—in a survey of native usage in Florida, Georgia, Alabama, Mississippi, Tennessee, Louisiana, Arkansas, and East Texas. The present report identifies the sources and the substance of the grammatical data gathered in the LAGS Project to suggest some of the information available to a grassroots grammarian: 1) the evidence sought directly in the standard interview procedure, 2) the range of incidental material transcribed in a single protocol, 3) the contents of a brief passage from a field record summarized in the protocol, and 4) the probable format of the data that will be organized as a regional contribution to an inductive grammar of American common speech.

I

Because massive grammatical evidence occurs in spontaneous conversation, it is easy to overlook the valuable data elicited through items in the work sheets. These forms are the systematically contrastive features that have been surveyed in other regional atlas projects, thereby providing information of an indispensible sort. Although a comprehensive grammar must do more than characterize the formal properties of a selected set of morphological and syntactic features, few complete, skeletal, or even partial paradigms of inflectional morphology can be expected in an unstructured interview. Atlas material provides a core of comparable data, and every survey aims to enlarge and improve upon the work from which it has emerged.

For the sake of efficiency, atlas projects survey morphology and syntax through the investigation of features observed in earlier research and exploratory fieldwork. In the LAGS Project, for example, a number of grammatical items came from a variety of sources.[3] Combined with the items used in earlier atlas surveys, this material comprises a wide range of grammatical evidence— the morphology and syntax of verbs, substantives, and modifiers, as well as the alternation and deletion of function words and some grammatical operations of contrastive stress.

Verbs. Forms and functions surveyed in LAGS include the principal parts of 33 verbs from several historical classes, preterit and participial variation among 26 other finite verbs, and 27 auxiliary verb forms. In addition to these, 29 forms in the syntax of verb negation are sampled. Person, tense, mood, voice, status, and aspect are included incidentally, as well as special instances of durative and perfective constructions.[4]

Nouns and Pronouns. Investigation of substantive forms (i.e., nouns, nominals, and pronouns) and constructions in the work sheets include singular and plural forms of 15 nouns, five plurals of nouns of measure, and three variable plurals. The possessive case was surveyed in the preliminary work sheets—"John's book" versus "John's own book" and "He buried his son" versus "He buried him a son"—but such reflexive genitives were unproductive. They are, however, included in the protocol when occurring in conversation. As the most fully inflected set of English substantives, the pronouns are closely covered.[5]

Modifiers. Adjectival and adverbial modifiers itemized in the work sheets are morphological, phrasal, and clause structures. Adjectives in the comparative degree are represented by the disyllabic form *pretty* (*prettier/more pretty*) and the present participle *loving* (*more loving/lovinger*) and in the superlative degree by past participle *grownup* (*most grown-up/grown-uppest*). The redundant *onliest* ("He was the onliest one to get sick") and superlatives of deprecation ("That was the sorriest dog of the bunch") are most effectively investigated incidentally. Free form alternation among adjectivals include *almost/nearly/nigh on to, gone/all gone, none/not a one/ne'er a one,* and *many/many a one.*

Adverbial modifiers include the alternation of bound forms and free forms,[6] as well as syntactic features of tense, aspect, and phase: *anymore/nowadays, by and by/soon, in the past/used to, a week ago Sunday/Sunday week, a week from Sunday/last Sunday week.* Inchoative aspect is marked at the clause level by *during the night/of a night;* durative aspect, by *right on/steadily.*

Function Words and Idioms. Several prepositions and conjunctions are targeted in phrasal items,[7] but the most complicated of these occur in idiomatic constructions that must be evaluated in terms of both grammatical and semantic distinctiveness.[8] The interpretation of semantic data requires close attention, and this is the most demanding sort of analytical work, involving an open-ended set of forms and constructions. Without close attention to word and phrase structure, however, the grammatical system cannot be effectively described.

Closely related to function words in the interpretation of grammatical and idiomatic constructions are the structural signals of prosody—stress, pitch, and juncture as they combine in the basic contours of intonation. These include substantive/verbal pairs *addréss/áddress, brúsh/brùsh, fréeze/frèeze,* and *whíp/whìp,* a verbal/adjectival pair *hàs grôwn úp/mòst grównúp,* a substantive/ adjectival pair *bôil/bôiled éggs,* a prepositional/adverbial pair *òn púrpòse/pût ìt ón,* an adverbial/verbal pair *râthèr cóld/wòuld ráthèr,* and a substantive/verbal pair with morphophonemic alternation *cálf/cálve.* Other prosodic features influencing the phonological structure of grammatical forms are the deliberately/rapidly articulated utterances *gîve mé/gìmmè* and *Mrs̀. Còopèr/Míz Cóopèr* (both as titles of a married woman).

II

In addition to the items covered in the work sheets, other grammatical forms are recorded in every protocol transcribed in the LAGS Project. Most of this morphological and syntactic information will not be immediately useful in the demarcation of regional and social dialects, but all of it is necessary in the composition of a regional grammar. The following examples are limited to the incidental protocol notation from a single field record.[9] These forms include base-form and inflectional morphology and syntactic structures at the phrase, clause, and sentence levels.

Morphology. The combinations of morphemes recorded in free conversation provide not only examples of lexical, semantic, and grammatical variation but also outline processes of word formation observable in the idiolect. These include combinations of free forms—nouns, verbs, modifiers, and function words—in the creation of nominal, verbal, and modificational constructions, as well as composition by analogy and phrasal simplification (the deletion of free forms):[10]

Nominal Constructions:
    Noun + Noun: dùskdàrk (late evening), hóglàrd, pónd câtfìsh,
        vélvĕt bèan;[11]
    Verb + Noun: bóilĭng mèat (sidemeat), kíssĭng kĭnfòlks, sprĕad-
        ĭng oùtĕr;[12]
    Modifier + Noun: hígh shèrĭff,[13] scáredў càt, tráshў pèrsòn;
    Analogous Compounds: dèerdòg (after birddog), cátfìsh stêak
        (after beef steak);
    Reduced Compounds: chúckwàgòn [steak] (small beef steak),
        [electric] líghtpòle, ráil[road] lìght (kerosene lantern);
    Reduced structure of modification: nòndáirў (ă nòndáirў from
        nondairy product);
    Infixed intensifier: tee-niny peas [tì:ná:nɨ pìiz];[14]

Verbal Constructions:
    Analogous Constructions: lighten up (after brighten up), pooch
        out and punch out (both after bulge out);
    Blend: scweaming [skwíəmən] (of a baby, squirming and
        screaming);

Modificational Constructions of Various Categories:
    Adjectival: trough-like (of gutters, trough-like things); swively
        [swíəvəlɨ] (from shrivel with derivational suffix, after sticky);
    worlds of them (many); protracted meetings [pətrǽktɨd mí:
        tɨŋz] (extended meetings, i.e., rivivals).[15]

Supplementary evidence of inflectional forms in the protocol
includes these constructions: [brέkfəsɨz] (breakfast, pl.), [mέ:
ngàətɨz] (men's garters), [wɒəspnέəst] (wasps' nest), [hǽɛv
stóɐld] (steal, pp.), and [ɒɔffɨst] (awful, super.)

Phrase Structure. Variation here includes contraction, deletion,
and lexical selection in nominal, verbal, and modificational structures. In this idiolect, the most frequently recurring of these
variant features is contraction and deletion in the auxiliary construction be(am/are/is/was) going + infinitive marker to. In
these sometimes catenative phrasal units, the inflectional suffix
-ing is reduced to vowel nasality and the infinitive marker is

deleted, resulting in the forms [gõū ~ gɔ̃õ] followed by the unmarked infinitives:

I think I'm)going to try to learn [gõū́ trái tə̆|lɤ̆ɚ̆n];
They are going to stay [ðɛ̆ə gɔ̃õ stéɪ];
... I can asure you it's going to be sore [gõū́bí:|sóə];
I was afraid that fish)was going to eat me [wə̀z gõū́ í:t mì];
Daddy would have selected ones[watermelons], you know, that
   he would have picked out for different people that he was
   going to give to [wə̆z gɔ̃õ gívtȕu]... and we'd always get
   one of those.

All of these contrast with the recorded finite form of going:

... if she's not going[.] [ìf ʃî:z nàt góʊə̆n].

Other instances of deletion include an inflectional suffix (it
melt[s]), a verb auxiliary (they [have] run some tests), and a
preposition (You could smell them from here [to] yonder). A more
complicated problem of deletion concerns article the preceding
only, recorded three times in the protocol:

That's only land that I've really had experience with, sandy
   land;
Just this one time is only time we had to carry water;
That's only place [it was found].

In these instances the phonological and syntactic environments
are virtually identical, with the article position occurring between
fricatives (s/z) and the back vowel of only and following a linking
verb in an ostensible predicate adjective construction. The article
is also deleted before onliest in the same environment:

That's onliest woman that I've ever seen smoke a pipe, but she
   did.

In the uninflected forms above there is an adverbial sense: only
[kind of] land, only [when] we had to carry water, and only place

[*where it was found*]; but *onliest woman* is an explicit structure of modification, i.e., adjective + noun.

A semantic consideration at the level of phrase structure grammar involves the uses of the modifier *old*. In the work-sheet phrase *good old days,* the sense of the remote past is clear, as is the notion of approbation. Eight other phrases recorded in the protocol are more complicated:

Indicating age, without emotional overtones:
an old Negro woman [ən ôʉl nígə̀ wʊ̀mn̩];
Implying affection in recollections from the past:
our little old porch [lîəl ôʉl póətʃ];
a great old big pile (of sand) [gr̂eet òʉ bîg páɪl];[16]
big old cans (of lard) [bîg ôʉl kǽɛnz];
a little old thing (a cigarette roller used by her late husband during World War II) [lîəl òʉl θíŋ];
Implying playful disapprobation without reference to time:
old moonshine whiskey [òʉl mʉʉnʃàːɪn hwîəskɪ];
old badman [ðə̀ ôʉɫ bǽɛd mǽɛn] (a haunt, the boogerman);
old peckerwood [òʉ pɛ́kə̀wʊəd] (a joking term of abuse);

The affectionate and playfully disparaging use of *old* is quite common in Southern folk speech, as, for example, *sweet little old thing* or *little old peckerwood* for a child and *good old boy* for *one of the boys* or any misunderstood reprobate. The grammatical interpretation of the form *old,* however, will require a delicate interpretation of semantic structure in Southern folk speech.

Clause Structure. Examples here from the Aimwell protocol include copula deletion, subject-verb agreement, word order, and functional shift, specifically, the adverbial usage of verbs and adjectives as phrase and clause modifiers. The lone instance of a deleted copula occurred in a discussion of the use of whips in urging horses on, but never with mules:

Oh, mules slow anyway [óːʉ‖mjʉʉlz|slôʉ ɛ́nɪ̀weɪ].

In addition to the work-sheet items concerning subject-verb agreement, these structures of predication were recorded:

There was four other men.	[ðɛə wəz fóə ʌðə mɛ́ən]
Don't that sound stupid?	[dɔ̀ʉn ðǽɛt sáon stʉ́ʉpɨd]
That don't go way back.	[ðǽɛt dɔ̀ʉn góʉ|wéɨ bǽɛk]
The harnesses was hooked to that.	[ðə́ háənɨsɨz|wəz húkt tə́ ðǽɛt]

Also, a single occurrence of altered word order indicates an effort at emphasis: *Nevèr dìd wé hàve à ràil fènce* (after telling of various local rail fences).
Several instances of adjunctive structures are these:

He'd drink his [coffee] *black* (of coffee);
You had to cook that egg done, but not brown [of fried eggs for her son];
They would just come up volunteer [of crops not planted].

None of those is particularly distinctive in American English syntax, but a related utterance is considerably more complicated:

There used to just be bollweevils, real, real bad.
[ðɛ̀ə jʉ́ʉstə́ dʒʌs bî bɔ́oɯ wì:v̪z\|rí:ɯ\|rí:ɯ\|bǽɛd]

In this idiolect, the immediate underlying sentence, *the bollwee-vils here used to be real*[ly] *bad,* must be evaluated with an eye to the habitual use of *used to* as a sentence modifier with the grammatical and semantic meaning of *years ago.*[17] A grammarian of either the armchair or ivory-tower variety can readily point to the split infinitive, the colloquial adverbial use of *just,* and the uninflected adverbs (*real, real*) modifying *bad,* but only a dialect speaker with native competence can explain the relationship of this commonplace verb phrase to its adverbially usage in Southern folk speech.
Other sentences in this protocol that combine phrase and clause structure peculiarities are these:

Does lobsters do that? (i.e., crawl backward as crawfish do);
The tadpoles make the frogs (i.e., grow to become frogs as
  seeds make plants).

Sentence Structure. In addition to instances of eccentric syntax
already cited, relationships among clauses show several other
kinds of variation. These include deletion, contraction, rearrangement, and substitution among elements of the clauses and their
subordinators, as well as verb agreement in successive clauses.
Contraction (of the verb phrase *was supposed to come true*), deletion (of the subordinate adverbial-conjunction *for*) and the rearrangement of clauses are all illustrated in the following sentence
describing the folklore of the *pully bone: The one that got the
short piece of the bone, the wish was supposed to come true*
[ðə wʌ́n ðət gɑ̀t ðə ʃɔ́:ət| píːs|ə̀ ðə́ bə́ũn‖ðə́ wíəʃ|wə̌z spóstə̀|
kʌ́m trᵾ́ᵾ], i.e., *the wish was supposed to come true for the one
that got the short piece of the bone.*
   Substitution among subordinate conjunctions includes instances
of *that* for *when:*

   *You didn't ever see her that she didn't have that pipe in her
      mouth;*
   that for *of which:*
   Nobody ever killed a hog that you didn't get a piece;
   until for *that* (with excrescent repetition of the form):
   *He didn't get to go hunting very much this year because there's
      been so much crime until—the crime is increasing—until
      they don't have time* (concerning the curtailment of her son's
      deerhunting).

   Examples of shifting reference in the succession of clauses are
these:

   singular to plural:
   If you don't hem a snake up, they('re) not go(ing to) bother you
   [ɪf̀ jᵾᵾ dồːhê̂əm ə̌ snềɫk ʌ́əp ðèɫ nɑ̀t gə̂ə́ báːðə̌ jə];
   plural to singular:
   We have the great big black grasshoppers that eats things up.

III

As most of the examples listed in the preceding summary suggest, the best evidence for a comprehensive inductive grammar will be conversational data, whether gathered by linguistic geographers, sociolinguists, or descriptive grammarians. It should be just as obvious, however, that such material is difficult to organize. Even when roughly edited, none of the information is systematically contrastive because sentences are not, like phonemes or inflectional morphemes, members of clearly delineated and narrowly restricted sets. At the same time, sentences and their constituents provide information that covers the full grammatical range of an idiolect under investigation, and, although no atlas field record can possibly cover every element, the available sketch offers a step in that direction. To suggest how much information is gathered in a single interview, a short conversational passage is presented here from the Aimwell field record.

At Item #6, p. 24 of the LAGS work sheets (four hours and 42 minutes into the interview), the fieldworker, Gene Shaffer, asks:

F[ield worker]: What types of boats do people usually use to go fishing?

I[nformant]: Now, I'm just lost there. I don't know too much about boats. I really don't. Skiffs, they used to call 'em skiffs, you know.

F: Um hm.

I: Way back then, you know, when they were first begun having these little things to fish in, you know, and they call 'em skiffs, And rowboats, and now they just, eh, just boats is all I ju—.

F: Can you remember what the skifts and the rowboats looked like? How they were shaped?

I: Well, just like they are now.

F: Um hm.

I: Cause they, you know, they been those, this shape boat has been in for as as long as I can remember. Course, I remember what the, I remember seeing pictures of these boats, you know, way back when they used to make 'em. The Indians used, but.

F: Um hm.

I: But these shaped boats go back as far as I do.

F: Do they have flat bottoms or square fronts?

I: Yes, square, eh, eh, flat bottoms, but pointed on the end, you know, just like they do now.

F: Yeh, o.k.

I: My husband made, he and a friend of his made an aluminum boat one time.

F: Really? Aluminum? How did he do that?

I: They welded it together. And, oh, we fished a lot when Billy was small; before we moved away from here, we fished a lot. We'd go down on the Tombigbee River—that's the river down here.

F: Oh, yes.

I: Camp out at night.

F: Oh, that'd be great.

I: Yeh, that's a lot of fun. It really is. We caught—we went one time when Billy was five years old. We went one Saturday night, spent the night. We got up on Sunday morning, and one of their lines—you put out what you call trotlines.

F: What's that?

I: That's lines that you bait, and you go all the way across the river and have that line.

F: Oh.

I: There'd be one long line and then there's about, like, say every six feet, there would be a little short line down here with a hook on it, baited. And you go across the river and take that thing across the river and tie it to something on the other side. And it would be, it would be stretched all the way across the river.

So we had, one Saturday night, we went, and we had, and there was just a little willow tree that had, had grown up out of the river about this far, and it was just about as far as from here to that heater, from the bank. And they had finished with all the other lines—we just had a boat full of fish—so they got to this line and they could not pull the fish up. It had a fifty-six pound catfish on that little line, on that little willow tree!This man's wife and I had to wade out—it was shallow enough that we had to wade out—to take a trace chain for them to put on that fish to get this fish back in the boat.

F: Wow!

I: And we sold that. They brought that fish to town and dressed it and sold it to a market—to one of the markets here in town. Fifty-six pound! It was larger than either, either one of them. They were both—my husband was—well, he was tall. He was

really tall. Well, he was about as high as Billy, but he was—
he never weighed over 135 pounds. Real skinny. And this man
was a small man, too. So, we had to help them get that fish in
that boat. And, of course, he was cutting up so bad. I was
just—I thought sure I was go(ing to) drown. Fish was go(ing to)
eat me. And I've always been so afraid of those fins, you know.
They will just, oh, kill you.

F: Stick you.

I: They sure will, and it's very poisonous.

F: Oh, really? I didn't know it was poisonous.

I: I mean as far as infection is concerned. Yes, it will always
become infected, nearly, most always.

F: What would you put on something like that?

I: Well, methylate or mercurochrome or something like that. First
aid if you have anything at home. But usually, if you, if you,
if it's very bad, you go to the doctor with it.

F: Really? I'll have to remember that next time I catch one of those
things.

I: Yes, you do. If they fin you—and I can assure you it's go(ing
to) be sore, real, real sore. They just make a bad place, if
it's very bad.

This passage—including the remarks of the fieldworker—span
only four minutes and 50 seconds of a 485 minute field record.
To summarize all of its grammatical constructions would require
a text considerably longer than the present report. The verb
forms alone offer a substantial corpus of data.

At the morphological level, the passage includes 117 verb
forms—verbals (gerunds, participles, and infinitives functioning
as other parts of speech), auxiliary, marked, and unmarked forms
of 44 different verbs: *assure, bait, be, become, begin, bring, call,
camp, can, catch, concern, cut, do, dress, drown, eat, fin, finish,
fish, get, go, grow, have, help, kill, know, make, mean, move,
point, pull, put, remember, see, sell, spend, take, think, tie, use,
wade, weigh, weld,* and *will.*

The syntax of these verbs is most fully represented with seven
of the eight forms of *be* attested in the passage: *am, are, be, been,
is, was,* and *were.* With no occurrence of *being* in the text, the
41 instances of *be* exemplify (with the infinitive) 19 discrete elements of the verb paradigm:

As a finite verb:
   present tense: *am, are, is;*
   modal marked present tense: *is going to be, might be, would be;*
   past tense: *was, were;*
   phase marked past tense; *∅ been, has been, have been;*
As an auxiliary verb:
   as a present tense marker: *is going to be;*
   as a past tense marker with an intransitive verb: *was going to drown;*
   as a past tense marker with a transitive verb: *was going to eat me;*
   as an aspect marker with an *-ing* verb base: *was cutting up;*
   as an aspect marker with an *-en* verb base: *is concerned;*
   as a voice marker in a verb phrase: *would be stretched;*
   as a voice marker in a catenative construction: *were begun having.*

As in some of those examples—*∅ been, were begun having,* and *that's lines*—the syntax of the verb phrase must be interpreted within the context of the situation, the structure of both the narrative and the communication process. The first two of these occur in halting syntax at the outset of the passage, where unfamiliarity with the topic, boats, is mirrored in several other syntactic aberrations as well:

   they call 'em skiffs for *they used to call 'em . . .* or *called 'em skiffs; now they just, eh, just boats is all I ju—*for *now they are just called boats; that is all I call them, just boats;*
   I remember what the, I remember seeing. . . . The Indians used but for
   I remember seeing pictures of the boats that the Indians used, way back when they used to make them.

None of those citations could be rightfully included in a statement concerning morphological or phrasal deletion or in a description of clause patterns unless the context of the situation was identified. Similarly, the apparent lapse of subject-verb agreement in the clause *that's lines* preserves the concord of the discourse at the expense of the clause. The fieldworker placed the plural *trotlines* in the singular with his question *What's that?* The informant replies *That's lines that you bait.* Elsewhere, the fieldworker's remark interrupts a compound verb phrase to replace the conjunction:

> I: *We'd go down on the Tombigbee—*
> F: *Oh, yes.*
> I:—[And] *camp out at night.*

Later, the informant interrupts herself to preserve the suspense of her story *We caught* [a 56 pound catfish once], to clarify details *Well, he* [her husband] *was about as high* [tall] *as Billy* [her son], *but he was—he never weighed over 135 pounds. Real skinny* [but he was real skinny],[18] and to express her excitement in the situation, *I thought sure I was go(ing to) drown [and the] fish was going to eat me.*

All of this suggests not only the necessity of identifying situational styles but also of characterizing both the subject matter of the discourse and the informant's ability and willingness to discuss the topic. Attitude is difficult to define, but to ignore the psycholinguistic implications of a situation invariably leads to an imperfect representation of grammatical forms. The problem is not easily resolved, but a grassroots grammarian must always be willing to sacrifice elegant description for accurate explanation.[19]

IV

In the composition of a national grammar, the role of LAGS and other regional surveys is predetermined by the division of labor within the field of descriptive linguistics. Linguistic geography gathers the data, describes the regional and social patterns, and indexes a corpus for other kinds of analysis and description. To produce a complete and coherent statement, descriptive grammar must provide integrated rules to refine and codify the discursive and nontechnical summaries of linguistic geography, as, for example, the substance of the present report.

The LAGS Project was organized to develop summary descriptions of 750–800 native idiolects in the Interior South and to find social and historical correlations among those idiolects in the identification of dominant and recessive forms, features, and patterns. The passage from the Aimwell record, for example, comprises less than one per cent of the retrievable information, the field record of that single idiolect. Consistent with its primary goals, the LAGS Project will produce two collections and three documents. The basic collection is the complete set of tape-recorded interviews, from which will be derived the Linguistic Atlas of the Gulf States. The atlas will be published in the format of 1000 fiche of microphotography, including a reproduction of all protocols (in narrow phonetic notation with substantial marginalia) and as much connected discourse (in broad phonic and conventional orthographic notation) as time and space permit. The LAGS handbook will follow the second edition of Kurath et al., *A Handbook for the Linguistic Geography of New England* (1972), in form and content.

The three descriptive documents will follow the models of Kurath, Atwood, and Kurath and McDavid,[20] with the order of publication reversed and the contents reflecting the advantages of the tape-recorded corpus. Rather than a morphological statement limited to verb forms, it should be possible to identify all inflectional patterns investigated in the work sheets for nominals and modifiers and to note the recorded processes of contraction, deletion, rearrangement, and substitution. The word geography should reflect both the phonological and grammatical analyses that precede it, separating differences of phonology (e.g., *spigot/ spicket*) and differences of function words (e.g., *quarter of/to/til/ until*) from the proper study of the subject, i.e., lexical and semantic forms.

All of that material should provide useful information for a regional component in a national grammar, but more will be needed to complete the work, even within the province of Southern speech. The ultimate baseline contribution of a regional survey would be an encyclopedic description of morphological and syntactic constructions in the conversational passages of the interview, as well as the systematically elicited items. This would give substance to a Grassroots Grammar of the Gulf States, a modern extension of Joseph Wright's *The English Dialect Grammar.* Whereas that work provided the historical backgrounds of English grammar from its Indo-European sources through the Nineteenth Century, a volume today could begin with Wright and place the regional speech within the context of the English language of the Twentieth Century. By means of the descriptive methodology developed during the past three decades,[21] an exhaustive index of morphological and syntactic structures could offer the very information that Mencken sought.

With all of that completed, data gatherers in the Gulf States will yield to the rule writers of descriptive grammar. That work properly done will carry LAGS research into the next century, and, perhaps, the grammarians can celebrate the centennial of Mencken's call with the publication of the comprehensive inductive grammar of the common speech of the United States. Looking to the immediate and distant future, a prudent seeker of information, assistance, and wise counsel heartily wishes James McMillan a happy birthday and many more of them.[22]

NOTES

1. "My call for a comprehensive inductive grammar of the common speech of the United States, first made in a newspaper article in 1910, has never been answered by anyone learned in the tongues, though in the meantime philologists have given us searching studies of such esoteric Indian languages as Cuna, Chitamacha, Yuma, and Klamath-Modoc, not to mention Eskimo." H. L. Mencken, *The American Language/ An Inquiry into the Development of English in the United States,* the Fourth Edition and the Two Supplements, abridged, with annotations and new material, by Raven I. McDavid, Jr. With the assistance of David W. Maurer (New York: A. A. Knopf, 1963), 509.

2. See "Tape/Text and Analogues," *American Speech* 49 (1974): 5–23, for some of the implications of the tape recorder in conventional linguistic geography. The tape-recorded interview is designated *field record* and the narrow phonetic transcription of forms elicited from the work sheets is designated *protocol* in the LAGS Project. For a summary of progress through 1974, see "The Linguistic Atlas of the Gulf States: Interim Report Two," *American Speech* 49 (1974): 216–24. Interim Report Three will summarize the work completed through 1976, the termination of field work and the plans for editing the atlas.

3. The principal sources are these: E. B. Atwood, *The Regional Vocabulary of Texas* (Austin: University of Texas Press, 1962), Raven I. McDavid, Jr., and Virginia McDavid, "Grammatical Differences in the North Central States," *American Speech* 35 (1960): 5–19, J. LeComte's "A Vocabulary Study of Lafourche Parish and Grand Isle Louisiana," and William R. Van Riper's "Linguistic Atlas of Oklahoma," as reported by A. L. Davis, Raven I. McDavid, and Virginia G. McDavid, *A Compilation of the Work Sheets of the Linguistic Atlas of the United States and Canada and Associated Projects,* 2nd ed. (Chicago: University of Chicago Press, 1969), for finite verbs, adjectives, and adverbs; James B. McMillan, "Vowel Nasality as a Sandhi-Form of the Morphemes -*nt* and -*ing* in Southern American," *American Speech* 14 (1939): 120–3, and "Phonology of the Standard English of East Central Alabama," University of Chicago diss., 1946, for items concerning morphophonemic alternation, consonant vowel assimilation, simplification of final consonant clusters, and vowel nasality in sandhi forms; and the Dialect Survey of Rural Georgia for items concerning deleted articles, auxiliaries, and prepositions, as well as the habitual investigation of verbs in all three principal parts. For information on the plan and progress of the Dialect Survey of Rural Georgia, see Lee Pederson, Grace Rueter, and Joan Hall, "Biracial Dialectology: Six Years into the Georgia Survey," *Journal of English Linguistics* 9 (1975): 18–25; Pederson, "The Plan for a Dialect Survey of Rural Georgia," *Orbis* 24 (1975): 38–44, Pederson, Dunlap, and Rueter, "Questionnaire for a Dialect Survey of Rural Georgia," *Orbis* 24 (1975): 45–71.

4. These include 1) the principal parts of *ask, begin, bit, blow, break, bring, catch, climb, come, dive, do, drag, dream, drink, drive, drown, eat, fight, freeze, give, grow, hear, help, ride, rise, run, see, shrink, sit, swell, swim,* and *write;* 2) finite forms of *be, borrow, burst, cost, do, draw, grease, hang, kneel, know, launch, lie, make, shrivel, stab, sweat, teach, throw, tear, wake,* and *want;* 3) the auxiliaries *be/am/is/ was/were, can/could, do/does/did/done, get/gets/got, go/goes/going, has/have/had, may/might/might could/maybe could, shall/should, take/ took/taken, will/would, dare, ought,* and *used;* 4) verbal phrases of negation, the full and contracted forms of *aint, am not, are not, aren't, cannot, can't dare not, dassn't, does not, doesn't, do not, don't, haint, has not, hasn't, have not, haven't, ought not, oughtn't, should not, shouldn't, used not, usen't, didn't used, was not, wasn't, will not, won't,* and *would not;* 5) besides the inceptives listed above (*go* and *take,* as in "goes to drinking" or "takes to gambling"), the durative aspect

(marked by the prefix *a-* to present participles) and the perfective aspect (marked by auxiliary *done*, as in "I done told you," as opposed to adverbial use in "He was done dead").

5. These include *as he is/as he be/as him, as I am/as I be/as me, he and I/him and me, it is I/me, it is he/him, it is her/she, it is them/they, you and I/me and you*, and *you/you-all* (singular and plural), *who/who-all (who-all is/who-all's); hers/hern, his/hisn, ours/ourn, theirs/theirn, whose/who-all's, you-all's/your*, and *yours/yourn; those/them* (boys), *what/what-all, himself/hisself, themselves/theirselves*, and the relatives *that/which/who/what/Ø.*

6. These include *backward/backwards, forward/forwards, real/really, almost/like to/like to have, anyplace/anywhere/anywheres, apt as not/ probably/like as not, at home/home/to home, kind of/kindly/rather/sort of.*

7. These include *all at once/all to once, down/in/over/out/up in* (a given place), *fall off/off of, fall off/out of* (bed), (the wind is) *out of/ from/to* (a direction), (put wood) *in/into* (the stove), (it has buttons) *on/ on on to it, quarter of/til, to/until* (the hour), *half past/after* (the hour), *toward/towards, sick to/at/on/in/of* (the/one's) *stomach.*

8. In addition to those listed above are *for to/to/in order to* (tell me), *as if/as though/like, because/since, by the time/time, as far as/all the farther/the farthest/all the fartherest/all the furthest, unless/without* (you go too), and *whether/as.*

9. This 485 minute tape recorded interview was conducted by Gene Shaffer, May 5–6, 1976, in the community of Linden in Marengo County, Alabama. Forty miles due south of Tuscaloosa County, Marengo is bound on the west by the Tombigbee River, scarcely 20 miles from the Mississippi border, 90 miles due north of Mobile, and 75 miles west of Montgomery. Linden is at the center of the county; the informant's birthplace and childhood residence, Aimwell, is 12 miles to the south and west. She is a 56-year-old widowed housewife, a fourth generation native of the county. She completed two years of high school, married a lumber inspector, and several years later gave birth to a son, who is presently the sheriff of Marengo County.

With her husband having worked in the principal local industry (pulp wood), family travel in the Interior South, and her son's current position of authority, the informant is a good representative of Type II (common speaker) B (worldly, i.e., nonrustic or provincial within the context of Marengo County). According to her position in the community, the field-worker assigned a heuristic social classification of upper middleclass; from the referents of Hollingshead's Two Factor Index of Social Position, middle to lower-middle class status should be assigned at a national level of ranking.

Phonologically, her speech is clearly a modernized, western extension of the East Central Alabama dialect described by McMillan (1946), including 19 of the 20 distinctive dialect features summarized in his conclusion. Only the unconstricted diphthong [ɜɪ], as an allophone of /ɜ/, as in *bird,* is unattested in the protocol. Although the substitution of /d/ for /z/ before the alveolar nasal /n/, as in *wasn't,* was not recorded, her pronunciation of *clumsy* [kḷʌ̃mᵈɔ̆ɪ.] suggests the pervasive influence of nasal consonants on contiguous fricatives in West Central Alabama as well.

10. The notation here is broad phonic, one of five transcriptional forms used in the LAGS Project, identified in "Tape/Text and Analogues," *American Speech* 49 (1974): 5–23.

Broad phonic transcription is a system of notation that records all distinctive vowel and consonant units with various diacritical marks. These include the 32 vowels and 98 consonants identified for the *Linguistic Atlas of New England* and reproduced for the LAGS Project in Lee Pederson, Raven I. McDavid, Jr., Charles W. Foster, and Charles E. Billiard, *A Manual for Dialect Research in the Southern States* 2nd ed. (University: University of Alabama Press, 1974), pp. 243–4. This provides not only binary notation of all glides (diphthongs and triphthongs), but also variation in the articulation of consonants. Only the diacritics of length, voicing, devoicing, nasality, and syllabification (i.e., syllabic consonants) are presently used. Thus, a narrow phonetic transcription of the word *mountain* [mã̯õ‹nt?ŋ̆] would be represented in broad phonic transcription as [mã̃õnt?ŋ̩]. Such a system can be refined or simplified according to the idiolect or dialect in question, so long as the distinctive features are identified.

11. These are described as black beans that "stung you" when you picked them; they were prickly (like okra) and were fed to cows to improve milk production.

12. Among the snakes identified by the informant—*rattlesnake, chickensnake, ratsnake, water moccasin, black moccasin,* and *kingsnake*—was the cobra-like reptile that raises and spreads its head when threatened. Two different pronunciations were recorded [sprɛ́dṇàəɾḷ] and [sprɛ́dṇàətə], both of which share phonological features of the phrases recorded in Mathews (*DA*), *spreading adder* and *spreading viper:* the alveolar stops [ɾ~t] in the final syllable of each after *adder*) and preceding syllabic [aə] of each (after *viper*). The first form, if not

misspoken, might be interpreted *spreading idol,* but the second seems a popular etymology, a *spreading outer.* Varieties of snakes were not, but should have been, systematically investigated in LAGS fieldwork.

13. The informant notes that local blacks call the county sheriff the *high sheriff,* another relic form that endures in black folk speech. As in one of the few authentic indigenous ballads from the Gulf States, *Stackerlee (Stagolee, Stackolee),* "The high sheriff told his deputies/ 'Get your guns and come with me; we go' go to town right now/Get that Stackerlee/He's a bad man;/That mean old Stackerlee.'"

14. As an intensifier, i.e., *t-in-iny,* it seems to be an instance of infixing with [-i:n-] having the reduplicative morphological function of *bitty* in *little bitty,* perhaps derived from *teeny* in *teeny weenie* or *teeny tiny,* as in the popular tune of a decade or so back concerning, "Teeny-weenie, Yellow-Polka-Dot Bikini." If so, this is another instance of the process described by James B. McMillan in his paper, "Infixing and Interposition in English," presented at the ADS annual meeting, December 29, 1975.

15. See Mary Celestia Parler, "'Lay-by Time' and 'Protracted Meetings'," *American Speech* 10 (1945): 306–7. Here is an instance of a word rarely occurring in LAGS interviews because the item was not included in the work sheets. Other constructions in this interview, rarely investigated in general surveys also were recorded: *honky tonk* [hɔ̃ɔ̃ŋkɨ̃ tɔ̃ɔ̃ŋk] (which was identified as a *Negro joint* [nɪ́grɔ̃ dʒɔ́ənt] located on the county line), *an iron stab* [ən ɑ́ɪən stɑ́ɔb] (i.e., an iron stake), *rolly pollies* (small gray armored insects variously called milk bugs, doodle bugs, or pill bugs, which when threatened roll themselves into balls), *keep it clean* (of cotton plants, i.e., free of weeds), and other morphological forms related to rural life. At the same time, this middle-aged informant reflects the contemporary vocabulary in a number of phrases that were elicited from the basic work sheets, e.g., *Georgia Cracker* (as a friendly term for all Georgians), *hoosier* (only in the phrase *Hoosier Hot Shots,* who were the rural counterparts of Spike Jones and his City Slickers in the 1940s and 50s), *instant grits, leisure suit, pants suit, piglet* (for a newborn pig), *run some tests* (in the hospital), and *sweet corn* (yellow corn imported from Florida, as opposed to locally raised *corn on the cob* and *yellow field corn*).

16. I.e., *big old → old big.*

17. Instances of *used to* as sentence modifier in the protocol include these: *We, used to, when we lived out in the country, we had neighbors; Used to, when there were trains around....* At a "deeper level," no

doubt, this sentence modifier is derived from *used to be,* but such speculation requires the native competence of the dialect speaker to reduce the observation to credible rules.

18. The problem of pronominal reference here might be more ambiguous outside the rural South. The ensuing comment *he was cutting up so bad*—after references to the son, the father, and the other small man, as well as the fish identified earlier in the neuter gender—is here only superficially vague. In several LAGS records, the intimate use of the masculine pronoun is commonly used, whether the antecedent is a fish, a plant, or a bean: *Oh, the pinto bean, he's a spotted little feller.*

19. Current investigators of urban speech, for example, would be much more convincing if they provided texts.

20. Hans Kurath, *A Word Geography of the Eastern United States* (Ann Arbor: University of Michigan Press, 1949); E. Bagby Atwood, *A Survey of Verb Forms of the Eastern United States* (Ann Arbor: University of Michigan Press, 1953); Hans Kurath and Raven I. McDavid, Jr., *The Pronunciation of English in the Atlantic States* (Ann Arbor: University of Michigan Press, 1961).

21. In addition to the aforementioned descriptive work of Atwood, Kurath, McDavid, and McMillan, other useful models include Eugene A. Nida, *A Synopsis of English Syntax* (Norman, Okla.: Summer Institute of Linguistics, 1960), George L. Trager and Henry L. Smith, Jr., *An Outline of English Structure* (Norman, Okla.: Studies in Linguistics, Occasional Papers, 3, 1951), and W. Freeman Twaddell, *The English Verb Auxiliaries* (Providence: Brown University Press, 1960), as well as several secondary sources, such as W. Nelson Francis, *The Structure of Modern English* (New York: Ronald Press, 1958) for phrase structure taxonomy, Archibald A. Hill, *Introduction to Linguistic Structures: From Sound to Sentence in English* (New York: Harcourt, Brace and World, 1958) for a taxonomy of phonological syntax, and Roderick A. Jacobs and Peter S. Rosenbaum, *English Transformational Grammar* (Waltham, Mass.: Blaisdell, 1968) for transformational taxonomic structures.

22. Afterword: the composition of this essay, in the summer of 1976, led to the revision of LAGS plans to organize the atlas legend and index in a dictionary format, after the microfiche publication. When McMillan was asked about the proposed presentation, he said, "I have always thought that was the best way to publish linguistic atlas material."

LEXICOGRAPHY

Further Aspects of Short-Term Historical Lexicography

R . W . B U R C H F I E L D

1.1. Professor James McMillan, to whom I respectfully and in friendship offer this paper, is aware that the new *Supplement to the O.E.D.* is being prepared in the confusing circumstances of a shifting and expanding language. Unlike Dr. Johnson, who said that his "purpose was to admit no testimony of living authors," we have as our sources for the most part the works of living writers, or at any rate of writers who survived into the twentieth century. Unlike Dr. Johnson and Sir William Craigie (in the *D.A.E.*) we have set no *terminus ad quem* to our work, but deal with words, and admit quotations from the latest sources, up to the moment of correcting the galley proofs.

1.2. The penalties of this policy are fairly obvious. We are repeatedly having to make decisions about the inclusion or exclusion of words, when the easier course would simply be to put them all in a pending tray. For very recent accessions to the language, such works as *The Barnhart Dictionary of New English since 1963*[1] are a useful guide, and we often find that the evidence we have ourselves collected in the *O.E.D.* files, added to Barnhart's, provides a reasonably firm basis for decision-making. For instance, in Volume II (H-N) of *A Supplement to the O.E.D.,* we included the words *miscode* "to code incorrectly" (1965) and *monetarism* "the economic doctrine or theory of a monetarist or of monetarists" (1969) on the basis of the joint evidence—our own would barely have been sufficient to justify the expenditure of time on a search for further examples.

1.3. Two items, chosen more or less at random, will give some idea of how difficult decisions about the exclusion or inclusion of words often are. The word *middlescence* (first recorded use in 1965) "the period of middle age" just qualified for inclusion in Volume II of the Supplement as a new member in the sequence *juvenescence* (1800), *adolescence* (c 1430), and *senescence* (1695). Our quotation files contained several examples of its use, and also of the corresponding adjective *middlescent,* from North American and Australian sources, but none from Britain or from any of the other English-speaking areas. The currency of both words is probably not very great even in the United States and Australia, and neither is listed in the Barnhart Dictionary nor in *Webster's Third.* Nevertheless the primary test of admissibility, namely the existence of "sufficient" printed evidence, was satisfied, and the words were therefore included in the *Supplement.*

The other word is *impregnable* in the sense "capable of being impregnated (as an egg)." It is recorded in *Webster's Third,* but when we dealt with words in *impr-* we had no examples of this new use, and the position remains unchanged in 1976. My scientific colleagues examined the relevant abstracts and indexes and various textbooks on embryology, including avian embryology, and did not find the word in print. Their view was that if anyone needed such a word, *impregnatable* would be the obvious form— as Fowler suggested in *Modern English Usage* in 1926. We therefore concluded that *impregnable* was not sufficiently current and should be omitted.[2]

Time will tell whether these comparatively minor decisions about inclusion and exclusion are right. But the problem remains that at the level of historical lexicography with which my staff and I are involved the interval between Supplements is likely to be in the region of half a century, and it is therefore tempting to be as inclusive as possible provided that "sufficient" printed evidence exists.

1.4. The edited material is bound to reflect the imperfections or the biases of the reading programme undertaken at the pre-editorial stage. For example, our quotation files lacked convincing evidence of the currency of the word *Anglophone* "an English-speaking person" when we were working on the letter A in 1965, and it was therefore omitted from our first volume; but in 1971 when we reached the latter part of the letter F our files contained adequate material for the corresponding word *Francophone* "a French-speaking person," and it was therefore included. Such inconsistencies are bound to arise in a work of this magnitude, and they are an important feature of the *O.E.D.* itself.

1.5. It is likely (though I have not put it to the test) that the proportion of transient words in use is about the same at all periods, including the present time, but, for the period down to about the middle of the nineteenth century, sufficient time had elapsed for the editors of the *O.E.D.* to be able to judge whether a given item had had too brief a period of recorded use to justify its inclusion in the Dictionary. Such problems of inclusion or exclusion are harder in "short-term historical lexicography"[3] i.e., the treatment on historical principles of the vocabulary of a period as short as or shorter than a hundred years, than in the *O.E.D.,* because the patterns of permanence and transience have not had sufficient time to emerge.

1.6. Not surprisingly, the editors of the *O.E.D.* seem to have found themselves in difficulties about the choice of items when dealing with the new vocabulary that was coming into the language as they proceeded with the editing of the Dictionary, i.e., in *their* period of short-term historical lexicography. In the list that follows I have set out essential details of Main Entries in the *O.E.D.* in the range *V-Vaz* (published in October 1916) in which the earliest example falls within the period 1880−1916.

1.7. This list, indicative of the kind of bric-à-brac that lies scattered about the *O.E.D.,* is important in that it shows a set of *ad hoc* principles at work when the quotations before the editorial staff of the time were drawn from recent sources. It can hardly be argued that the 58 words listed below are drawn from the works of major literary authors: only *vapulatory* is cited from a writer of distinction (James Russell Lowell), whilst the remainder are drawn from a miscellaneous array of late Victorian or Edwardian newspapers or journals (*Westminster Gazette, Athenæum, Academy, St. James's Gazette, Pall Mall Gazette, Expositor*), from

word	date of first record	number of examples (an asterisk sig- nifies "cited only from another dictionary")	type of source or actual source	label
vacatable, adj.	1895	1	*Westm. Gaz.*	—
vaccarage	1895	1	*Linc. N. & Q.*	rare
vaccinable, adj.	1899	1*	—	—
vacciniform, adj.	—	—	—	(In recent Dicts.)
vaccinine	—	—	—	(In recent Dicts.)
vaccinogenic, adj.	1889	1	medical textbook	rare
vaccinogenous, adj.	1899	1*	—	—
vaccinoid	1880	1	medical textbook	—
vady, adj.	1880	1	Mrs. Parr	south-w. dial.
vag, v.	1891	1	C. Roberts	U.S. slang
vagarian	1891	1*	—	rare^{-0}
vagarisome	1883	1	*Bazaar*	—
vagarist	1888	1	*The Voice (N.Y.)*	rare
vagarity	1886	1	*N. & Q.*	rare^{-1}
vagrant, v.	1886	1	Miss Broughton	rare^{-1}
vagrantism	1908	1	sociological textbook	—
vague, v.[2]	1880	3	*Cornh. Mag.* Mrs. C. Praed	rare
vallated, adj.	1888	1	*Science*	rare^{-1}
Valliscaulian, sb. and a.	1882	2	*Athenaeum,* religious textbook	—
valorization	1907	1	*Amer. Polit. Sci. Rev.*	U.S.
valval	1891	1*	—	Bot.
valvulate, adj.	1881	1	biology textbook	rare
valvulitis	1891	3	Dict., medical textbook	Path.
vamp, sb.[2]	1884	2	J. F. Hodgetts, *Academy*	—
vamping, sb.	1881	1*	—	Mining
vandalously, adv.	1890	1	*Tablet*	rare^{-1}

(continued)

word	date of first record	number of examples (an asterisk signifies "cited only from another dictionary")	type of source or actual source	label
vaneless, adj.	1889	1	P. H. Emerson	—
vanessid, a. and sb.	1911	2	*Encycl. Brit.*	Ent.
vanillism	1884	2	*St. James's Gaz., American*	Path.
vanner[2]	1888	3	*Referee, Pall Mall G.*, manual on horses	—
vanning, vbl. sb.[2]	1892	2	*Athenæum, Times*	—
vapography	1898	1	*Pop. Sci. Monthly*	—
vaporograph	1903	2	*Month*	—
vapourgraph	1903	1	*Sat. Rev.*	—
vapulatory, adj.	1886	1	J. R. Lowell	rare[-1]
varanid	1896	1	zoology textbook	Zool.
variancy	1888	1	*Macm. Mag.*	rare
variationist	1901	1	musical textbook	—
varicated, adj.	1891	1*	—	Zool.
variedness	1897	1	*Expositor*	rare
variegator	1891	2	Dict., *Expositor*	rare
variolitization	1890	1	*Q. Jrnl. Geol. Soc.*	Geol.
variolization	1891	2	Dict., *Edin. Rev.*	Med.
variotinted, adj.	1903	1	A. M. Clerke	—
Varsovian, adj.	1902	1	S. Merriman	—
vasal, adj.	1891	2	Dict., medical textbook	—
vascularize, v.	1893	2	medical textbooks	—
vascularly, adv.	1890	2	*Nature, Westm. Gaz.*	—
vasculiform, adj.	1887	1	zoology textbook	—
vasculose, sb.	1883	2	*Science*, botany textbook	—
vasectomized, ppl. a.	1900	1	*Lancet*	—
vasectomy	1899	1	*Lancet*	Surg.

(continued)

Continued from page 119.

word	date of first record	number of examples (an asterisk signifies "cited only from another dictionary")	type of source or actual source	label
vasifactive, adj.	1882	1	*Jrnl. Microsc. Sci.*	Biol.
vasotribe	1903	1	*Lancet*	Surg.
vassalic, adj.	1897	2	history textbook	—
Vaticanize, v.	1890	2	religious works	—
vaticinatory, adj.	1883	1	religious work	rare⁻¹
vaudouism	1884	2	*Spectator, U.P. Mag.*	—

minor or popular writers like Rhoda Broughton, Mrs. Louisa Parr, and Rachel M. Praed, or from a small range of medical or botanical, etc., journals, textbooks, and dictionaries. The range of North American sources cited is almost ludicrously small.

1.8. One rough-and-ready way to test the effectiveness of the choice in such a set of items is to see how many of them were still current enough to be listed in *Webster's Third New International Dictionary* (1961). Less than a half of them survive this test:[4]

vacatable	vanillism	vasal
vacciniform	vanner	vascularize
vaccinoid	vanning	vascularly
vag	vapography	vasectomized
valorization	varanid	vasectomy
valval	variationist	vasifactive
valvulate	variegator	vassalic
valvulitis	variolitization	
vamp	Varsovian	

2.1. Against this pattern of *ad-hoc*ness what can one do with words that have made their way into our files in a much shorter period than that of 1880 to 1916, namely in the period since 1966,[5] when the drafting of B words was completed for *A Supplement* *to the O.E.D.?* A similar exercise is attempted in *The Barnhart Dictionary of New English since 1963*, and the Edwardian period had its "Barnhart Dictionary" in J. Redding Ware's *Passing English of the Victorian Era: A Dictionary of Heterodox English, Slang, and Phrase* (1909). I have little doubt that the survival rate of much of the vocabulary listed in these two dictionaries, and the permanent value of these two works as "literary instruments," will be no better than that of the sample of *V-Vaz* words cited above from Volume XII of the *O.E.D.*, and for the same reasons.

2.2. In 1975–76 our "oligotropic"[6] collecting of quotations happened to be based on a number of North American sources (as well as of British ones) and these included selected journals and books of the oil industry, *The National Observer* (U.S.), *New Yorker, American Speech,* and *Scientific American*. These sources generated a layer of vocabulary that had escaped record in the *O.E.D.* and in *A Supplement to the O.E.D.,* Volume I (A–G). My assistants and I edited a group of 27 such items from the letter B in May and June 1976, and the edited versions follow in section 3. A number of them naturally turned out to be chiefly restricted to North America (*backhoe, bad mouth, barf, bedroom community, beltway, birder, boff* and related words, *boonies,* and *bugger*). Almost all of them, after investigation, were found to date from before 1966: only *bean-bag chair* (1969), *bioethics* (1971), *biofeedback* (1970), and *bounce dive* (1974), proved to be genuine "new" words. Many of the words were traced back to sources twenty or thirty years before 1966, and a few, e.g., *barrio* (1841), *Black English* (1734)[7], and *black lung* (1837), to a much earlier period.

2.3. Scientific and technological developments produce new vocabulary all the time, and the same is true of many other spheres of modern life. One of the most productive sources of new vocabulary in the period 1975–76 is the language used by addicts of the Citizens Band Radio in North America. The craze has not yet spread to Great Britain[8] despite its popularity in North America, and it is too early yet to assess what permanent accessions to the language might emerge. Articles, TV documentaries, and other accounts of CB are appearing now all the time,[9] but notwithstanding these, the documentation in our files (August 1976) is insufficient to justify entries for even the commonest of the terms used, e.g., *bandit, breaker, front door, green stamps, negatory,* and *smokey bear.* We are doing something about this, and our files on the subject will soon build up. At the level of the *O.E.D.,* where illustrative examples are obligatory, there is need for constant vigilance and endless primary research whenever a new activity emerges in any part of the English-speaking world.

3.1. Edited versions[10] follow of 27 words in the letter B for which a sufficient amount of printed evidence had accumulated in the *O.E.D.* files since Vol. I of *A Supplement to the O.E.D.* had been prepared.

B. III. B.O.P., blow-out preventer (stack).
1934 *Proc. World Petrol. Congress 1933* I. 361/1 In the U.S.A. two forms of rotating B.O.P.'s were developed. These packed off between the square kelly and the casing and gave a positive control. **1966** A.B. CAMERON in P. Hepple *Petroleum Supply & Demand* 39 One recently reported BOP improvement eliminates the need for multiple high-pressure hoses. **1975** *BP Shield Internat.* May 5/3 Typical tasks include re-establishment of guide wires, inspection and repair of the BOP.

back-acter (bæ·k,æktəɹ). Also **-actor.** [f. BACK *a.* + ACT *v.* + -ER[1], ACTOR.] An excavating vehicle in which the scoop is rigidly attached to the lower end of a short hinged arm at the end of a boom and is pulled towards the vehicle in operation; = BACKHOE (below).
[**1928** W. BARNES *Excavating Machinery* ii.50 The action of a back-acting shovel is .. the reverse of a standard shovel, as it digs towards the machine like a drag line.] **1957** J. H. ARNISON *Pract. Road Constr.* iii.52 The shafts for the manholes may be cut out by manual labour, and the main trench by mechanical plant such as a back-acter [*printed* -acker] or trencher. **1963** M. J. TOMLINSON *Foundation Design & Constr.* ix.526

Types of mechanical excavator available are the skimmer, face shovel, backacter (backhoe), dragline, drag-scraper, grab, and loading shovel. *Ibid.* 537 Small hydraulically operated tractor-mounted backacters are being used to an increasing extent for narrow and shallow trench excavation. **1971** *Sunday Express* (Johannesburg) 28 Mar. 13/3 (Advt.), Fully hydraulic excavator with back-actor R22000.

backhoe (bæ·khōᵘ). Chiefly *N. Amer.* [f. BACK *a.* + HOE *sb.*[2]] = BACK-ACTER (above).
1928 *Engineering & Contracting* LXVII. 193/3 A new gasolene powered shovel... In changing from shovel to clamshell, back hoe or dragline service, no additions or changes are necessary in the operating machinery. **1942** *Pit & Quarry* 60 One of the 3/4-cubic yard Northwest gasolene shovels used at this plant can be equipped with a back-hoe whenever a deep pocket is encountered. **1950** *Engin. News-Record* 23 Nov. 32 (*heading*) Something new in big-sewer excavation is started in Chicago when a .. long-boomed backhoe digs deep trench. **1956** H. L. NICHOLS *Mod. Techniques Excavation* iv. 11/2 The hoe (backhoe or dragshovel) is the dozer's principal competitor for small cellar work. **1963** *Engineering* 14 June 807 The machine performed well in the dry conditions, as backhoe, loader and bulldozer. **1971** *Islander*

(Victoria, B.C.) 18 Apr. 12/3 The contracting firm had marshalled a large compressor, two dump trucks, a backhoe and a crane. **1974** *Greenville* (S. Carolina) *News* 23 Apr. C. 2/4 (Advt.), Backhoe operators, pipe layers and laborers wanted.

bad mouth. *U.S.* [f. BAD *a.* + MOUTH *sb.*] **A.** *sb. phr.* Malicious gossip or criticism (see also quots. 1930 and 1948). Cf. *MAUVAISE LANGUE. The statements in quots. 1948 and 1972 are highly speculative.
1930 *Dialect Notes* VI. 79 *Bad mouth,* n. phr. To suggest an evil contingency is supposed to bring it about. Such a suggestion is referred to in the expression, 'Don't put bad mouth on me.' **1948** L. D. TURNER in *Pubn. Amer. Dial. Soc.* IX. 81 The indebtedness of the Gullahs to the African languages is also unmistakable . . ; *a bad mouth* 'a curse', being the Vai expression [daₑ ɲaₑ maₑ] 'a curse', lit. 'a bad mouth'. **1970** H. E. ROBERTS *Third Ear* 4/1 *Bad mouth,* the telling of stories that may be true, but which reflect adversely on a person's character or reputation. **1972** D. DALBY in T. Kochman *Rappin' & Stylin' Out* 177 [Listed as a probable Africanism in American English.] *Bad-mouth,* 'slander, abuse, gossip' (also as a verb). Cf. similar use of Mandingo *da-jugu* and Hausa *mugum-baki,* 'slander, abuse' (lit. 'bad mouth' in both cases).
B. *v. trans.* (Usu. **bad-mouth** or **badmouth.**) To slander, to malign, to run down, to talk badly about (a person).
1941 J. THURBER in *Sat. Even. Post* (U.S.) 5 Apr. 9/2 He bad-mouthed everybody. **1960** J. D. MACDONALD *Slam Big Door* (1961) vi.96 What . . reason would he have to bad-mouth Jamison? **1965** 'S. RANSOME' *Alias his Wife* iv.35 Bad-mouthing customers, picking fights, making himself obnoxious. **1966** *Guardian* 19 Mar. 6/6 This fellow at dinner last night was really bad-mouthin' you. **1969** *Listener* 31 July 159/1 Edgar tried to think of a way to badmouth this immense son leaning over him like a large blaring building. **1973** *Black World* Jan. 58/2 What could they do? Badmouth them in the poolhalls, barber-shops and churches? **1975** *New Yorker* 29 Sept. 76/3 They bad-mouth Georgina to their friends, and they insist to one another that they tolerate Georgina only because she is their well-loved Felipe's wife.

baggies (bæ·giz), *sb. pl.* [f. BAGGY *a.*] Baggy shorts, esp. as used by surfers (see quot. 1967[1]).
1963 *Surfing Yearbk.* 40/2 *Baggies,* over-sized boxer trunks, which are considerably longer in the legs, while retaining the standard waist size. **1965** *S. Afr. Surfer* I. III. 38 They [*sc.* Australian surfers] come bounding down the gangplank like kangaroos with boards under their arms and baggies in their pouches. **1967** *Britannica Bk. of Year 1966* 802/1 *Baggies,* trousers (as denims or chinos) raggedly cut off for use as shorts or swim trunks. **1967** *Surfabout* IV.III. 14/2 Peter Troy was the 'gemmie king' of the group of young local surfers, all complete with bleached hair and baggies. **1973** *Daily Pennsylvanian* 9 Oct. 6/1 (Advt.), Baggies, cuff pants, plain colors and plaids.

barf (bāɪf), *v. N. Amer. slang.* [? Imit.] *trans.* and *intr.* To vomit.
1960 WENTWORTH & FLEXNER *Dict. Amer. Slang* 20/1 *Barf,* to vomit. Some student use. **1963** T. PYNCHON *V.* i.35 Behind her she heard someone barfing. **1967** *Amer. Speech* XLII. 228 [University of Connecticut] It made me want to barf. **1971** D. HEFFRON *Nice Fire & Some Moonpennies* vi.51 He barfed all over shiny Ted's shiny old suit! All this dog-puke all over his shiny lap. **1975** *Canadian Mag.* 30 Aug. 22/4 They all begged his pardon and barfed in the sink when he tried to bring up the contractual link. **1976** *Whig-Standard* (Kingston) 20 Feb. 6/5 Top people like Peter Lougheed, John Turner and Fred Shero, people that we Canadians can imagine as prime minister, without barfing our bickies.

barong tagalog (barǫ·ŋ tagā·lǫ̀g). [Tagalog.] In the Philippines, an embroidered shirt for formal use. Also *ellipt.* **barong.**
1941 F. HORN *Orphans of Pacific* ii.37 This

shirt, called *barong tagalog*, is often of a pastel shade, and is made of organdy-thin piña cloth ... It is invariably embroidered, sometimes elaborately, sometimes very simply. **1952** *Manila Chron.* 15 Mar. 5 Members of all Lions Clubs in the Luzon area are enjoined to participate in the affair and to come dressed in *barong tagalog* and *balintawak*. **1955** *Travel* Oct. 7/1 In the *barrios*, or villages [in the Philippines], you may catch sight of.. men wearing the *barong tagalog*, the embroidered shirt worn outside the trousers. **1965** *Sunday Mail* (Brisbane) 7 Mar., In response to Sir Robert Menzies' plea for a new cool style of formal evening wear for men, the Consul General for the Philippines in Sydney .. is recommending the 'barong tagalog'. **1966** MRS. L. B. JOHNSON *White House Diary* 25 Oct. (1970) 434 Lyndon was presented with a barong tagalog—the thin embroidered shirt with open collar worn outside the trousers. **1970** *Reader's Digest* (Austral. ed.) Aug. 14/2 *Barong*, the light, embroidered open-neck shirt of the Philippines. **1973** *Times* 8 May (Hongkong Suppl.) p.vi/5 The most important commodities shipped through Hongkong are textiles (especially made-up articles of embroidered damask of the kind that go to make the Filipino national dress, *barong tagalog*).

barrio (bæ·rio, bari·o). [Sp., f. Arab.] A ward or quarter of a city or town, or a village, in a Spanish-speaking country; also a Spanish-speaking quarter of a city or town in the United States. Also *attrib.* or as *adj.*
    1841 G. BORROW *Zincali* I.i.xii.199 The quarters (barrios) where they now live with the denomination of Gitános. **1899** A. LAST tr. *P. Baranera's Handbk. Philippine Islands* 45 Each town, or township, is divided into wards or *barrios*, the headsman of which is called *cabeza de barangay*. **1900** *N.Y. Sun* 19 Mar., I shall hold you responsible for the peace and good order of the town and the barrios. **1912** R. K. BUCKLAND *In Land of Filipino* xiii.134 Nicolas thought we should enjoy a picnic up the river to a little *barrio*,

the inhabitants of which, bound in a way to him by a sort of feudal system prevailing among the Filipinos even to this day, would furnish us with refreshment and entertainment. **1931** C. BEALS *Mexican Maze* ix.156 Here and there, a *barrio* or ward still retains the name of its ancient *calpulli*. **1937** C. BENITEZ *Philippine Social Life & Progress* xviii.386 Though the barrio is a political subdivision of a town, it is also a social grouping, because almost always it is also a neighborhood community. **1955** [see BARONG TAGALOG]. **1965** C. D. EBY *Siege of Alcázar* (1966) 14 The one-story brick shanties of Las Covachuelas, the northernmost *barrio* of Toledo. **1967** *Economist* 16 Sept. 983/1 Roughly half the adult males in the capital [*sc.* Santo Domingo] are out of work with the proportion reaching 90 per cent in some of the poorer *barrios*. **1969** J. MANDER *Static Soc.* v.144 Yet the two *barrios* did not live in total apartheid. **1969** *Time* 4 July 14/1 *Barrio*, literally 'district', the Spanish-speaking quarter of a U.S. city. **1971** *Daily Colonist* (Victoria, B.C.) 2 Feb. 3/7 An overnight curfew brought calm to the East Los Angeles Mexican-American barrio Monday. **1972** *N.Y. Times* 1 June 18/8 Most of the Protestants of a tiny Puerto Rican barrio 20 miles outside San Juan gathered for a gay send-off for their pastor. **1973** *Black Panther* 21 July 7/3 From the ghettos, barrios and slums of our cities,.. a people's party must arise! **1974** *Amer. Speech 1971* XLVI. 299 Barrio Spanish serves the Chicano in communicating with Mexican nationals as well as with Spanish-speaking people in general.

bean, *sb.* **8. bean-bag chair,** a malleable chair with a circular base and sack-like shape, partially stuffed with plastic granules so as to mould itself to the shape of the user.
    1969 *Better Homes & Gardens* Nov. 129 Bean Bag chair, upholstered in black Arpel and filled with polystyrene beads. **1970** *American Home* Sept. 70/2 Bean-bag 'chairs' come in for plenty of rough-housing. **1970** *New Yorker* 28 Nov. 155/1 A child-sized version of

the beanbag chair. **1973** *Washington Post* 13 Jan. F.1/9 (Advt.), Upholstered beds, heaters, bean bag chairs. **1975** *New Yorker* 20 Oct. 37/1 The dentist's taste in furniture ran mostly to things like orange beanbag chairs and black Formica Parsons tables.

bedroom 3.c. Used *attrib.* of a community, town, or suburb:=*DORMITORY *sb.* 1 c. Also *absol. N. Amer.*
   1940 *Sat. Rev. Lit.* 18 May 16 The Bostonians themselves were leaving Boston and its high taxes for the comfortable 'bedroom' towns in the suburbs. **1948** DAWSON & GETTYS *Introd. Sociol.* (ed.3) 219 There are industrial suburbs where work and residential quarters are side by side; there are 'bedroom suburbs' far removed from the city noise and smoke. **1970** *New York* 16 Nov. 42/2 Semi-professional bedroom towns spread up the hilly ridges. **1975** *Globe & Mail* (Toronto) 2 June 5/3 The provincial Government is doing its best to force Oshawa to be a bedroom community. **1976** *National Observer* (U.S.) 7 Feb. 20/4 Suffolk and Nassau counties.. are affluent bedrooms for New York City. *Ibid.* 3 Apr. 15/2 The Harveys have lived in this bedroom community, where the lawns are like carpets, for several decades.

beltway (be·ltwēⁱ). *U.S.* [f. BELT *sb.*[1] + WAY *sb.*[1]] A road that makes a complete circuit of a city, a ring road.
   1952 *Sun* (Baltimore) 22 Jan. 16/3 Preliminary construction on the proposed beltway circling the city through Baltimore county is expected to get under way. **1970** *Washington Post* 30 Sept. D.6/2 (Advt.), By road: Beltway to Exit 37. **1972** *Real Estate Rev.* Winter 92/1 Broad beltways now encircle ten of the nation's largest cities. **1973** *Times* 13 Aug. 10/7 The beltway built round Washington to relieve traffic jams was jammed with traffic.

berm. 4.a. The shoulder of a road. *U.S.* **b.** An unsealed portion (usually in grass) of a pathway between the foot-path and the gutter (*U.S.*) or between the sealed portion of a road and the gutter (*N.Z.*).
   1926 *Mod. Lang. Notes* XLI.126 The new meaning to which I would call attention is that of the word *berm*, as used recently in my presence by a construction engineer and apparently well established in parts of America. *Ibid.* 127 The new meaning.. may be explained as follows: In highway construction the ledge or level ground at the side of the road, from the top of the ditch to the boundary of the highway. *Ibid.*, The same term is applied to the ledge at the side of a city street, on which is usually a sidewalk and often a strip of sod between the sidewalk and the curb. **1943** *Post* (Morgantown, Va.) 23 Feb. 2/7 Motorists had to 'feel' their way along, keeping an eye on the center line or berm in order to keep on the road. *Ibid.* 20 Sept. 2/8 The truck ran off onto the berm and then cut back onto the concrete. **1959** I. JEFFERIES *13 Days* v.61 The tail of the truck caught the last barrel, spinning me half-way on to the berm. **1964** *Amer. Speech* XXXIX. 293 The designation for that strip of grass and weeds between the sidewalk and the curb.. seems to be most commonly called *tree lawn* or *parking strip* ... The Akron term is *Devil strip* or *Devil's strip*. There are a few, however, who think it vulgar or profane (although they recognize it), and to them it is the *berm*. **1970** *N.Z. Listener* 14 Dec. 62/3 When I bought my home in Lower Hutt I signed a paper sent by the City Corporation to say I would keep my berm cut. **1971** *Evening Post* (Wellington, N.Z.) 19 Aug., The animal ranger at Porirua.. experienced difficulty with horses being ridden on berms and footpaths instead of the road. **1971** M. TAK *Truck Talk* 11 *Berm*, the shoulder of the road.

bioethics (bəio,e·þiks), *sb. pl.* const. as *sing.* [f. BIO- + ETHICS (s.v. ETHIC *a.* and *sb.*).] The study of the morality of present-day science and its social implications, esp. in biology and medicine.
   1971 *Science News* 30 Oct. 294 Andre Helligers, professor of obstetrics and gyne-

cology and director of the newly established
Kennedy Institute for Human Reproduction
and Bioethics at Georgetown University in
Washington, said his guess is that 'operations
like the one at Georgetown will become in-
stitutionalized and more wide spread'. **1971**
Nature 3 Dec. 272/2 To bolster them comes
'bioethics', a *mélange* of Teilhard de Chardin
and ecological concern. **1976** *National Observer* (U.S.) 24 Jan. 9/3 Dr. Warren T.
Reich, senior research scholar at Georgetown
University's Kennedy Center for Bioethics,
believes that all the forms and the proposed
legislation have some shortcomings, but he
welcomes their effect. 'It's a movement that
is . . helping to sensitize physicians and others
to the complexities of dying.'

biofeedback (bəiofī·dbæk). [f. BIO- +
*FEEDBACK.] The technique of using
the feedback information of a normally
automatic or involuntary physiological
response, with the intention of acquiring
voluntary control of the response.
1970 *Look* 6 Oct. 91/3 In addition to her
laboratory work, Dr. [Barbara] Brown is now
occupied with the chairmanship of the Bio-
Feedback Research Society, which she helped
found a little over a year ago. **1971** *Prediction*
Mar. 18/3 Canadian drug-users, we are told,
'are taking a keen interest in electronic Yoga
or bio-feedback training (BFT) which is the
subject of extensive university and underground research in the States. The training
consists of using an electronic "black box"
to teach a subject how to manipulate the electrical activity of his own brain.' **1972** *Illustr.
London News* Dec. 47/1 A new technique,
known as biofeedback, is being developed
which may enable people to bring their automatic bodily functions under greater control.
1975 *Nature* 31 July p.xx/3 Biofeedback is a
learning technique enabling the individual to
gain control of physiological functions using
electronic instruments that detect and feed
back information on body functions. **1976**
Daily Colonist (Victoria, B.C.) 17 Mar. 12/1
Biofeedback can control epileptic seizures in
patients who have become totally incapaci-
tated.

bionic (bəi,ǫ·nik), *a.* [Back-formation f.
*BIONICS.] **a.** Of or pertaining to bionics.
b. Of or pertaining to a type of electronic doll, introduced in 1975, representing a superhuman person in the
U.S. television show 'Six Million Dollar
Man', or to the character Steve Austin
in the television show itself.
1964 *Sciences* 1 Feb. 3 Next to Earth, Mars
appears to have greater bionic potential than
any other planet. **1970** *Encyclopedia Science
Suppl.* (Grolier) 115 The bionic approach to
this problem consists of studying organisms
that exhibit the desired characteristic of moving through water with the least amount of
resistance. [**1974** *Sunday Mail* (Brisbane) 11
Aug. 2/6 Last Sunday's episode of Channel
0's 'Six Million Dollar Man' showed exactly
why the producers find it prudent to break
into slow motion photography whenever it is
necessary to show bionics man, Steve Austin,
in super-human action.] **1976** *Daily Tel.* 30
Jan. 3/3 After the inquest . . Mrs. ——— said
. . 'There should be a warning at the end of
each programme telling children not to attempt the stunts carried out by the bionic
man.' **1976** *National Observer* (U.S.) 6 Mar.
6/2 A key feature of the Bionic Woman, I
discovered, was that her arms and legs can be
separated from her body. *Ibid.* 3 Apr. 10-B/1
Kenner's Six Million Dollar Man doll . . with
his 'bionic eye' and 'power arm', . . is clearly
something that children can never be. **1976**
Daily Mail 7 June 3/2 Actress Lindsay Wag-
ner, who does remarkable things as TV's
Bionic Woman, was asked yesterday to go
through the motions of heaving a car across
a London street.

biorhythm (bəi·oriðˑm). [f. BIO- +
RHYTHM *sb.*] The rhythm of physiological activity that can be discerned in
bodily functions which are by nature
recurrent or cyclic.
1960 *New Scientist* 29 Sept. 849 Hiberna-
tion . . proceeds in a biorhythm of the same
sort that causes Man to sleep and waken at
regular intervals regardless of his where-
abouts. **1966** *N.Y. Times* 24 Apr. VI. 12 Seve-

ral universities are currently completing studies validating three long-term cyclical patterns called 'biorhythms': a 23-day physical cycle, a 28-day emotional cycle, [etc.]. **1975** *Drive* New Year 83/2 The Japanese say these ups and downs are controlled by three immutable patterns, or biorhythms, which can be so precisely plotted that they are an important behavioural guide. **1975** *Sci. Amer.* Feb. 12/3 Since 1960 he has spent his summers as an instructor and investigator of 'all aspects of clock-controlled biorhythms' at the Marine Biological Laboratory at Woods Hole. Hence **biorhy·thmic** *a.;* **biorhy·thmically** *adv.*

1975 *Drive* New Year 83/1 A safety officer consults their individual biorhythmic calendars. *Ibid.* 85/1 He came to the startling conclusion that 70% of accidents happen on biorhythmically critical days.

birder (bɔ·ɪdəɹ). **4.** = **bird-watcher.* *N. Amer.*

1950 in WEBSTER Add. **1965** *Times* 22 Dec. 7/1 Bird watchers—known in America as birders. **1967** *Boston Sunday Globe* 23 Apr. B.59/2 Some time ago an assembly of Audubon enthusiasts rejected the term 'bird watchers' by which they had been commonly known, and adopted the designation 'birders'. **1974** *Globe & Mail* (Toronto) 23 Sept. 6/4 The elusive jaeger eluded birders yesterday in the first large-scale Toronto-based sweep of Lake Ontario for rare birds. **1976** *National Observer* (U.S.) 7 Feb. 8/5 Like a birder searching for rare specimens, I look for evidence of the mad architect wherever I go.

Black English. [f. BLACK *a.* + ENGLISH *sb.* 1 b.] A technical linguistic term for a group of related social dialects of English spoken by communities of American Blacks, characterized by a self-consistent and systematic grammatical structure and by intonational patterns and a choice of vocabulary that are not usually employed by white speakers of standard American in the same regions. Quot. 1734 is a casual use.

1734 *S. Carolina Gaz.* 30 Mar. 3/2 To be Sold... Four young Negroe Men Slaves and a Girl, who.. speak very good (Black-) English. **1969** W. LABOV (*title*) The study of Black English. **1969** *Internat. Herald Tribune* (Paris) 6 Nov. 14/3 The seemingly ungrammatical version.. of 'Twas the Night Before Christmas' is actually a translation of Clement Clarke Moore's familiar poem into what linguists call Black English. **1970** D. DALBY in *N.Y. Times* 10 Nov. 47/5 Distinctive forms of black English have developed and survivied on both sides of the Atlantic. Striking similarities reflect their common origin in West Africa. **1971** *Black World* June 7/1 The reality and significance of the difference between Black English and standard English was played down by assimilation-minded Blacks and liberal whites. **1971** *Language* XLVII. 205 Speakers of Black English know that in more formal situations they must increase the number of overt, surface occurrences of the copula. **1972** *Ibid.* XLVIII. 480 Most of those who have dealt with Negro Non-standard English, or Black English, or 'the language of the inner city', have not been linguists. **1972** J. L. DILLARD (*title*) Black English. *Ibid.* 24 There is much reason to believe that structural and historical differences between Black English and the English spoken by most other Americans have practical consequences which take them out of the realm of purely academic concerns.

black lung. [f. BLACK *a.* + LUNG.] **a.** A lung severely darkened by the deposition of inhaled carbon particles. **b.** (Also *black lung disease.*) A disease caused by this, formerly called *anthracosis* and now known as *anthracosilicosis* or (*coal miners'*) *pneumoconiosis.*

1837 *Med.-Chirurg. Trans.* XX. 234 The first specimen of black lung which I remember to have seen, was taken in 1824−5 from the body of a patient of the Royal Dispensary. **1838** *Edin. Med. & Surg. Jrnl.* XLIX. 490 The third [appearance] is what has been called the black lung of coal-miners, and may more shortly be defined *anthracosis.* **1869** *Trans. Path. Soc. Lond.* XX. 41 (*heading*)

Black lungs from a case of colliers' phthisis. **1930** *Jrnl. Path. & Bacteriol.* XXXIII. 1100 Jousset (1928) has recently attributed to silicosis the most important place in the production of the 'black lung' of coal-miners. **1952** *Brit. Jrnl. Industr. Med.* IX. 105/2 A black lung or 'anthracosis' in a coal miner is often accepted as a normal finding. **1969** *Newsweek* 16 June 44/2 Promoting mine-safety legislation.. to protect employees against the dread black-lung disease, which annually disables thousands of miners. **1976** *Sci. Amer.* Jan. 30/3 The Government is.. spending about $1 billion a year as compensation to coal miners who have contracted black-lung disease. **1976** *National Observer* (U.S.) 13 Mar. 2/2 Black-lung benefits for coal miners would be liberalized under a bill passed by the House and sent to the Senate.

blow-out. 3.c. A rapid, uncontrolled uprush of fluid from an oil or gas well. **1916** A. B. THOMPSON *Oil-Field Devel. & Petroleum Mining* x.457 Heavy mud mixtures are an additional safeguard against 'blow-outs'. **1924** L. C. UREN *Textbk. Petroleum Production Engin.* x.304 The gates are ordinarily kept open, but in the event of a threatened blow-out are closed about the drill pipe, preventing further escape of the well fluid. **1968** *Daily Tel.* 16 Nov. 1 Lifeboats saved 47 men from the gale-lashed North Sea after a 'blow out' on a gas-drilling platform. **1974** *Sci. Amer.* May 76/3 The oceanic microlayer.. absorbs the brunt of oil spills, including oil released from blowouts on the ocean floor.

Freq. *attrib.* in **blow-out preventer,** a heavy valve or assembly ('stack') of valves usu. fitted at the top of a hole during drilling and closed in the event of a blow-out to control the flow; abbrev. *B.O.P.* (above). **1916** A. B. THOMPSON *Oil-Field Devel. & Petroleum Mining* vii.367 An apparatus which is largely employed with rotaries is what is called a 'Blow-out Preventer'. **1962** *Economist* 15 Sept. 1046/2 The blow-out preventers and the drill bit itself can be lowered. **1970**

New Scientist 29 Oct. 221/1 Massive blow-out preventer valves are tested every 24 hours. **1975** *Offshore Progress—Technol. & Costs* (Shell Briefing Service) 7 For safety and operational reasons, the blowout preventer stacks must be installed on the seabed, rather than on the drilling platform.

body, *sb.* **30. body language** (see quots. 1972); = *KINESICS. **1926** *New Republic* 24 Feb. 19 The arabesque or body-language of Picasso. **1966** *Psychol. Abstr.* XL. 1252/2 Language corporel et théorie de l'information. (Body-language and information theory). **1970** J. FAST *Body Language* (1971) i.11 To understand this unspoken body language, kinesics experts often have to take into consideration cultural differences and environmental differences. **1972** *Britannica Bk. of Year 1971* 733/1 *Body language,* the gestures and mannerisms by which a person unwittingly communicates his feelings to others. **1972** T. McHUGH *Buffalo* xiii.152 Buffalo also express themselves in 'body language', assuming certain positions or moving in a particular way. **1974** *Language Sciences* 37/3 Nonlinguistic mechanisms, such as paralanguage and body language.. can also alter or confirm the communicative distances already set up.

boff (bǫf). *U.S. slang.* [perh. f. *box office.*] **a.** A box office or show business 'hit'. **b.** A belly laugh. **c.** A gag or line designed to elicit a belly laugh. **1946** *Time* 21 Jan. 70 Such trade phrases [from *Variety*] as 'boff' (a variation of sock or punch) for smash hit. **1946** *Hollywood Quarterly* July 364 A wave of reaction throughout the industry against.. any type of cartoon except those based on the 'boff' or belly laugh. **1948** *Commonweal* 27 Dec. 250 For sixteen years the Jack Benny program has marked the ending of the Sabbath and the beginning of a two-hour secular ritual of gags, boffs, and yaks. **1950** *Sat. Rev. Lit.* 17 June 36 Exhibitors throughout the United States are unanimous in reporting that less than a dozen names still retain their old box-office 'boff'. **1955** *People* (Austral.) 26 Jan. 21/1 A classic example of what is known in the laugh trade as 'the boff' (the great gust of laughter) following a split second after the point of the gag is seen. **1961** BOWMAN & BALL *Theatre Language* 34 *Boff*. 1. A box office; by extension, box-office appeal, drawing power, and hence (of a production, of theatre business) tremendously successful. Also in the forms *boffo* and *boffola*. 2. A hearty laugh, especially one even heartier than a belly-laugh, and usually in the form *boffo*.

boffo (bǫ·fo), *a. U.S. slang.* [f. as prec.] Very successful; such that it produces a loud laugh, entertaining. Also as *sb.,* = BOFF a,b (above).
   1946 *Atlantic Monthly* Apr. 140 Nothing lavish was intended here since the term epochal until recently was understood to be a degree slightly above terrific and a shade below boffo. **1950** *Time* 30 Jan. 84 Though prices were advanced (90¢ for $1.20), the results were boffo: standing room only, bigger popcorn sales and a whopping $300,000 gross. **1950** *Sat. Rev. Lit.* 4 Nov. 27 Mr. Agee defined the four main grades of laughter that Chaplin, Turpin, Langdon, and Lloyd worked for and evoked: the titter, the yowl, the belly laugh, and the boffo. The boffo, he said, is the laugh that kills. **1958** *Spectator* 21 Nov. 629/1 Life would be socko, boffo, unbearable. **1961** [see prec.] **1971** *IT* 2-16 June 11/3 Broadway scalpers are having a field-day with tickets for Gotham's latest boffo smash, *Oh! Albania!* **1973** *Daily Colonist* (Victoria, B.C.) 29 July 2/2 Dave Barrett got off some boffo lines and had them chuckling. **1974** *Publishers Weekly* 16 Sept. 53/1 The suspense and the laughs are served up expertly and the finale is a genuine boffo.

boffola (bǫfōᵘ·lă). *U.S. slang.* [Extended form of prec. two words.] = BOFF above.
   1946 F. WAKEMAN *Hucksters* (1948) 88 It'll sound all right. Good jokes, laughs, I'll pack the script with boffolas. **1947** *Ethyl News* Nov. 20 The gag-men strain for 'boffolas' (jokes producing belly laughs). **1949** *Time* 23 May 30 The new boffola of the Soviet screen is *Meeting on the Elbe.* **1955** *New Republic* 28 Nov. 20 This is invariably followed by from fifteen to thirty seconds of 'canned' laughter, the hysterical kind ordinarily reserved for the very biggest boffolas. **1961** [see BOFF]. **1967** *New Yorker* 19 Aug. 86/2 For every sorrow there's a boffola. **1976** *National Observer* (U.S.) 20 Mar. 20/2 The trademark of this approach to comedy .. is that Lear goes for the boffola, the belly laugh, and uses disease and tragedy as props toward that end.

boonies (bū·niz), *sb. pl. N. Amer. colloq.* [Hypocoristic form of *boondocks* *BOONDOCK.] The boondocks, an isolated or wild region.
   1956 *Amer. Speech* XXXI. 190 If .. any of them [*sc.* U.S. Marine Corps trainees] had been caught *crapping out* [*sc.* loafing] during the day, the whole platoon may get .. a forced march the following morning through the *boonies* (woods, jungles, etc.). **1968–70** *Current Slang* (Univ. S. Dakota) III–IV.14 *Boonies,* rustic backwoods. College students, both sexes, Minnesota. **1971** W. HILLEN *Blackwater River* xii.115 Several miles into the boonies from the main ranch. **1971** *Last Whole Earth Catalog* 57/2 That's not what I mean. I mean out in the boonies, where you'd take a trail-bike, or something. You know. Cross-country. **1974** *Daily Colonist* (Victoria, B.C.) 6 Nov. 4/6 Back from what the pseudo-sophisticates .. are wont to call the 'boonies'. **1975** *New Yorker* 19 May 8/3 (Advt.), Closer to the docks than to the boonies, this dark, sawdusted café is still cashing in on the late-sixties soul-food bonanza.

bounce, *sb.* [1] **6. bounce dive,** a dive of short duration to the sea bed.
   1974 *Petroleum Rev.* XXVIII. 672/3 Several types of diving techniques are available: surface demand (SD) and swimmer's air-breathing apparatus (SABA); bell diving

(bounce dives); saturation diving and diving from lock-out submersibles. **1975** *BP Shield Internat.* May 17/1 You can make a bounce dive—down and up again. It will take a diver about an hour to get ready and to get there and he may spend about 20 minutes on the bottom. **1976** *Offshore Engineer* May. 37/1 Certainly for conventional exploration drilling from jack-ups and semi-subs, bell diving, mostly done as bounce dives, will continue as normal in shallow waters to perhaps 200–250m.

bugger (bɒ·gəɹ), *sb.*[2] [f. *BUG *v.*[1] + -ER[1].] One who 'bugs' by means of a concealed microphone or recording apparatus. **1955** H. COBURN in *Front Page Detective* June 65 Deputy Midyett, in charge of recording instruments .. was .. 'the chief bugger'

of Maren County. **1966** W. W. TURNER in *Ramparts* Nov. 51, I was a burglar, wiretapper, bugger, and spy for the F.B.I. **1967** R. M. BROWN *Electronic Invasion* xi.143 The so-called 'expert' buggers more often than not are led to believe that the transistors are malfunctioning or that a circuit wire has broken loose. **1969** J. M. CARROLL *Third Listener* 167 (*heading*) The bugger's lexicon. **1973** *Sunday Express* 22 July 16/3 No doubt the buggers would have made a mess of it as they did at Watergate. **1974** *Japan Times* 23 Nov., The particular medium Coppola has chosen for scrutiny in his film is bugging ... Coppola's .. film has for its protagonist a drab, plodding bugger named Harry Caul. **1976** *National Observer* (U.S.) 6 Mar. 9/1 (*letter to editor*) It's a damned good thing that the Watergate buggers didn't have to make a fast getaway.

NOTES

1. Edited by Clarence L. Barnhart, Sol Steinmetz, and Robert K. Barnhart (Bronxville, New York, 1973).

2. Evidence of its currency presumably exists somewhere as the word is treated in several American dictionaries as well as in *Webster's Third*.

3. A phrase that I used in a paper prepared for a Festschrift now in the press (for publication in 1977) for the Dutch linguistic scholar, Dr. Felicien de Tollenaere.

4. It is perhaps of interest as showing what the reductive process must necessarily be in the standard small (desk) dictionaries that only eight of these are listed in the *Concise Oxford Dictionary* (ed.6, 1976): *vacatable, valorization, vamp, vasal, vascularize, vascularly, vasectomized,* and *vasectomy.*

5. A few quotations for some of the items had made their way into the quotation files from earlier reading, and the editing process itself naturally produced others.

6. *Oligotropic* 'collecting nectar from only a few kinds of flower.'

7. Admittedly an isolated early example.

8. Apparently the Home Office has ruled that Citizens Band equipment is illegal in Britain, under Statutory Instrument No. 61, 1968

(I quote from a report in *Electronics Today International,* July 1976, p. 10).

9. For example, W. Neely, "Radio S-e-m-i," *Playboy* (Canadian ed.) 22 Nov. 1975, pp. 103, 124, 155–7; G. Ewens and M. Ellis, "Call of a (Distant) Road," *Truck,* June 1976, pp. 16–17; and an unsigned article, "CB4UK," *Electronics Today International,* July 1976, pp. 10–14. Glossaries and handbooks include Robert L. Perkowski and Lee Philip Stral, *The Joy of CB* (Matteson, Ill., 1976); Lanie Dills and Dot Gilbertson, *The "Official" CB Slanguage Language Dictionary* (New York, 1975); Jethro K. Lieberman and Neil S. Rhodes, *The Complete CB Handbook* (New York, 1976).

10. I am indebted to several of my *O.E.D.* colleagues for assistance with the preparation of these entries, especially Mrs. L. S. Burnett, A. M. Hughes, Dr. J. B. Sykes, Mrs. Adriana P. Orr, and Miss V. M. Salusbury. Dr. Frederick C. Mish also kindly sent some examples from the G. & C. Merriam citation files.

Use of Computers in One Lexicographical Project: *DARE*

FREDERIC G. CASSIDY

Professor James B. McMillan (Jim to his friends) has always been a scholar who quietly insisted on exactness of analysis in language study. As a consequence he has never written on any subject without illuminating it. With the illumination have been mingled gleams of humor, the other happy faculty of a good teacher. It is a pleasure to add this small offering to a volume in Jim's honor.

This short account does not pretend to survey the use of "computers"—various electronic devices—in past or present dictionary making. The *Random House* and *American Heritage* dictionaries have already advertised their modernity through their uses, and others—Barnhart, Merriam, the *Dictionary of the Older Scottish Tongue* to mention only a few—have availed themselves of some of these aids. Indeed, any dictionary which makes no use whatever of computer devices today must be a rarity. But the extent of use—what is done with what machines—remains quite varied. The computer can at least do some of the lexicographer's drudge-work, but it does not threaten to displace him, and never will. The experience of the *Dictionary of American Regional English* (*DARE*) with computer methods, the common ones and some being applied for the first time, may be of interest for the future.

Because *DARE* was planned from the beginning to cover the entire United States and to have a historical aspect, it was foreseen that the corpus of data would be very large and that, to produce the dictionary within a reasonable time, computers must be used wherever fruitfully applicable. But in 1965, when *DARE* was launched, most computer processing was still numerical or mathematical; computer users had not done anything significant with massive alphabetical projects. Whereas the computer, as its name implies, was accurate and fast with calculations, it was burdened and slow with the irreducible mass of words essential to lexicography.

So *DARE* met head-on the paradox of efficiency: efficiency comes only through improving on the relative inefficiency of any first attempt.

The things *DARE* hoped to do by use of computer methods were:

1. To bring together the geographical and social facts about current American regional and non-standard usages, and to combine and display these in various ways.
2. To do actual editing on the CRT (cathode ray tube) screen, displaying the evidence in the form of quotations, choosing and combining these, filling in definitions and other features, and thus actually writing up final entries on the screen and transferring them to tape for printing.

These first plans have been greatly modified in the light of experience. Expense in money and in time has driven us back to manual editing. On the other hand, we have developed a CRT mapping program which furnishes a better basis for decisions about usage, both geographical and social, than has existed hitherto.

The *DARE* data base falls into two distinct parts: oral responses by informants interviewed in 1002 communities in 50 states (put together in what we call the "Data Summary") and examples of usages drawn from all sources else, especially the Dialect Society's collections and similar publications, but also a wide range of other oral and printed sources (put together in what we call the "Main File"). These are distinct as to the kind of computer processing they permit.

Since the country-wide interviewing was done with a question-air in which each question was exactly phrased and the field-worker was instructed to ask it in that form, the responses to questions successfully answered should be nationally compar-able. Needless to say, this ideal was not fully attained. Under field conditions the fieldworker occasionally departed from the exact text of the question, informants sometimes answered at cross-purposes when they misunderstood the question or chose to respond jocularly or flippantly, and some responses remain as mysteries the fieldworker did not clear up at the time—and which we cannot resolve now. These, with non-answers, must be dis-counted. Nevertheless, for the greatest number of questions there are more or less comparable answers, the whole constituting a rough synonymy: all or most of the ways in which Americans today respond to these specific questions. Since there were 1847 questions, and many multiple responses, the total number of answers runs close to two and a half million.

Each of these responses is directly referable to the individual who made it, and each individual is identifiable by a code con-sisting of two letters for the name of the state plus his or her personal number. Thus OK016 is informant no. 16 from Oklahoma (representing the community of Boley, Okfuskee County), IL103 is the 103rd Illinois informant (representing St. Elmo, Fayette County) and so on. Geographical distribution of any answer can thus be shown by listing these codes, or by displaying them on a map. (Here the CRT has proved most useful as will be described later.)

The individual's code, however, represents not only his or her community's place on the map, but a series of biographical facts, the most important of which are age, sex, race, degree of edu-cation, and community type. (Further biographical facts—family background, occupation, travel, hobbies, etc.—can be found in the questionairs.) The problem was to have the capacity to store, combine, and retrieve, for every response, the *area* and the *social correlates* of its use, so that the editor writing up the word could

know, first, whether it is regional—found in general use in a
limited part of the United States; second, whether it is used
mainly by certain types of people—for example, young city Negroes, speakers having little education, old rural females. It was
obvious that only the computer would be able to store such a
large number of items—the responses and the social facts about
each informant—and to sort and combine them upon command.
This is the kind of thing which, done by non-mechanical means,
would be extremely slow and extremely expensive.

Leaving aside the normal troubles of computer use—failure to
anticipate all possibilities and provide for them in the program-
ming; changes of hardware (machines) when one is committed to
a particular model, thus requiring a conversion in which some
feature may be lost or become garbled; mistakes made by the
machine, which though few are real; machine breakdowns; com-
petition for machines; the tendency of computer people to think
and work in terms of stages, so that inaccuracies in one kind of
detail may be tolerated until the final run while some other kind
of detail is being dealt with—leaving aside these normal time-
wasting and expensive troubles, one may generalize by saying
that *unless* the projected dictionary or glossary is very large or
complex, one had better stick to the long-established manual
methods in lexicography: the quotations or other data, item by
item on slips of paper, being filed in the familiar alphabetical
way until the time for editing comes, at which time the sorting
by meaning category or date can follow. This method may possibly be improved, for medium-sized or ongoing projects, by
using punch cards instead of slips, sorting and filing them on
one's own machines under immediate supervision. To send a
large number away to a processing center invites loss or mis-
handling, or requires extra record-keeping.

What makes the computer appropriate for *DARE* is our attempt
to get at the geographical and social basis of usage. The "usage
labels" in general dictionaries are usually too short, too conven-
tionalized, too traditional (with a dubious load of inherited preju-
dices)—that is one of the great weaknesses of these dictionaries.

They do better with usage *notes* than with labels, but cannot usually afford space for more than a few.

DARE has compiled for the first time—and it took a nation-wide program of fieldwork, and five years (1965–70) to do it—a very large body of coded data on currently spoken American English. No dictionary before now has had a data base with similarly comparable items. The final volume of *DARE* will present a great part of this assembled material to the reader who wants to go beyond the treatments of individual words in the preceding volumes. It will contain every question of the questionair, with all the responses given to each question, tabulated with their frequencies in descending order; for those responses made by only eight or fewer informants, the individuals' codes will be given.

For example, question H70: "When people bring baked dishes, salads and so forth to a meeting place and share them together, that's a _____ meal". This will be followed by the 131 different responses given to it, in descending order of frequency. Thus: *potluck* 429, *covered dish* 371, *picnic* 52, *covered dish supper* 33, *potluck supper* 27, *dinner on the ground* 19, *carry-in* 16, *buffet* 11, *tureen supper* 10, *tureen dinner* 9, *basket dinner* 8, *casserole* 8, *hot dish* 8, *smorgasbord* 8, *church supper* 6, *covered dish luncheon* 6, *get-together* 6, *tureen* 6, *dutch* 5, *pitch-in* 5, and so on. Seventy-three responses were unique, fifty-six were given by two or more informants. This kind of list will make it easy to see whether a response is clearly local—e.g., *pitch-in*, which was found only in southern Indiana—or not as clearly so—e.g., *smorgasbord*, which was spotted through the North (MS, RI, PA, NY, IN, ID, CA) and upper South (MD, DC), but not found in the South, South Midland, or Southwest. (It should be understood that spontaneous responses are taken to represent current local use; other words may be *known* but not currently used. To say that any term was *found* does not mean that other terms do not exist—only that they were not given as spontaneous responses to *DARE* fieldworkers.)

The reader will find each of the above terms treated in alphabetic sequence in the first volumes of the dictionary; if he wants to see them listed together with their frequencies and the informants' codes, he can turn to the Data Summary volume. (For still further detail, the scholar may use our computer tapes on line to an appropriate computer and retrieve any item with its relevant data. As a final recourse, one may consult the 1002 original questionairs individually in the *DARE* offices in Madison.)

The sorting, filing, combining, and printing capacities of the computer have been essential to the production of the Data Summary, which presents our five years' collection of spoken American English immediately in useful form. Using the index to this material, the dictionary editor can immediately trace any item to its source, namely, the informant or informants who so responded. But this material has also been programmed for display on the CRT screen through our "interactive program." By use of a base map distorted so that each letter-space on the screen represents one *DARE* community, no more and no less, one can display in a few seconds the distribution of any response—a mapping capacity which one would never attempt by manual methods because it would be intolerably tedious and slow. The maps so displayed—if we want to keep them—can be printed out very rapidly.

These "distorted" maps deserve a word more. On them the size of the states is dictated not by their actual areas but by population and settlement history, since it was chiefly on this basis that the *DARE* communities were chosen. Thus the more populous states' areas on the map are expanded, while the less populous may shrink away to very little. Southern California bulges out into the Pacific Ocean, while Alaska, with only two communities allotted, is smaller than Hawaii, with three. Nevertheless, states are kept in their proper relative positions, their shapes are simulated, and with a very little practice one can recognize them. The map thus reflects population and community distribution, hence the informant distribution, which is relevant to language use as mere area is not.

On these maps, and through the interactive program (which connects the screen in our office by telephone line to the Univac 1110 at the Madison Academic Computing Center, University of Wisconsin), our staff member can examine each response for six

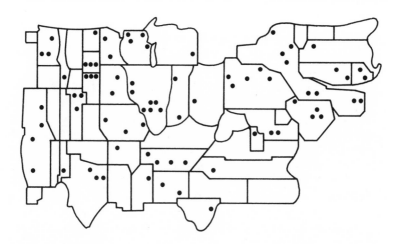

Response Distribution

Question 402—Response 3—"Acreage"
Number of Responses-79

kinds of distribution: by area, age, sex, race, degree of education, and type of community. Since the codes are given in the Data Summary responses by eight informants or less, and these can be read directly, the operator does not map them. But he maps everything else to look for possibly significant distributions and notes his findings on a check-slip for the editors. The non-significant maps are dismissed from the screen at the push of a button; the significant ones are printed out—and the best will eventually form a section in the dictionary. The operator works systematically from question to question throughout the series, but he can also call up individual responses at any time upon an editor's request. With the map the computer tabulates and percentualizes the responses so that cross-relations between any of the six features—for example sex and education or race and community type—may be seen. These figures should make it possible for scholars to quantify, and where appropriate to test statistically, claims about the distribution of expressions.

This system gives the editors a sound basis for statements about usage, at least where the evidence is plentiful. For example, the general expectation might be that certain words are used by rural and older Negroes, hence chiefly in the South, others by urban and younger Negroes, hence chiefly in the North. If the data, upon analysis, run counter to expectation but are evidently valid, we write a usage note calling attention to this and correcting it. Our usage statements should take into account both geographic and social factors often unknown or ignored before. In this respect, at least, computer processing adds a useful tool. It took several years and considerable expense to produce, however, and requires the kind of data base which dictionaries in general do not have.

Materials in *DARE*'s Main File could not be handled in the same way: they are far too miscellaneous. Examples of usage are both oral and written; some are simple references to sources, others are full quotations; some were collected by scholars of language, others by members of the general public. The computer could not be expected to do more with this kind of miscellany than to put them in alphabetical order, sort homographs by parts of speech, and chronologize those which were dated. This has been done—imperfectly—for the letter A, on which editing is going forward actively. At least it puts printout sheets of quotations and references before the editors, along with the index to the Data Summary, and from these two he or she builds the treatment manually—or writes the Dictionary. These treatments or "write-ups" will have to be "keyboarded" with significant typographical codes and scanned to tape from which the printing machines will be run.

What of our hopes to edit the material directly on the CRT screen and return it to tape? While perfectly possible, this proved to be too difficult and expensive and had to be abandoned. Unless the editing were done in factory-like shifts, which would have made editorial cooperation virtually impossible, each editor would need a separate screen, and the material in process of writing-up would often sit inactively on the screen for many minutes while the editor checked on a source, sought an additional example, or did a dozen other necessary things—meantime paying to have the machine running. We could transfer the basic data to cassettes, rather than be on line, and feed it to the CRT through another machine (which we have) and after editing feed it back again to cassettes—but the cost of buying five such sets of machines and keeping them working proved excessive. In any case, the coding of our tapes for the printer would have required a process analogous to keyboarding, so little would have been gained. We have therefore returned to conventional manual editing, which now, with practice, is being systematized. It should be possible to increase the speed as we get into the rest of the alphabet.

What then has *DARE*'s experience with computers to suggest that may be of use for other lexicographical projects? In Matthew Arnold's phrase, we have been "chastened by experience"—but that was perhaps to be expected. We got off to a bad start when the CDC machine to which we were committed was pulled out of the Computing Center. The program associated with it would not run on other machines, and had to be converted. Time and money lost. The author of our program left the project, and his successors failed conspicuously to make it run. Much more time and money lost. Losing confidence in the University computer organization, we tried to get our work done off-campus but were denied permission. At last we found a man who could and did make our program completely over and produce the material processed as we wanted it. But during all the conversions, errors were introduced and parts of the data lost. More time and money spent for special proofreading and for redoing some of the input.

If the project had been small, presumably the processing could have been finished quickly with one person or only a few involved. The massiveness of the *DARE* corpus—the very factor that gives it value for the editor—was against this. To the computer people it was an uncomfortably big job—the type they were not used to, were not particularly interested in, and which they pushed off to the last. Their time estimates were regularly overoptimistic, their promises too easy. *DARE* lost fully a year and a half through all these annoying delays.

Use of the computer in any way requires fore-planning. Everything one expects it to do must be built into the program—no room for serendipity. The computer replicates error as willingly as truth—which is a virtue of sorts, but means that proofreading must be done exactingly with the first input and the temptation of easy replication resisted. With alphabetical projects, the simpler mechanical operations are most needed—and these the computer performs very well—sorting, updating, and the like, when human errors are not introduced. Punched cards are very dependable, and devices exist to prevent or overcome human error with them. Optical scanning is less accurate but still very useful. The CRT is especially good for correcting or revising draft copy. With telephone connections one is potentially in touch with computer installations in dozens of other cities—but every communication is expensive. The ideal is to own one's own machines, powerful enough for the job in hand but not more, and thus to control one's own electronic slave rather than be in the hands of outsiders. This shifts the expense, and may reduce it, but does not eliminate it; the cost of control must be balanced against other costs.

DARE, specifically, has found it prohibitively expensive to edit on CRT screens. However, our investment in processing the Data Summary so as to have immediate access to any responses, to be able to map these on the CRT screen for geographic and social distributions and print copies of these maps at will, is well justified. This special kind of dictionary, based on data collected so as to be comparable and processable in just this way, will be able to give better information on usage than has been available hitherto. Perhaps the chastening is inevitable—it is the "vanity of human wishes" to hope that life and lexicography can be trouble-free. If a good *Dictionary of American Regional English* can come out of it, the use of computers—in some ways—will have been justified.

Dictionary Reviews and Reviewing: 1900–1975

ROBERT L. CHAPMAN

A look at dictionary reviews is precisely appropriate for a volume honoring Professor James B. McMillan, because he wrote what is in my opinion the very best of the genre. Before commending his review as a model, I will examine selectively the history of dictionary reviewing in this century, singling out some of the themes, tendencies, and issues that emerge; then I will cite McMillan's review and propose what I hope to be some very slight improvements of his method.

1. History

First, a few gross numerical facts about dictionary reviewing during the first three-quarters of this century (or rather approximations, since the count is not exact). Magazines, professional journals, and metropolitan newspapers (New York, Boston, San Francisco, and Springfield, Massachusetts), printed about 250 reviews of thirty-two dictionaries during that period. I use "review" here with a certain latitude: these totals include news stories signaling the publication of dictionaries (most of them based entirely on the publisher's claims); they also include all critical notices, from about 30 words to the grand champion 11,000 word jeremiad with which Dwight Macdonald greeted *Webster's Third New International (NID3)*. I use "dictionary" empirically as guided by the occurrence of reviews, to compass general dictionaries of English in all sizes, including those made for children in school, and dictionary supplements. A fuller version of this paper might cover bilingual dictionaries, dictionaries of special vocabularies, and even such curiosities as the Bernstein *Reverse Dictionary.*

Not surprisingly, the number of reviews matches with the number of new dictionaries, the bumper decade in both respects being the 1960's, when nine books received seventy reviews. To adopt a purely computational approach for a moment, it is perhaps worth noting that the average number of reviews per book has been stable during the 1920's, '30's, '40's, '50's, and '60's at about nine (although of course not each new book got its average nine reviews). The figure was lower by about half during the first two decades of the century and during what has passed of this decade.

The number of dictionaries reviewed increases from one in the 1920's (the *OED,* of course), to four each in the '30's, and '40's, to five in the '50's, to nine in the '60's, to eight already in the '70's. These figures apply, however, only to books which are more or less generally reviewed, in, say, four or more places. Another group of dictionaries nearly as large (twenty-nine against thirty-two) was reviewed essentially *only* in the *Subscription Books Bulletin,* and hence only for librarians. In this category go fully sixteen books during the 1930's, and six each during the '40's and '50's. They are chiefly school dictionaries, including collegiate, and subscription books sold only by mail and with certain tie-ins. But the category also includes C. T. Onions' *Shorter Oxford,* H. C. Wyld's remarkable *Universal Dictionary,* and the *New Century Dictionary.* To this should be added that as far as I can tell, several good dictionaries apparently went unreviewed: *Funk and Wagnalls Standard Dictionary, International Edition;* the *Penguin Dictionary;* Walter Avis's *Dictionary of Canadianisms;* Barnhart's *World Book Encyclopedia Dictionary;* and the *Holt Intermediate Dictionary.*

These figures show, I think, that periodical editors have been somewhat erratic and negligent in bringing both good and bad dictionaries to the notice of their readers. In particular they have ignored the books designed for schools, arguably a crucial category for the national intellectual weal. I will say more later about what I think they should do and what I think academic dictionary critics should do in order to encourage better standards and enhance open discussion of these important books. The record of the linguistics journals, by the way, is perhaps the worst of all when it comes to appraising general dictionaries.

Now, abandoning the merely numerical, let us sample the reviewing record.

Funk and Wagnalls New Standard Dictionary of 1913 was generally praised for its practicality, as its editor Dr. Isaac K. Funk would have wished. The *New York Sun* admired its "marvelous ingenuity" in typography, and no one in the early years seems to have objected to its having two separate pronunciation systems. In 1934, however, the *Subscription Books Bulletin* (*SBB*) withdrew its full recommendation because the manner of updating the chronological list of events made it less useful than it should have been. In 1937 the *SBB* complained mildly about the practice of inserting new entries in the standing type pages by deleting and cutting earlier entries and by sometimes using smaller type. Finally, in 1948, the *SBB* checked the publisher's claims of responsible updating against a list of new words taken from issues of the *Britannica Book of the Year* and other sources that appeared during the previous decade and found that the *New Standard* was in fact seriously out of date. They proclaimed it "badly in need of thorough and complete overhauling."[1]

The *NID2* had appeared, of course, in 1934 to very general acclaim, and elicited about a dozen reviews. Some stress was put on its deliberate compromise between the claims of the scholar and those of lay persons. Eric Holmyard, for instance, said that " 'Webster' though thoroughly deserving the epithet scholarly is designed for the educated, practical citizen of the world"; and happily concluded that "the dictionary-maker is no longer 'a harmless drudge'; he is a vital factor in the advancement of learning and the progress of civilisation."[2] Thomas Knott, who was General Editor of the *NID2* under William Allen Neilson, recalled the decision that "Scholarship per se would not be enough; [the dictionary] must also be made intelligible to the general reader, to the business man, even to the boy and the girl in the 8th grade."[3]

This emphasis on the needs of the scholar vis-à-vis the ordinary citizen came about because the immediately previous great dictionary had been the *OED*, finished in 1928, and greeted with tributes like this: "[It is] the very reverse of pedantic, [but is] one of the greatest monuments to the patient persistence of scholarship and one of the most sterling illustrations of that strange piety which only scholars can understand."[4]

Hence, over against the *OED*, the two great American unabridged books were praised as being both sound and utilitarian. Their "encyclopedicness," in spite of the purely generic model of the *OED*, caused at the time no adverse comment.

Having mentioned how reviewers in the *SBB* chided Funk and Wagnalls for somewhat misrepresenting the up-to-dateness of the *New Standard* in 1948, I must mention how the same fate overtook the *NID2* in 1946, although it was then only twelve years old whereas the F and W was a somewhat type-stricken thirty-five. E. J. Kahn, Jr., wrote an amusing piece for the *New Yorker*, called "An Entirely New Book." Commencing with a misprint on p. xxi, he badgered the Merriam-Webster editors until he quite deflated their claim that the latest printing was entirely new. Only the Addenda Section, in fact, could claim that.[5]

Edward L. Thorndike's *Thorndike-Century Junior Dictionary* of 1935 had twelve reviews. It was praised for the "simplicity and directness" of its definitions, which "follow the rule that definitions for young people must be longer than those for adults, rather than shorter."[6] W. Wilbur Hatfield described it as "really for children."[7] Book-review editors and educators thus appear to have recognized the portent of this opening gun in "the Thorndike revolution" that purportedly converted American dictionaries from being stuffy, stilted, and pedantic into being direct, vernacular, intelligible, and free of the archaic and obsolete.[8] The reviewer for *Catholic World*, however, perhaps expressing a less liberal attitude, taxed the *TCJD* with "many examples of unsound pedagogy, defective English, inaccuracies, and unfortunate, if unintentional, bigotry."[9]

During 1936–1938 reviewing was dominated by the appearance in fascicles of Sir W. A. Craigie's *Dictionary of American English on Historical Principles* (*DAE*). The first fascicle drew nine reviews, including one by H. L. Mencken, who found that its only defect was the use of printed sources only.[10] Reviewers of the separate fascicles were generally favorable, and tended to greet the dictionary more as a readable, browsable transcript of American history and culture than a record of the American stamp on the language. This tendency continued as the four volumes appeared during the years 1938–1944. Sterling North, for instance, called it "an alphabetically arranged poem in prose which contains our cultural heritage."[11] Horace Reynolds called it "a cyclopedia of Americana and history of the American mind."[12] The adverse judgment which clouded the reception of this first of the *OED* "period dictionaries" appears to have begun with Edmund Wilson's *New Yorker* review of Feb. 19, 1944. Wilson granted that "many subjects are quite brilliantly developed," but went on to assert that the book "inevitably suffered as a result of being compiled by a Britisher." Craigie "was out of touch with many natural sources of information and had his own special views on the importance of certain words in the history of the American people."[13]

Scholarly criticism of the *DAE* began with the first part of Troubridge's "Notes on *DAE*" in December 1945.[14] By early 1951, eleven pieces detailing mistakes and omissions in the *DAE* had been published in *American Speech* alone.

The lexicon most widely yet perfunctorily reviewed during the 1930's was *Macmillan's Modern Dictionary* of 1938. All reviews were brief, and all praised it for its current, popular style, its omission of synonyms and antonyms, of pictures, of obsolete words. SBB recommended it "for quick reference."

The second broadside in the "Thorndike revolution" was fired in 1941 with the *Thorndike-Century Senior Dictionary,* which profited from the consultancy of Craigie, Kemp Malone, Leonard Bloomfield, Miles Hanley, and Louise Pound. The reviews again stressed the directness and simplicity of defining language, and explained the use of the Thorndike-Lorge and Buckingham-Dolch semantic counts. *Time,* which dubbed the *TCSD* "the man in the street's dictionary," noted rather tamely its pioneering use of the schwa as a useful shortcut.[15]

The prime lexicographical event of the postwar 1940's was of course the publication of Random House's *American College*

Dictionary (*ACD*), edited by Clarence L. Barnhart, in late 1947. Its reception was overwhelmingly cordial, as a book of its quality surely deserved. The best appraisal was that of Carlton F. Wells in the *Saturday Review* of January 24, 1948. Professor Wells, who was head of the freshman composition program at the University of Michigan, declared it up-to-date, clear, accurate, and authoritative. He found it free from "mere traditionalism and editorial crotchets."[16] To check in areas of competence beyond his own he consulted colleagues in natural and social science and in medicine. His only cavil was at the "overdetailed treatment of some entries."

The *DAE*'s successor, *A Dictionary of Americanisms,* edited by Mitford M. Mathews, attracted a most distinguished group of reviewers in 1951. The poet Randall Jarrell wrote as he said not a review but "an appreciation," and went on to stress the riches of the book for a knowledge of America.[17] James R. Newman lamented that the *DA* came out so quickly after the *DAE,* which it meant to correct and extend. He called it "... a valuable apparatus; the expenditure of a little more care and time might have made it a better one."[18] Edmund Wilson had thought the *DAE* an overhasty job; both critics probably had in mind the two-generation span of the *OED.*

The *Times Literary Supplement* professed not to understand why the book had been done so soon after the *DAE,* either not understanding or giving no credence to the American view that Craigie's ignorance of the country made him a poor choice as editor.[18] Bergen Evans observed that the British editor was well and truly replaced by Mitford M. Mathews, a native of Alabama.[19] The historian D. W. Brogan, the period's chief interpreter of America to the British, reviewed the *DA* for the *Spectator* of September 28, 1951. Brogan did not comment on the appearance of the *DA* so soon after the *DAE,* Craigie's "great enterprise." As a historian ought, he placed the *DA* in its proper relations with yet earlier dictionaries of Americanisms (Bartlett's, Farmer's, Thornton's) and with the work of G. P. Krapp, Louise Pound, and Dr. Mencken [*sic*]. He likened American English, without condescension I think, to the "vulgar eloquence" that Dante called nobler than the learned Latin tongue. As to the historical method in lexicography, Brogan observed that the use of printed material only was a palpable drawback, citing first appearances from a song and a movie sound track. Like most other reviewers, he ended up commending and enjoying the book more as a clue to the national temper than a dictionary *per se*.

Early in 1951 Doubleday published the *Thorndike-Barnhart Comprehensive Desk Dictionary*, last of the "revolutionary" series with which E. L. Thorndike himself was associated, since he had died in 1949. The book was hailed with twelve reviews, including one by the literary critic Malcolm Cowley which was typical of the general approbation. Cowley admired the "painstakingly simple" definitions, which follow the rule that a definition should be simpler than the term defined. He illustrated the *CDD*'s superiority by comparing its definition of "acne" with that of *Webster's Collegiate*. He praised Porter Perrin's usage notes, and quoted with approval the one for "linguistics":

> The outstanding trait of a linguist's approach to language is detachment—contrasting with the emotion often shown by non-professional users in defending or disapproving matters of speech. A linguist accepts such locutions as "I seen him yesterday," "He ain't got none," "That book is hern" as facts of the language— as well as words like *phagocyte* and *sternutation*. This does not mean that he uses any of these locutions himself or recommends them to others, but he notices that certain people use them and he observes and defines their place in the language.[20]

Robert Wallace's article in *Life* (see note 8) surely gave a particular dictionary and a particular editor, Clarence Barnhart, the widest national fame since Frank Vizetelly had pontificated in the *Literary Digest* and until the late Philip Gove became notorious in 1961. Wallace used the theme of "revolution in lexicography" to organize his review: "for $2.75 you will get a piece of a revolution." The Thorndike *Junior* and *Senior* and the *CDD* constituted the first phase, he said, the *ACD* the second, and the third, triumphal (and never realized) phase would be the use of Thorndike's radical insights in a new unabridged book.

The World Publishing Co. of Cleveland, after years of producing dictionaries reviewed only in the *SBB*, and consistently not recommended, at last achieved critical respectability and notice with the two volume *Webster's New World Dictionary* of 1952. S. Stephenson Smith, writing in the *Library Journal,* called it more modern, scientific, and usable than the *NID2.* He made a spot check of 400 items omitted or not properly covered in existing dictionaries, and found *WNWD* to be "a really satisfactory job, measuring up to modern lexicographical ideals."[21] The *New World* editors Joseph Friend and David Guralnik prepared the College edition of 1953, which had eight reviews, generally favorable. Mitford Mathews of the *DA* called it a "good piece of work."[22] W. H. Jackson in a newspaper notice lauded it for not cramping the growth of the language, but "legitimizing, so to say, new and newly developed words which have reason behind them."[23] Edward Calver, head of freshman composition at Wayne University, gave the book a very careful review using quantitative criteria, and partly dissented from the general praise. He said the editors had not corrected the mistakes of the two-volume edition, and showed a "clearly low-brow" tendency.[24]

Funk and Wagnalls New Practical Standard Dictionary of 1954 was noticed chiefly because it came out in combination with the *Britannica World Language Dictionary* as a subscription package. One reviewer of the *NPSD,* W. E. Garrison, praised it as "A thoroughly good dictionary with a wide coverage of new words, many of which are given place on the sound theory that it is the lexicographer's business to record actual usage whether he likes it or not."[25]

The reviewing history of *Webster's Third New International Dictionary* (*NID3*) has been exhaustively treated by several scholars, and summed up very handily by Raven McDavid in his article, "Dictionary Makers and Their Problems,"[26] hence needs no synopsis here. It stands out beyond that of all other dictionaries quite discontinuously: there was not merely more notice, there was immensely more, and most of it ill-informedly unfavorable.

In 1964, the fifth edition of the *Oxford Concise Dictionary of Current English,* originally edited by the brothers H. W. and F. G. Fowler, elicited four reviews, including one by B. Hunter Smeaton of the University of Calgary, who since then has been the fairly regular reviewer of dictionaries for the *Library Journal*.[27] Smeaton also recommended the *Funk and Wagnalls Standard College Dictionary* (*SCD*) "with considerable enthusiasm."[28] The *SCD* was not at all widely reviewed, and in fact no "college" dictionary since the *ACD* has received much notice.

During 1963 and 1964 several consumers journals, especially *Consumers Reports*, resumed the appraisal of dictionaries which had begun with an article by Charles Van Doren in 1958. Six separate articles appeared, including two by Allen Walker Read and one by James Sledd. Consumerism in reference books continued with an article in *Mechanics Illustrated* of January 1971. The unsigned piece treated encyclopedias primarily, and began its three-paragraph section on dictionaries with some dubious advice: "You can hardly go wrong when purchasing a dictionary." By this perception it made no real distinction between the *NID3*, the badly outdated *Funk and Wagnalls New International*, and the semi-unabridged Random House "Unabridged Dictionary." The writer perhaps meant that you can hardly go wrong if you buy books of a reputable publisher and check the copyright dates and claims of revision very carefully.

The launching of the *Random House Dictionary: the Unabridged Edition* (*RHD*) in 1966 and 1967 followed a publicity fanfare that stressed the high cost of the book, the pioneering use of electronic data processing (essentially to speed the filing and work-distribution processes), and its up-to-the-day modernity. Since this was the first big book after the *NID3*, and the use of the attributive "unabridged" demanded comparison, book review editors made its reception rather a gala occasion.

The critical discussion of the *RHD* was in fact more complex than that of the *NID3*, where the one theme of permissiveness and corruption overwhelmed all others. Only a single major reviewer, the UCLA bibliographer J. M. Edelstein, chose to deal with the *RHD* primarily as the "latest event in the long history of the corruption of the language ... [and] the downward trend toward anarchy ... [based on] a philosphy of language which supports not the precise and exact, but the vague and the ambiguous."[29] Joseph Wood Krutch might be seen as obliquely of this camp, although in his *Saturday Review* article of October

14, 1967[30] he complained at the "permissiveness" revealed by the *RHD* editor Jess Stein in a *TV Guide* article, expressing relief that the dictionary was more conservative than the editor.

Two reviews called the *RHD* to account for the claim of being unabridged, at 260,000 entries. *Choice* designated it more an expanded version of the *ACD*,[31] and the *SBB* recommended the attributive "semi-unabridged."[32] Two reviews complained that some of the staff-composed illustrative quotations were quite useless in realizing a defining context. The *SBB* inquired what help in comprehension came from "His feeling verged on *infatuation*."[33]

Anthony Burgess, along with Granville Hicks, was dubious about the entering of so many terms which even by the publication date of the book had become archaic. He instances "mod" and "rocker," observing "how waxwork they all look set there."[34] The *SBB* calls this tendency a "concentration on modish terminology."[35]

Most reviews of the *RHD* were laudatory in varying degrees, but one negative theme emerged fairly clearly, in particular among the literary and belletristic reviewers. The book was taxed as being too positivistic and impersonal, and not sufficiently literary, historical, and humanistic. E. E. Wardale had alluded to the issue in his 1928 review of the *OED*, comparing it with dictionaries of the Johnson sort:

> The essential difference between a dictionary made on such lines and one made on modern principles needs no emphasizing. Not only is the personal element eliminated, but the more exact knowledge of the earlier stages of the language and fuller acquaintance with our older literature have made fuller accuracy possible in the historical treatment.[36]

Now critics like John Ciardi, Anthony Burgess, Roger Du Bearn, and Granville Hicks lamented the loss of an authoritative personal voice *and* a lack of concern for word-history and for literature. Ciardi said that the etymologies were skimped, and failed to show the semantic development that somehow inheres in each word. This betrayed "a click-click let's-get-on-with-it mind" with its "tone of tidy but shallow efficiency." Proper lexicographers, said

Ciardi, must "love words and have a feeling for them as living forces."[37] By "living" he meant somehow containing their whole semantic history for the poet to use for profundity and complexity of reference. Granville Hicks objected to the method of ordering the senses within a given definition, because it took no account of semantic history.[38]

Roger Du Bearn wanted an even more extensive record of the semantic cluster adhering to any given form. He asked how one can enter "Allyn" as a girl's given name without recalling that Allyn and Bacon published an excellent Latin Grammar. And how can one set down "Lundy" merely as a boy's surname, without then mentioning "the excellent ship wreckers established on Lundy [Island]."[39] Dictionaries, said Du Bearn, should show what words do "for the poetry of life." The *RHD* defined without "any intrusion of elegance or wit such as ruined Dr. Johnson's reputation for seriousness. It could be dismissed as "obese and anti-literary."[40]

Anthony Burgess's review, quite remarkable for elegance and wit, likewise singled out an anti-literary bias, and the lack of literary quotations. He wanted the reader to keep Johnson's "quirky pioneering masterpiece [at hand], just to remind us that there was a time when a man could contain a language."[41]

Kurt Vonnegut's page-one review in the *New York Times Book Review* section of October 30, 1966, is notable chiefly for its insouciance and playfulness where lexicography is concerned, and for an amusing characterization of the *RHD*'s usage notes: "Schoolmarmisms tempered by worldliness."[42]

The 1960's were capped with yet one more notable clutch of dictionary reviews, when the *American Heritage Dictionary* (*AHD*) was published in 1969. Pre-publication releases, and the well-known story of James Parton's attempt to take over the Merriam-Webster company, had cited a "language of confrontation" between the at least partially prescriptive AHD and the fatally permissive *NID3*. In spite of this potential drama, the critical reception was relatively tame, and the occasion to scarify the *NID3* over again was not taken. Most attention was paid to the usage notes based on polls of the usage panel. B. Hunter Smeaton approved of these and of the fact that "usage is re-

enthroned'' in the book.[43] Rochelle Girson, book review editor
of the *Saturday Review*, hoped that the notes might help "to fill
the lacunas in the teaching of grammar and composition that
American education in recent years has been all too guilty of."[44]
The logician Willard V. Quine was somewhat dubious of the
usage-by-vote procedure, but brightly counseled that those 300
usage notes can be a guide: avoid all those usages, he said,
since they are all questionable, having been quesioned.[45]

Quine, and B. Hunter Smeaton as well, particularly praised
the genuinely new and imaginative etymological system of the
AHD, which depends on a list of Proto-Indo-European roots in
the back matter. Quine said that "it is to the publisher's eternal
credit to have catered so generously to an abstractly scientific
interest on the part of a small fraction of the many expected
buyers."[46] On balance he preferred the *AHD* to the *RHD* (college
edition).

The first publication of the 1970's was the Second Edition of
WNWD (college edition), 1970. The remarkable thing about the
response to this excellent book is its extreme muteness. At the
level I have been examining it elicited only two reviews, for a
total of 470 words.

Oxford dictionaries have dominated reviewing in this decade.
The initial volume of R. W. Burchfield's *Supplement to the OED*,
1972, was greeted by thirteen reviews, including an exceptionally
well-informed treatment by Professor Fred C. Robinson of Yale.[47]
In particular he takes note of the *NID3* and the exploitation of
its fate by the publishers of the *AHD*, and is gratified that in virtually every case the supplement vindicates the *NID3*'s judgment.

George Steiner wrote a haunting and idiosyncratic essay showing how the *Supplement* contrasts with the magisterial and potent
OED itself. Now, he said, the "center of linguistic gravity," "the
core of energy," has passed away from England, and the *Supplement* shows the force of English to be "registered in [*NID3*] and
Eugene Landy's Underground Dictionary."[48] The new supplement, he concluded,

> is a political, social, even more than a linguistic statement. It seeks
> to close the ancient, strategically effective gap between "British

English" and the uncouth, vaguely menacing babel of the semi-literate or largely oral world.[49]

Steiner's thesis constitutes the farthest and boldest attempt of any reviewer to appraise a dictionary in such a general cultural-historical context.

The theologian Martin Marty continued the good tradition of canny dictionary reviewing in the *Christian Century*, hitherto embodied in the literary editor Winfred E. Garrison, with an essay greeting both the *Supplement* and the *OED Compact Edition* of 1971. Dictionary editors might quarrel with Marty's conservatism and premises about what is "official," but they must admire his reverence:

> The OED has near-canonical status at our house. When new words work their way into American dictionaries, we are tempted to wait a few decades to see when Oxford accepts them; only then have they officially entered the language.[50]

The *OED Compact Edition* was graced with a panegyric review in the *New York Times Book Review* by William F. Buckley, and with equally laudatory notices by five other reviewers. The third Oxford dictionary of the 1970's was the Second Edition of the *Oxford Illustrated Dictionary* of 1975 (original edition 1963). This new edition got much more attention than the original, which had signaled a quiet reversal of Oxford's policy of not dealing in pictures nor in proper names. The British response showed that the anti-encyclopedic bias which once had rather clearly distinguished British lexicographic practice from American has now been fairly dissipated. Anthony Burgess had rumbled a bit in his review of the *RHD*, saying that unwillingness to distinguish between a dictionary and an encyclopedia "becomes somewhat embarrassing here," but now Mary Warnock, writing in the *Times Literary Supplement*, concedes that "a mixture of a dictionary and an encyclopedia is familiar enough . . . , [this is] an English Larousse."[51]

The last of the four Oxford dictionaries so prominent in the 1970's was the Third Edition of the *Advanced Learner's Dic-*

tionary of Current English of 1974. Although it had only two reviews, and both of these in library journals (*Booklist* and *Choice*), the notable thing is that it was finally acknowledged at all outside of the dictionary offices and the occasional article on grammar, where its system of structural patterns, its labeling of nouns as count or non-count, and its careful indication of the stylistic values of its entries have been admired for years.

Reviews of the *American Heritage School Dictionary* of 1972 are worth mentioning because in them and in the publicity surrounding publication the issue of sexism in dictionary definitions first became prominent. Florence Forst, writing in *ETC.*, observed that the dictionary counters masculine sexism by a high proportion of reference to females in the illustrative quotations, and not only in the stereotypical mothering and nursing sorts of roles, and also has more women and girls in its pictures.

The Doubleday Dictionary for Home, School, and Office was published in 1975 and received three reviews, in addition to a *New York Times* news story. The *Booklist* notice, like the other two, was generally favorable, but took notice of a "curious policy," the exclusion of offensive racial and religious epithets.[52] Janet Domowitz, seemingly without ironic intent, praised the book as "with it."[53] B. Hunter Smeaton, by this time our most experienced and regular reviewer, taxed it with a "terseness which defeats the major purpose of a dictionary (or am I wrong in believing that this is to tell us what words mean?)" He found the very small print to be also of no help.[54]

That is, roughly, the history of dictionary reviewing for the past 75 years.

2. Method

Mario Pei, at the beginning of his review of the *RHD*, said that in all candor one cannot review a dictionary—"It is only after months and years of use and consultation that one can pass final judgment."[55] Then, of course, Professor Pei broke out of his own paradox and went on to review one.

Still, James B. McMillan's omnibus review of "Five Dictionaries," published in *College English* for January 1949, is the best job of dictionary reviewing extant, not particularly because he was a seasoned consulter of all five, or because it is extraordinarily well expressed and lucidly organized, though it is, but because he used a method based on analysis and comparative sampling.[56] Letting the form of a dictionary determine the form of his article, he attends to every feature of the books, assessing the quantity of information, the quality of information, and the effectiveness of presentation. Where general matters of "style" and policy are concerned he shows the differences among the books and takes account of the reasons for preferring one policy or another. For instance, after choosing *ACD* for the relative richness of its pronunciation variants, he says,

> Teachers who for pedagogical reasons prefer a minimum of variant pronunciations or who for philosophical reasons prefer an "authoritative" pronunciation to a reporting of current usage, will, of course, reverse my ratings of the dictionaries on this point.[57]

Where the day-to-day standard of editorial performance is concerned, rather than a specific policy decision, he makes a number of comparative samplings. He prints the five definitions of "dumb" and the five etymologies of "feign." He shows how the usage labels vary on "movie," "razz," "tycoon," and "plug." When he finally picks the *ACD* over the others, the case and the premises have been so well deployed that the aggrieved editors and publishers could hardly have refuted them.

Among the other reviews considered here, the ones that come closest to McMillan's standard of clarity and persuasiveness are that of the *ACD* by Carlton F. Wells, that of *WNWD* by Edward Calver, and in general the series of notices in the *SBB*. These latter have been the responsibility of a Subscription Book Committee of about thirty librarians, well distributed by region and professional area. Often a particular review is prepared by a library professor and a class in reference books. Sampling is used, but not as systematically as one might expect. The reviews, when one has read numbers of them, are too quantitative and not sufficiently qualitative.

The *SBB* deserves great credit for, within limits, reviewing *all* dictionaries. In eight cases during the period under consideration, the *SBB* gave a verdict of "not recommended" to dictionaries re-issued from old plates with false or dubiously justifiable claims of revision, up-to-dateness, authority, etc. Some of these had hoary histories of many editions under many pretentious titles, and the *SBB* painstakingly traced these incarnations. No other reviewing medium has been so useful in guarding buyers against shoddy goods.

Beyond commending the McMillan review as a model, I have four suggestions to offer toward a still better method. First, it would be desirable, if it does not prove too clumsy, to constitute a reviewing team something like the technical advising team most dictionaries use. These cooperating authorities would examine definitions in their own fields, and give their ratings to the reviewer. Carlton Wells did this for his appraisal of the *ACD,* and I suggest it should become the practice in all serious reviewing.

Second, reviewers should use a random sampling device that covers the book from A to Z, so that the total average performance may be assessed. This might be something as simple as "the tenth main entry on every twentieth page" (not including abbreviation, cross references, and the like). This would yield about fifty entries, and if the reviewer has more time he should go to every fifteen pages, or every ten pages.

Third, very close attention should be paid to the quality of these fifty or more definitions. They should be painstakingly analyzed for, to use McMillan's criteria, accuracy, completeness, clearness, simplicity, and modernity. To these should be added two further criteria. One is "substitutability"; that is, can the definition take the place of the term in a usual context, and be adequate both as to meaning and syntax. The other might be called "lexical integrity": can each term used in the definition (except of course for taxonomic description) be found in the dictionary?

Fourth, the "referential integrity" should be tested by tracking down a number of cross-references. This is an excellent gauge of editorial thoroughness and the effectiveness of systems. John Ciardi gave a splendid example of this quest when he began with the term "mokko" in the *RHD* and tracked it through, turning up among other things an anomalous plural notation and a misprint, apparently, for "koggai."[58]

My general point here is that after policies are determined, what a dictionary staff primarily does is, precisely, definitions. The value of the book lies finally in the excellence of its definitions, so it is these which should be most carefully and judiciously studied and compared.[59]

I urge my colleagues to take a larger part than they have in the regular and comprehensive reviewing of dictionaries, preferably using the method sketched above, based on McMillan's practice. We should review *every* dictionary that emerges, and do what we can to suppress or improve the bad ones. Someone (McMillan himself?) should do the job today on four college dictionaries that he did in 1949 on five. Editors of scholarly journals and of popular magazines should be pressured to print these reviews.[60] I am convinced that some good effect might be achieved, certainly the improvement of future editions, perhaps even some slight alleviation of the seeming trend toward illiteracy.

NOTES

1. *Subscription Books Bulletin* 19 (July 1948): 46.
2. *Nature* 134 (October 1934): 603.
3. *American Scholar* 4 (May 1934): 372.
4. *Nation* 124 (June 15, 1827): 660.
5. *New Yorker* 22 (October 5, 1946): 67–79.
6. *Chicago Daily Tribune* February 9, 1935, p. 14.
7. *Elementary School Journal* 36 (December 1935): 313.
8. For an entertaining account of the "revolution" see Robert Wallace, "A is for Aardvark: Thorndike-Barnhart Comprehensive Desk Dictionary," *Life* 30 (February 12, 1951): 125–35.
9. *Catholic World* 141 (May 1935): 250.
10. *Books,* October 4, 1936, p. 2.
11. *Book Week,* February 6, 1944, p. 2.
12. *New York Times,* January 23, 1944, p. 1.
13. *New Yorker* 20 (February 16, 1944): 81.
14. *American Speech* 20 (December 1945): 265–76.
15. *Time* 37 (March 17, 1941): 73.
16. *Saturday Review* 31 (January 24, 1948): 19.

17. *Nation* 173 (December 29, 1951): 570.

18. *Times Literary Supplement,* October 5, 1951, p. 630.

19. *Saturday Review* 34 (April 28, 1951): 8.

20. *New Republic* 124 (April 16, 1951): 27–8. Perrin's usage note on "drunk" was much cited for its pith and wit. Perrin discusses some of the common euphemisms, and concludes tersely, "But *drunk* is the word."

21. *Christian Century* 71 (1954): 584.

22. *Library Journal* 76 (1951): 2002.

23. *School Review* 61 (September 1953): 369.

24. *San Francisco Chronicle,* April 28, 1953, p. 19.

25. *New Republic* 128 (April 20, 1953): 21.

26. Ed. Virginia McDavid, *Language and Teaching: Essays in Honor of W. Wilbur Hatfield* (Chicago: Chicago State College, 1969), pp. 70–80.

27. *Library Journal* 89 (1964): 2069.

28. Ibid., p. 232.

29. *New Republic* 155 (November 26, 1966): 26.

30. Pages 19–21.

31. *Choice* 3 (October 1966): 616.

32. *Booklist and Subscription Books Bulletin* 63 (April 1, 1967): 805.

33. Ibid., p. 806. The other complainer was Granville Hicks in the *Saturday Review* 49 (October 22, 1966): 49–52.

34. *Encounter* 28 (February 1967): 70.

35. *Booklist and Subscription Books Bulletin* 63 (April 1, 1967): 806.

36. *Nineteenth Century* 103 (January 1928): 102.

37. *Saturday Review* 52 (May 24, 1969): 39.

38. *Saturday Review* 49 (October 22, 1966): 50.

39. *American Scholar* 36 (Summer 1967): 454.

40. Ibid.

41. *Encounter* 28 (February 1967): 71.

42. Page 56.

43. *Library Journal* 94 (1969): 4512.

44. *Saturday Review* 52 (September 27, 1969): 25.

45. *New York Review of Books* 13 (December 4, 1969): 3.

46. Ibid.

47. *Yale Review* 12 (1973): 50–56.

48. *New York Times Book Review,* November 26, 1972, p. 17.

49. Ibid.

50. *Christian Century* 89 (1972): 1115.

51. *Times Literary Supplement* May 3, 1975, p. 604.

52. *Booklist* 71 (1975): 1204.

53. *Christian Science Monitor,* January 25, 1975, p. 9.

54. *Library Journal* 100 (1975): 110.

55. *Nation* 203 (December 19, 1966): 675.

56. The five are the *ACD,* the *Funk and Wagnalls College Standard,* the *Winston,* the Merriam-Webster *Collegiate,* and the *Macmillan Modern.*

57. McMillan, *op. cit.,* p. 216.

58. *Saturday Review* 52 (April 12, 1969): 12–14.

59. Another model of close inspection of definitions is McMillan's "Of Matters Lexicographical," *American Speech* 45 (1970): 288–92.

60. A look at these footnotes will give a good indication of the periodicals that have fairly faithfully reviewed dictionaries. It seems to me that *Language* and other linguistic journals should be importuned to publish such reviews.

On Redefining
-oriented

MARY GRAY PORTER

The siting of temples, churches, and other religious structures so that they faced the east, or some other point of the compass, was a widespread practice throughout the ancient and medieval world. It is surprising, then, that the English verb *orient,* borrowed from French, appears so late: 1727–41 is the *Oxford English Dictionary*'s earliest attestation for the transitive *orient* "to place or arrange (anything) so as to face the east...." Illustrations of other senses of the verb date from more than a century later, and the only example of the intransitive verb "to turn to the east, or (by extension) towards any specified direction" dates from 1896. In addition, the *OED* offers several examples of *orientate* in the same senses as *orient,* the earliest from 1849.

Also from the middle of the nineteenth century come the *OED*'s illustrations of figurative uses of *orient;* the earliest for *orientate* with the same figurative meanings occurs a few years later (1866). *Webster's New International Dictionary Second Edition* (1934), *Webster's New World Dictionary of the American Language* (College Edition, 1960), and *The American Heritage Dictionary of the English Language* (1969) are representative of dictionaries defining the verb *orient* as "to cause to become familiar with or adjusted to facts, principles, or a situation" (*AHD*). *The Century Dictionary* (New York, 1906), edited by William Dwight Whitney, had earlier emphasized the mental, as opposed to the geographic, orientation, and defined both *orient* and *orientate* as "take one's proper bearings mentally."

Some dictionaries have recognized the need for *oriented, adj.*

as a separate entry. *Webster's Third* defines the adjective *oriented* as "directed, related" and adds the illustrative quotation "this book, value-*oriented* throughout..." *Chambers Twentieth Century Dictionary* (New Edition; Totowa, N.J.: Littlefield, Adams & Co., 1972) has a single entry "*oriented, orientated*, directed (towards); often used in composition as second element of *adj.*" The definition of *oriented, adj.* in the eighth edition of *Webster's New Collegiate Dictionary* (1973) makes it explicit that the direction or orientation is not a spatial one but a mental one: "intellectually or emotionally directed <humanistically ~ scholars>." *The Doubleday Dictionary for Home, School, and Office* (Garden City, N.Y.: Doubleday & Co., Inc., 1975), edited by Sidney I. Landau and Ronald J. Bogus, makes two useful contributions to a more precise definition in its entry under *oriented, adj.:* "*1* Directed toward; interested in: *oriented* to the arts. *2* Directed or centered: used in combination: a *child-oriented* family."

The definitions of *oriented* proposed below are based on a collection of more than 1800 quotations taken principally from American publications of the 1970s (newspapers and magazines of general interest and circulation); others have been excerpted from works of earlier date or more restricted circulation. Nor should television be forgotten; news announcers and talk-show guests have supplied several of the quotations, and the number could surely have been increased if the time available for watching television had been greater. Finally, I am indebted to Frederick Goossen for assistance with some music-oriented quotations and to several people who have added to the mass of citations: John Algeo, Dennis E. Baron, I. Willis Russell, Peter Tamony, and to the *Jubilar* of this festschrift, James B. McMillan.

Combinations of the type of *x-oriented* express the same senses as *oriented* followed by a prepositional phrase. The most frequently used prepositions are *to* and *toward(s)*, but no claim of statistical significance is made for the slightly higher frequency of *toward* in the small collection of citations. They appear, in fact, to be interchangeable. A school of the performing arts is described as being "oriented *toward* production and *to* history and criticism of film as art'' *(Town & Country,* Sep. 1974, p. 67/2). Another writer differentiates two meditation systems on the basis of their orientation: ''his meditation is oriented *to* rest. TM is oriented *toward* dynamic activity and creativity'' *(Ladies' Home Journal,* Mar. 1974, p. 174/2). The frequency of other prepositions trails far behind that of *to* and *toward(s).* Only two instances of *around* were noted: ''a computer program oriented *around* blood-and-guts pathology'' *(Atlantic,* Nov. 1974, p. 75/2) and ''new towns oriented *around* the automobile'' *(Family Circle,* Mar. 1975, p. 2/4). One other preposition, *on,* is in fairly common use in connection with physical or geographical orientation, but only two occurrences in other contexts were found: The public makes use of television, radio, newspapers, and magazines, and ''does not usually orient itself *on* a single one of these media'' *(Kulturbrief: A German Review,* Bonn: Inter Nationes, Oct. 1974, p. 5/1–2). ''The American-Swiss Association, Inc. collected a small library of French, German, Italian, and Spanish films, generally oriented *on* Swiss folk customs and culture'' *(Accent on ACTFL,* Sep. 1972, p. 24/1–2). Compare *activity-oriented (Journal of Rehabilitation,* Sep.–Oct. 1964, p. 27/1; *World,* 22 May 1973, p. 20/3), *automobile-oriented (Saturday Review,* 3 Apr. 1971, p. 62/3; *New York Times,* 7 Apr. 1974, p. IA9/1), *creativity-oriented (Psychology Today,* July 1973, p. 62/3), *history-oriented (PMLA,* May 1974, p. 559/2), and *production-oriented (U.S. News & World Report,* 16 Oct. 1972, p. 18/2; *Business Week,* 9 Mar. 1974, p. 158/3).

Virtually all the collocations of *orient(ed)* with a prepositional phrase and combinations of the *x-oriented* type express the general notion of ''turned, literally or figuratively, toward something that serves, for example, as a guide, destination, aim, or focus of interest or liking.'' It is rare that *oriented* is used when there is a turning away or an aversion. My citations furnish only three examples: *anti-pleasure-oriented (Ladies' Home Journal,* May 1973, p. 40/3), *counter-oriented,* and *oriented against.* Present-day Americans would not have modern plumbing ''if the rural American of 1900 had been as *counter-oriented* to the ongoing thrust of technology as certain romantic elements are in 1973'' *(Atlantic,* Apr. 1973, p. 94/1). If the orientation *toward* is absent or nonexistent, *not* is commonly used to negate the adjective; the prefixes *non-* and *un-* occur less often. *Non-* is consistently prefixed to *x-oriented* combinations (see the entries in the glossary under *non-*). *Un-,* in its single occurrence, is prefixed to *oriented:* "this jazz-unoriented girl" (*Esquire,* May 1972, p. 157/1).

In the majority of cases the first component of *-oriented* combinations is a noun or substantivized adjective; in other instances the adjective clearly retains its adjectival quality. Phrases composed of an adverb and *oriented* ("highly oriented," "technologically oriented") have not been considered. Other parts of speech are rare: one occurrence each of a pronoun (*me-orientated*), a verb (*sell-oriented* [*Saturday Review,* 11 Dec. 1976, p. 89/1]), and a letter (*r-oriented,* where *r,* the intrinsic rate of increase of a population, is one of the terms in the basic equation of population biology [*Analog,* Oct. 1976, p. 69]). Often the first part of an *-oriented* combination is a compound or cluster of words. Groups like Planned Parenthood are *family-planning-oriented* (*Saturday Review,* 11 Mar. 1972, p. 43/1); some stockbrokers are *small investor-oriented* (*Washington Post,* 22 Nov. 1970, p. B6/5); and a variety program on Japanese television is *youth-and-rock-oriented* (*TV Guide,* 1 May 1971, p. 7/2). There appear to be few constraints on the composition of the first element—and occasionally no restraint at all: "Genuine mate wanted . . . Eastern college seacoast, mountain, non-urban-oriented" (classified ad in *New York Review of Books,* 21 Feb. 1974, p. 35/1).

Much of the difficulty in defining *oriented* results from the great increase in the frequency of its occurrence, especially in the 1960s and '70s. The earlier dictionary definitions of the verb *orient* in its figurative uses seem to limit its direct object to words referring to persons. The recent vogue, welcomed and encouraged, if not initiated, by computer-oriented technicians and Madison Avenue, has led to the use of the adjective *oriented,* alone or in combination, as a modifier of nouns with an ever increasing variety of referents; to an apparently unrestricted choice of first elements of *-oriented* combinations; and to ever decreasing precision and clarity in the connection between the first element and the modified word.

The definition of *oriented, adj.* given in *Webster's Third,* "directed, related," raises several questions: directed *toward?* or directed *by?* related in what way? Many of the quotations in the glossary show clearly how the modified noun and the first element of the -*oriented* combination are related; others show how context-dependent the meaning of *oriented* can be. And in some, the verbal context does not furnish the information that is needed to determine the nature of the relationship. What, for example, is a *Presbyterian-oriented* college? Is it a college supported, partially or wholly, or owned, by Presbyterians? By the Presbyterian Church? Or is it one that espouses and teaches the tenets of Presbyterianism? About all that is clear is the existence of some kind of link between the college and the Presbyterian Church (or Presbyterians or Presbyterianism). Wilson Follett (*Modern American Usage,* 1966, p. 204) has already objected to this lack of clarity in connection with what he terms "the additives -*wise, -wide, -conscious, -minded, -oriented*": "they generally link the neighboring ideas wrongly or feebly.... The appearance of meaning may be given, or the meaning may be supplied by someone with the facts;... around the central word there is nothing but a haze of possible connections."

The definitions of -*oriented* suggested here are an attempt to clear away some of that haze. They are based primarily on those occurrences where a single meaning emerges, more or less distinctly, out of the "haze of possible connections." Other -*oriented* words are ambiguous, but their range of ambiguity always includes the meaning suggested by less ambiguous citations. Ambiguity is especially common in vogue uses, where the main function of *x-oriented* words apparently is not so much to convey meaning as to be fashionable. The million words of running text contained in the Brown University Corpus (1961) include, in addition to *oriented, disoriented, reoriented,* and *socially-oriented,* only eleven combinations of the *x-oriented* type: *action-, college-, crisis-, family-, goal-, Hamilton-, people-, policy-, success-, well-,* and *world-oriented.* Although little significance can be attached to the specific number of -*oriented* items found by someone searching for them in comparison with the number of such items that occur even in 1,014,232 words of text, the trend since 1961 seems clear. Many of the approximately 675 items collected for this study, a few of which occur more than fifty times, owe their existence to the *-oriented* vogue of the '60s and '70s.

The frequent occurrence and the often obscure meaning have led to playful uses of *orient* and its derivatives. There are a few puns in which the *orient* derivative is used because, like Mount Everest, it is there, and because it makes possible some kind of connection or association with the Orient. "New Orientation" is the heading of a letter in which a reader offers his recipe for an "Oriental-style omelet I devised" (*Gourmet*, July 1976, p. 1/3). A two-piece evening outfit showing the influence of Chinese costume is advertised: "Our skirting gets oriented to the tunic..." (*New Yorker*, 7 July 1975, p. 20/1). A writer for *W*, the society-oriented sister publication of *Women's Wear Daily*, was unable to resist the combination of the *oriented* vogue, the influence of Chinese dress and art, and the coincident release of the movie *Murder on the Orient Express:* "Marc Bohan of Dior is on the Orient Express. He's well-oriented.... Bohan uses China as a theme of his fall collection" (*W*, 18 April 1974, p. 19/1).

Vogue words, like other fads, and jargon are susceptible to parody, especially when used in conjunction with trendy subjects such as the counterculture and ecology. Carter A. Daniel has taken a few slaps at educationese in his neo-Socratic dialogue "Anopheles": "But elimination and/or deactivation of low-enrollment programs should occur only after careful ICLM-oriented analysis over a time continuum..." (*AAUP Bulletin*, Aug. 1976, p. 155/2). One can only regret that this handsome specimen of the style is marred by the abbreviation *ICLM;* "induced course-load matrix-oriented analysis" would have been a beauty. What purports to be "Buckminster Fuller's Repair Manual for the Entire Universe" proposes the construction of a "geodesic earth-roof" 450 nautical miles from the surface of the earth; it would "function as a permanent obstruction to divine intervention, thus facilitating the development of a me-orientated semieternal world-around control system," whatever that may mean (*National Lampoon*, Jan. 1972, p. 46). In the nuptial vows described by Peg Bracken on page 125 of *The I Hate to Cook Almanack: A Book of Days* (New York: Harcourt Brace Jovanovich, 1976), "ecology-oriented goal attainment" may not contribute much to a dictionary definition of -*oriented,* but the diction must be admired. The bride and groom and their baby "proceed to some body of running water—ocean, river, park fountain, or open drain—to stand barefoot and read aloud to each other from *Portnoy's Complaint* and *Jonathan Livingston Seagull* as they pledge their continuing co-operative efforts at ecology-oriented goal attainment, with background music by The Funky Chicken."

Definitions and Selected Illustrations

1. Turned toward the specified direction or toward the specified object; positioned with the axis running in the specified direction

   Examples of ambiguous combinations in which -*oriented* could have this sense are: *earth-oriented, left-oriented.* An *earth-oriented* satellite, for instance, is turned so that its antenna and sensors are pointed toward the earth. The primary meaning, however, seems to be a satellite whose uses are related to the earth (mapping, surveys of earth resources, terrestrial communications), not to space. Similarly, it is no doubt true that the asymmetries of *left-oriented* corkscrews, potato peelers, and other implements mirror those of regular corkscrews, etc., but it is less certain that they are turned toward the left; 'intended for the use of left-handers' is probably the primary sense.

   beach-oriented: 1973 Jan *Woman's Day* 176/3 "deluxe golf- and beach-oriented resorts" —**north-south oriented:** 1974 June *Sci Amer* 116/3 "Place it tenderly in the properly north-south oriented pyramid." —**pool-oriented:** 1975 Feb *Town & Country* 114/2 "the pool-oriented, somewhat formal Casa Grande [hotel]" —**sky-oriented:** 1975 Sep 19 *W* 34/2 "[He] was an astrology expert who believed that mares yield better foals if they look up at the sky.... Hall-Walker quickly started building his sky-oriented stables." —**south-oriented:** 1974 June *Southern Living* 124/2−3 "The south-oriented room was pleasant enough." —**water-oriented:** 1972 Mar *Amer Home* 68/1 "Business executives can tie up alongside water-oriented offices." 1974 June *Town & Country* 45/3 "Water-oriented community with three separate marinas" —**woods-oriented:** 1975 July *Town & Country* 10/2 "beach front or woods-oriented homes"

2. a. Familiar with, adjusted or adapted to *x*
aviation-oriented: 1971 Feb *Pop Photog* 118–119 "Most people looking at the picture are not aviation-oriented, and find it difficult to recognize objects from unusual angles." —**cartoon-oriented:** 1972 Apr *House Beautiful* 142/4 "today's cartoon-oriented child" —**child-oriented:** 1972 June *Sports Afield* 78/2 "a patient, child-oriented old horse" —**city-oriented:** 1971 July *Esquire* 96/1 "I'm a city-oriented man." —**farm-oriented:** 1973 Dec *Field & Stream* 84/3 "any farm-oriented person in the county you plan to hunt" —**theater-oriented:** 1974 Nov 2 *TV Guide* A3/2 "Most of our cast is theater-oriented... so that we don't expect the hour length to put undue strain on the cast." —**traffic oriented:** 1972 Nov–Dec *Horse Lover's Mag* 24/1 (picture caption) "Unless your horse is well trained and traffic oriented it's best to ride with the traffic flow."

  b. Suitable for *x*
grape-oriented: 1972 July *Amer Home* 62/3 "The Davis professors have devised a zoning system for the state based on 'degree-days,' over and under a particular grape-oriented temperature."

  c. Getting one's bearings or sense of place in the world from *x*
affiliation-oriented: 1972 Mar 11 *New Yorker* 75/1 "In the sociologists' jargon, the Hawaiian adult continues to be affiliation-oriented, as he was in pre-Cook times, as against achievement-oriented."

3. Inclined toward *x*
Several related senses can be grouped together under a general heading "inclined." Paradoxically, the various sub-meanings cannot always be rigorously separated, although they are usually readily discernible. In the case of *black-oriented,* for example, the context is the deciding factor. A movie referred to as "this black-oriented escapist piece" might well be one intended to appeal to blacks in the audience, but because the whites, not the blacks, are depicted as stereotypes, I have taken *black-*

oriented to mean 'told from the black viewpoint' and have entered it under 3b.

    a. Inclined by nature, temperament, or training toward *x*
   action-oriented: 1971 Feb *Harper's* 68/1 "But he was action-oriented, his instinct was to do something." —*Specif,* inclined to take action to alleviate social ills 1970 Nov 1 *Parade* 24/1 "Today's teenagers are much more socially conscious, much more action-oriented than their predecessors of ten years ago."
—**human-services oriented:** 1972 Nov 11 *National Observer* 10/4 "The 'new breed' of officer . . . should be human-services oriented in his motivation." —**law-oriented:** 1972 July 10 *Time* 71/3 "But the prejudiced Lutherans . . . tend to be 'law-oriented' rather than Gospel-oriented. Law-oriented Lutherans show a distinct need for religious absolutism and a marked intolerance for change."
—**lid-off-the-id-oriented:** Inclined to "take the lid off the id"; disposed to deal with sexual matters uninhibitedly 1971 Mar *McCall's* 14–16 "[J, the author of *The Sensuous Woman*] is immensely romantic, hugely practical . . . and completely lid-off-the-id-oriented." —**litigation-oriented:** 1976 June 9 *Wall St Jour* 1/6 "the militant, litigation-oriented Environmental Defense Fund" —*mañana*-**oriented:** 1970 Nov 14 *Sat Rev* 54/3 "individuals with low self-esteem and *mañana*-oriented life-styles" —**nonbusiness-oriented:** 1972 Aug *Harper's* 34/3 "the predominately nonbusiness-oriented Maoist managers" —**nonmarketing-oriented:** c1972 Robert Heller *The Great Executive Dream* (NY: Dell Pub Co, Inc, 1974) 55 "The standard sneer against 'non-marketing-oriented' companies is that they have merely called the sales manager a marketing manager." —**research-oriented:** 1971 Jan *South Atlantic Bulletin* 17 "our research-oriented Ph.D.'s" 1974 July 20 *TV Guide* 3 "My research-oriented taste buds wanted to conduct a dispassionate analysis of the 75-cent banana split." —**violence-oriented:** 1972 Jan 22 *Sat Rev* 61/2 "violence-oriented leftists"
    b. Favorably disposed toward *x;* biased, slanted, or tilted in
      favor of *x;* portrayed from the viewpoint of or in terms of *x*
Administration-oriented: 1973 Dec 3 *Newsweek* 8/3 (letter) "News shows would be Administration-oriented." —**black-ori-**

ented: 1972 June 24 *New Yorker* 18/3 "THE LEGEND OF NIG-
GER CHARLEY—The whites are the stereotypes in this black-
oriented escapist piece." **—consumer-oriented:** 1975 Jan 16 Ray
Scherer "NBC News" "The Agriculture Committee will be less
farming- and more consumer-oriented." Nov—Dec *Columbia
Journ Rev* 22—23 " 'consumer-oriented' groups such as the Center for Science in the Public Interest" **—Eastern-establishment
oriented:** 1974 Oct 26 *TV Guide* A3/1—2 "The two-hour program... will 'not be liberal, Eastern-establishment' oriented."
—McGovern-oriented: 1972 Oct 14 *Sat Rev* 70/1 "the McGovern-
oriented liberal college students" **—pop oriented:** 1971 Feb 18
Rolling Stone 23/1 "Radio Monte Carlo... is pop oriented enough
to play Ike & Tina Turner." **—right-oriented:** Pun on *right* "conservative" and "correct" 1972 Mar 13 *US News & World Report*
38/2 "the viewpoint of some of the 'right'-oriented people"

   c. Tending toward *x;* resembling *x,* having some of the characteristics of *x*

Basie-oriented: [William "Count" Basie, American jazz mu-
sician] 1972 Nov 4 *Sat Rev* 92/3 "a Basie-oriented sextet"
—country-oriented: 1969 Apr *High Fidelity* 50/1 "a country-
oriented album" 1973 Aug 11 *TV Guide* 15/2 "25 per cent of
all records sold in the U.S. are country-oriented." **—live-oriented:**
1973 Aug 2 *Rolling Stone* 22/4 "Plans are to do a live album or
at least a live-oriented album with live vocals and a minimum of
overdubs." **—religious-oriented:** 1976 Apr 10 *National Observer*
6/4 " 'religious-oriented' books (including biographies of sports
superstars)" **—rhythm and blues-oriented:** 1975 Sep 5 *New Times*
56/2 "the rhythm and blues-oriented 'Spinning Wheel' " **—Summerhill oriented:** 1972 Apr *Atlantic* 130/2 (ad) "SUMMERHILL
ORIENTED SCHOOL AND SUMMER CAMP—Modified free
school approach"

   d. Characterized by the predominance or prominence of *x*

brush-oriented: 1973 Apr *Field & Stream* 218/3 "Because of his
brush-oriented environment, the few open parks sprinkled throughout [the blacktail deer's] range are danger zones." **—horn-
oriented:** 1970 Nov 30 *Rock* 24/2 "Taking some roots from Chicago, the horn-oriented sound is clear, tight and moving." **—warp
oriented:** 1973 Apr *Amer Home* 32/3 "In traditional tapestries...

the warp was completely covered up. My weavings are warp oriented.''

  e. 1) *Of persons,* interested in *x;* mindful of the importance of *x*

    2) *Not restricted to persons,* having a significant interest in or specializing in *x;* concerned with or dealing with *x* as subject matter

Without insisting on the inflexibility, or even the validity, of the following categories, I would suggest that the interest might be characterized as being, or being regarded by some as: (a) innate, inherent, permanent, or long-lasting; (b) preferential, the primary interest at the moment. It may be a preoccupation with *x* to the exclusion or detriment of other matters. Admittedly, the distinction between this and -*oriented* in the sense of 'favorably disposed toward' is a fuzzy one. And, finally, (c) the interest might be considered excessive, obsessive, or perverse.

action-oriented: 1974 *The Best Science Fiction of the Year #3* edited by Terry Carr (NY: Ballantine Books) ix "the action-oriented pulp-adventure formulas of the past" —**atmosphere-oriented:** 1975 Aug 23 & 30 *Science News* 120/3 "an atmosphere-oriented symposium" —**data oriented** 1972 Lee Pederson in *Studies in Linguistics in Honor of Raven I McDavid, Jr* edited by Lawrence M Davis (Univ of Ala Press) 123 "The first lesson the dialectologist learns is to be data oriented." —**extraction-oriented:** 1975 Jan *Reader's Digest* 117/1 "Avoid dentists who are extraction-oriented." —**feces-oriented:** 1971 Mar 22 *National Observer* 21/3 "It is incredible how the people who show up on Dick Gibson's various shows manage to be, almost to a man, so sex- or feces-oriented." —**foot-oriented:** 1973 Dec 3 *Newsweek* 17/3 "Making America more foot-oriented, less heated in winter . . . will involve the pain of readjustment." —**marriage-oriented:** 1974 Dec *Atlantic* 132/1 (ad) "SINGLE BOOKLOVERS gets the mature, cultured, marriage-oriented acquainted." —**results-oriented:** 1976 Apr *Psychology Today* 36/1 "a straightforward, results-oriented therapy geared toward getting the individual to cope with his immediate environment" Dec 28 *Wall St Jour* 9/2 (ad) "New position available for a results oriented individual" —**Star Trek oriented:** 1974 Nov *Analog* 165/1 "KWEST-CON

74 (Star Trek Oriented Convention), Kalamazoo, Michigan"
—**women's lib-oriented:** 1971 Jan 23 *TV Guide* A2/2 "a women's
lib-oriented lady doctor"

4. Directed toward, aimed at, intended for *x*
   a. Having *x* as goal, purpose, objective, ideal, or guiding
      principle
achievement-oriented: 1972 June *Esquire* 144/2 "failure, the
worst of social diseases among the achievement-oriented" —
conservation-oriented: 1971 June 26 *Science News* 437/2 "conservation-oriented grazing and timber management practices"
—**exploitation-oriented:** 1973 Nov 16 *New Times* 7/4 "such exploitation-oriented films as *Bloody Mama* and *The Trip*" —**growth-
oriented:** 1: Having economic growth as aim or goal 1975 Dec 9
Wall St Jour 31/4 (ad) "Growth orientated company" 1976 Jan
12 *Harper's Weekly* 19/5 "the growth-oriented sort of cowboy
economy" —2: Of stocks, intended to produce increase in value
rather than present income 1972 Nov *Town & Country* 162/3
"For a growth-oriented portfolio, stocks are expected to increase
in value at a rate of 13 to 15 per cent a year and yield a
dividend income of 2 per cent." —3: Having as purpose or
goal the development of the individual 1973 Mar *Psychology
Today* 74/1–2 "Participants [in encounter groups] saw themselves as . . . more growth-oriented than did non-participants."
—**high-volume oriented:** 1975 Mar *Better Homes and Gardens*
10/2 "Mass merchandisers . . . are high-volume oriented even in
auto service." —**reform-oriented:** 1972 Feb *Intellectual Digest*
98/2 "reform-oriented judicial opinion" —**social-action oriented:**
1971 Apr 29 *Crimson-White* (University, Ala) 1/3 "The war on
poverty began the attraction to volunteer, social-action oriented
programs."
   b. Intended or designed for the use, benefit, or pleasure of *x*
American-oriented: 1975 Nov *Town & Country* C20/3 "American-oriented silver and gold rums" —**Anglo-oriented:** 1974 María
Medina Swanson in *Responding to New Realities* edited by Gil-
bert A Jarvis (Skokie, Ill: National Textbook Co) 82 "the middleclass Anglo-oriented curriculum" —**family-oriented:** Intended for
the entire family, children as well as adults 1965 Apr 5 *Sponsor*

24/3 "Sen. Maurine Neuberger... questioned cigaret sponsorship of family-oriented shows." 1973 Aug *Town & Country* 120/3 "a... family-oriented amusement park" —**lay-oriented:** 1971 Dec *Esquire* 56/3 "*Today's Health*, the once-staid lay-oriented publication of the American Medical Association"

    c. Intended for the relief of *x*

acne-oriented: 1975 Apr 4 *W* 17/1 "sulfur—which is contained in many acne-oriented products"

    d. Intended or designed to appeal to *x*

affluent-oriented: 1971 Jan 10 *Washington Post* F22/1 "an affluent-oriented shopping center at Western and Wisconsin Avenues" —**black-oriented:** 1974 Nov 30 *TV Guide* 22/2 "two action-filled, black-oriented theatrical movies" —**tourist-oriented:** 1975 Feb *Esquire* 130/1 "The operation became large, brassy, pressurized, exchanging Creole authenticity for tourist-oriented glamour." —**youth-oriented:** 1970 Dec 2 *Rolling Stone* 1/2 "the youth-oriented shows" 1971 Jan 23 *Sat Rev* 60/2 "in *Yunost,* a youth-oriented journal" Aug 23 *Newsweek* 51/2 "such youth-oriented topics as communes and hitchhiking"

5. a. Based on, organized around *x*

aerospace-oriented: 1972 July 17 *USN&WR* 58/3 "the city's aerospace-oriented economy" —**course-oriented:** 1974 June 22 *National Observer* 10/5 (letter) "Medical-school teaching today is more patient-centered and problem-oriented than course-oriented." —**in-group oriented:** 1962 Jan−Feb *Jour of Rehabilitation* 10/2 "Social life appeared in-group oriented..." —**meat-oriented:** 1974 Feb *Sci Amer* 14/2 "the meat-oriented diets of the West" —**Nile-oriented:** 1970 Nov *Natural History* 22/3 "the Nile-oriented economy, which necessitated the maintenance of a sizable manpower pool for the short rush periods of planting and harvesting" —**print-oriented:** 1970 July 18 *Sat Rev* 44 "Their education is far too print-oriented..." Dec 19 *New Yorker* 64/3 "an off-screen, print-oriented public-relations campaign"

    b. (?) Based or headquartered in *x*

The evidence for this sense of *-oriented* is weak, both quantitatively and qualitatively. Only three occurrences were found.

Texas-oriented: 1976 May 23 *Family Weekly* 22/3 "A certain

business group, allegedly Texan or Texas-oriented, wanted Johnson as President." —**Virginia-oriented:** 1971 Oct 30 *National Observer* 4/3 "[He] is a director of many Virginia-oriented corpora-
tions..." —**Washington-oriented:** 1976 May 10 *Chron of Higher
Educ* 10 (subheading) "Statewide and multi-campus student units
have been gaining strength while Washington-oriented bodies
have fragmented much of theirs."

6. Related to *x;* connected or associated in some way with *x*
     The nature of the relationship is rarely evident. Both *-oriented*
and *-related* are used in the same sense in many combinations,
occasionally in the same passage; see, for example, *depression-
oriented* and *sports-oriented.*
     An interesting but baffling use of *defense-oriented,* not to men-
tion the adjectives flanking it, is: "Much of this has been said
before, but usually in a technological, defense-oriented, keep-up-
with-the-Russians tone of voice" (*Science News,* 12 Aug. 1972,
p. 101/2).
     age-oriented: 1975 June 1 *NY Times Book Rev* 3/2 "Walking is
a universal form of exercise, not age-oriented or bound to any
national heritage." —**combat-oriented:** 1972 Aug 21 *USN&WR*
51/1 "combat-oriented jobs as gunner's mate and torpedoman"
—**depression-oriented:** 1975 Apr 13 *NY Times Book Rev* 37/2−3
"Depression-oriented subject matter on the rise.... The... most
obviously depression-related [title] is 'Your Check Is in the Mail'."
—**export-oriented:** 1974 Aug 15 *Forbes* 25/1 "some 2 million American export-oriented jobs" —**job-oriented:** 1971 Jan 10 *NY Times*
NER40/4 "job-oriented college courses" —**machine-oriented:** 1972
Apr 8 *TV Guide* 34/2 "the impact of machine-oriented recrea-
tion in the Parks" —**mission-oriented:** 1970 Apr *Natural History*
70/2 "a 'mission-oriented' laboratory" 1971 Apr 8 *New Scientist
and Science Journal* 79/1 "under pressure of mission-oriented
goals" 1974 Nov 2 *Science News* 275/3 "mission-oriented research" —**non-complaint-oriented:** 1976 May 10 *Chron of Higher
Educ* 16/3 (repr from *Federal Register* May 3) "What are the
principal factors or criteria the Office for Civil Rights should
assess and apply in periodically establishing priorities to guide
its non-complaint-oriented activities?" —**people-oriented:** 1971

Nov *Sci Amer* 65−66 "It is clear that the mercalli intensity scale is people-oriented; anyone can estimate the intensity from his own experience during an earthquake." —**sports oriented:** 1976 July 18 *Tuscaloosa News* C8/1 "These could be... sports related camps. Those who attend sports oriented camps usually do so to try and improve their skill..." —**water-oriented:** 1971 Aug *Southern Living* 39/2 "His hobbies—fishing, sailing, and gunning for waterfowl—are water-oriented."

The De-definition of *-oriented*

As elusive as the sense of *-oriented* may be in some of the combinations cited above, it leaps immediately to the eye and mind when compared with the use of *-oriented* in those that follow. In a number of combinations, *-oriented* seems to be used not so much to convey meaning, or even Follett's "appearance of meaning," as to serve a function: the formation of adjectives. Often the *-oriented* could be dropped, leaving a noun used attributively. The "combat-oriented" entered under the definition 'related to' certainly approaches, if it does not cross, the boundary between meaning and non-meaning. How do *combat-oriented* jobs differ from combat jobs? Can a full-time mother or working wife who wishes to continue her education work toward a degree without enrolling in a traditional campus program? She can do so "without enrolling in a traditional *campus-oriented* program" (*Family Circle,* Aug. 1976, p. 30/1). Anyone willing to help stage a *"charity oriented* tennis tournament or exhibition" (*Town & Country,* May 1974, p. T5/1) would surely put forth the same effort for a charity tournament. A *"community-oriented* effort to conserve energy" (*New Times,* 22 Mar. 1974, p. 26/2) would probably conserve no more energy than a community effort. It would seem that society leaders could as well avail themselves of the services of a society public relations man as of a society doctor and would not need a *"society-oriented* P.R. agent" (*Harper's Bazaar,* Nov. 1972, p. 126/1). But perhaps that would not "jibe with my proper upbringing and *society-oriented* background" (*American Home,* Apr. 1976, p. 53/2). At the other end of the social scale can be found "an illiterate, lower-class, *peasant-oriented* woman" (*In-*

tellectual Digest, Aug. 1972, p. 17/2). According to an ad in the *Wall Street Journal,* 4 Jan. 1977, p. 17/4, "A Boston-based *transportation-oriented* authority seeks an Air Cargo Marketing Representative"; applicants can presumably present themselves at the offices of the transportation authority.

Adjectives related to the nouns (*economical, problematical, scientific*) appear to be adequate substitutes for noun + *oriented* combinations in the following: "The budget benefits too, because the more time-consuming casserole-type dishes... are usually *economy oriented*" (*Family Circle,* Sep. 1974, p. 126/1). "However, three problems cropped up, which makes such use [of extra-thin-base 35-mm films] *problem-oriented*" (*Popular Photography,* Oct. 1971, p. 138/2). With 181 pounds of experiments aboard, "IMP-J is one of the heaviest *science-oriented* satellites in the sky" (*Science News,* 20 Oct. 1973, p. 248/2).

In one occurrence of *Western-oriented, -oriented* seems to have as little meaning as it does in the examples cited above: "a 'people oriented' development strategy which not only increases agricultural and industrial production, but does so by involving the maximum number of workers (rather than through *Western oriented,* labor-saving technology)" (*NY Times Book Review,* 15 Dec. 1974, p. 19/4). In another instance, *-oriented* is charged with a greater burden of meaning than it is capable of bearing: "People tend to think of the national-park system as being *Western-oriented ...*" (*US News & World Report,* 24 Jan. 1972, p. 54/2). Here the meaning "located for the most part in the western United States" becomes apparent only after the end of the sentence is reached: "... and this is true from a standpoint of total acreage."

Some noun + *-oriented* combinations contribute to the English lexicon adjectival forms that are no doubt preferable to adjectives in *-ish,* whatever else may be said about them: "I have a friend ... who will give me recipes that are not *casserole-oriented*" (*Ladies' Home Journal,* Apr. 1974, p. 54/1). "[He] inflated his tough-guy, *gang-oriented* image by saying his mother was a prostitute" (*Reader's Digest,* Sep. 1971, p. 13/1). "[The performers] were all *quality-oriented*" (*Saturday Review,* 4 Dec. 1971, p. 38/2). And several companies have reacted to the booming

American wine market "in a very *quality-oriented* way" (*Vintage*, June 1972, p. 2/1). With the new television movie season approaching, it remains to be seen "how *quality-oriented* it can get" (*TV Guide*, 6 Sep. 1975, p. A8/1). To a German ear "basketball sounds so *university-orientated* with all those English terms" (*German Tribune*, 25 Feb. 1971, p. 15/2). Some glimmer of meaning comes through the haze in "that most intricate *gravity-oriented* machine of all, the human body" (*Reader's Digest*, July 1971, p. 153/2). But what is to be made of "the *nose-oriented* Stereo Realist [camera]," which forces the user "to squint into the tiny eyepiece with only *one* eye!" (*Popular Photography*, Aug. 1971, p. 63/1)?

Most, if not all occurrences of these combinations can be attributed to vogue usage. Even if it were conceivable that any speaker or writer of the English language would hesitate for a moment before using a "noun" as an "adjective," there would still remain an occasional adjective + -*oriented* combination with apparently the same meaning as the unadorned adjective: "a case of *psychosomatic-oriented* bronchitis" (*Greensboro, N.C., Daily News*, 23 June 1972, p. B3/2). The University of Texas was interested in a collection of historic photographic items "largely because of its *Victorian-oriented* nature, which dovetails with the university's interest in the literature of that era" (*Popular Photography*, Nov. 1971, p. 138/2).

From its first comparatively late appearance in English, *orient* has broadened its range of meanings from the geographical, the physical, the concrete, to the mental, the nonphysical, the abstract. Its participle, *oriented*, has acquired an adjectival life of its own. Its most frequent use has been in a large number of combinations in which -*oriented* covers a broad spectrum of sometimes overlapping senses. Particularly in the last decade or so, an -*oriented* vogue has led to an even greater frequency of use and range of meanings, to the point where -*oriented* in some words is devoid of meaning. The word faddists, however, have not found the semantic vacuum at all abhorrent and continue to toss their pet phrases about. At this point in the time continuum, it has become difficult to distinguish a serious use of -*oriented* from a parody-oriented use like "the high waste-production profile of the *urban-oriented* disadvantaged individual'' (*National Lampoon,* Jan. 1972, p. 63/1) or the pseudo-Socratic dialogue quoted earlier: ''Will you also concur that a decline in the *foreign-language-oriented* segment of a F.T.E. student's program, resulting both from paradigmatic alteration and elective trend, is a matter of concern?'' (*AAUP Bulletin,* Aug. 1976, p. 153/2).

Index
of Names

JAMES B. McMILLAN: ESSAYS IN
LINGUISTICS BY HIS FRIENDS AND COLLEAGUES
was composed in VIP Times Roman
by The Composing Room, Grand Rapids, Michigan,
printed by Thomson-Shore, Inc., Dexter, Michigan,
and bound by John H. Dekker & Sons, Grand Rapids, Michigan.
Production: Paul R. Kennedy
Book design: Anna F. Jacobs